A VERY ITALIAN SCANDAL

ANYA LONDON

Chapter 1

To say that Francesca Brook was out of her element was like saying summers in Death Valley were a touch toasty.

First time in Italy? Check.

First time her sister had snuck out for the night? Check.

First time chasing her down to a sex club? Check and, oh God, check.

Francesca glanced at the cracked screen of her phone for the fifth agonizing time, then at the building again. Her sister's location—as it was shared from her phone to Francesca's—could not be correct. Isa would never be here.

Maybe someone had stolen her phone? Took it with them to… to… No, impossible. No one who could afford entry to this place would bother stealing an outdated, six-year-old smartphone they had bought used—together with hers—online earlier that month.

Isa treasured that phone. She'd never let it out of her sight. It was the first time she'd ever owned a cell phone. For that matter, it was the first time Francesca had owned one too. She was still getting used to its many features.

She checked her sister's location again. *It can't be*

right. Out of all the places in Rome, what would her sister be doing *here*?

Painted the same peach sherbet color as the rest of the block, the exclusive club blended in well with the hotels and restaurants on the narrow street. Climbing plants scaled up one of its walls and hugged its facet in lush greenery, curving around its emerald-green shutters.

A massive arched door—original to the building, Francesca was certain—reflected the same fresh coat of emerald paint.

Two thick-necked giants, each one buttoned into a fancy suit that looked much too heavy for the hot August evening, flanked it on either side. She could make out their matching earpieces.

The shades had all been pulled tightly closed for the privacy of those inside, but glimmering gold light escaped around the rich fabric. A faint din of music emanated from within, mingling with voices and the clink of glassware. From somewhere near a window, she heard the celebratory pop of champagne followed by a peal of laughter and cheers.

She took an exploratory step closer, feeling each cobblestone through the worn soles of her Walmart sneakers.

The two bouncers gave her the once-over. Francesca faltered. Did she go and ask them to find Isabella inside? Could she trust them? *What if they ask for ID and—*

No, she couldn't chance it. She and Isa hadn't fled from Nevada all the way to Rome only to be sent back.

She craned her neck to scan the four-story, stone building from corner to corner. Could she see anything through the windows? *Darn. No.*

The discreet engraved sign set into the stone wall only said *Zohra*. Members knew what that implied. Nonmembers weren't welcome. Francesca wouldn't even have known about the place if Isa hadn't gone on and on about it last week after she'd read that magazine article, fascinated by the very concept of a sex club. Growing up in the Righteous Hearth community, they'd never even imagined such a thing was possible.

She squeezed her eyes tight, trying to remember what else Isa had shared about the club. The owner of Zohra—Francesca couldn't recall his name—owned a dozen sex clubs across several countries, but not a single one in Italy. His younger half-brother, Nate… Something, had taken it upon himself to open a Zohra in Rome. Isa had been fascinated. It didn't hurt that Nate was apparently Isa's type. Francesca had pointed out that he was fourteen years older than her little sister, but Isa didn't care. Her eyes had welded themselves to his photo. The girl had fallen in love.

But why would she leave their nonna's apartment to find the man in the middle of the night? Isa was eighteen, but not foolish. Francesca had enough problems. She didn't need to add chasing her sister across Rome to the list, and Isa knew that painfully well.

One of the bouncers approached, asked her something in rapid Italian. Although her mother spoke the language fluently, she had kept it out of Francesca's sparse homeschool curriculum.

She shook her head, unsure of the question.

He switched to English. "May I direct you somewhere?"

Francesca didn't doubt that she stuck out like a sore thumb. Dressed as she was in ratty jeans and a top she'd borrowed from her grandmother—she didn't have the cash or the time to go shopping, and she and Isa didn't bring any items with them when they'd fled Nevada—didn't exactly scream sex party guest.

Did she tell them she's looking for her sister? Or should she attempt to find her own way inside and drag Isa out?

She faltered.

The other bouncer now watched her too. To them, she was suspicious.

"I'm one of the cleaning crew," she said in English, grateful he knew the language.

He looked annoyed. "Don't just stand there gawking. Go around the back. Enzo will let you in."

"Ummm… which way is around the back?"

The guard rolled his eyes. "Come on. I'll take you."

She followed close behind as he strode around the corner of the building to where another giant guarded the much smaller side door. He tipped his chin at his buddy. "She's cleaning crew."

Enzo gave her the once-over too. "You're late. Hurry up. Sounds like a full house."

Well, that was shockingly easy. Guess their jobs were to keep the tourists and crashers out, and she didn't look like either one to them.

As she entered the hallway, Enzo didn't bother to see where she'd go. The two guards were chattering jovially with each other before the door even shut behind her.

Where would Isa be?

Francesca glanced down at her phone once more. So near… but how would she search across four stories for her sister?

Distracted, she didn't hear the approaching footfall.

The rushing waiter sidestepped her before they collided. His tray held tiny square desserts—each one a different pastel color. Some were topped with raspberries, others with gold foil. She hadn't seen such beautiful, extravagant sweets before in her life. She stared after him as he disappeared from sight.

Then followed him. Maybe he'd take her to the heart of the party, and that's where Isa would miraculously be, and she could grab her sister and leave before they drew too much attention.

She trailed the waiter into a ballroom lit by the silvery glow of crystal chandeliers above. Notes of heavy perfumes hung low in the air, mixed with the fresh scent of flowers from the overfilled vases. A live DJ played for the dancing crowd. Most were dressed to the nines—the men in suits, the women in shimmering ball gowns or exotic lingerie. Masquerade masks concealed their faces. Couples or small groups conversed on emerald velvet couches that had been placed around the dance floor. Some were making out, others cuddling.

Where are you, Isa?

Her sister would never willingly… well, Isa did escape to a sex club. Maybe she didn't know her as well as she'd thought.

A naked couple kissing in the corner, the man's hands all over the woman, jolted Francesca. She averted her gaze as heat flooded her cheeks. Her upbringing had kept her away from anything of the sort. The time she'd given in to desire had left her shamed, mutilated, and she felt out of place here, surrounded by laughter and flirting and music. A far cry from their strict church community in the barren desert plains near Rose Falls.

Francesca swallowed. She was twenty-five years old and starting her new life. She shouldn't be scandalized by two willing people kissing in public… naked…

Oh boy, where is Isa?

Not recognizing her sister in any of the chattering groups downstairs, Francesca focused on the ornate staircase leading upstairs. Two guards stood at its base.

"Ooookay," she breathed. "Okay. You're a cleaner. You need to go upstairs to clean."

She took a step forward. *Just be confident. Act like you belong.*

Both guards put up their hands as she approached.

"May I help you?" the bald one asked in English. Zohra was, after all, American-owned.

"They asked for some clean-up help upstairs."

He skimmed her from head to toe. "Who asked?"

"Ummm… Nate?"

The guards exchanged knowing glances. Francesca didn't want to even think what that meant.

"All right." The guard stepped back. "He's on two."

"Thanks."

Whew… she made it in. But how the heck was she ever going to find Isa in this labyrinthine building?

She took the stairs one at a time until she reached the second floor. The corridor branched into two here. Doors—some open, some closed—spread out to both her left and her right.

Checking her phone again confirmed it. Isa was close. Just a few steps. Either on this floor or on the one above… or the one above.

I guess here is as good a place to start as any.

Following the dot on her phone, she passed by wide-open doorways with naked couples writhing inside until she stood in front of closed double doors at the end of the hall.

She pressed her ear against the carved wood, listened.

If only that couple from two doors down would stop grunting so loud. I can't hear a thing.

She tried the door handle. Unlocked.

Okay. Here goes…

Twisting the brass doorknob, she slivered the door open—

And heard Isa's voice. "Just take off your clothes!"

Francesca's heart dropped straight to her sneakers. Preparing herself for the worst, she tossed open the door the rest of the way and trooped inside. "Isa?"

She involuntarily took two steps back at the scene playing out in front of her like in one of those soap operas she used to watch before television was banned by their church.

Her eighteen-year-old sister kneeled on the gargantuan bed—she'd never seen a bed that large before—in just her bra and underwear. She had painted her lips a bright ruby red, the lipstick smeared across one corner of her mouth.

She faced a man—Nate, Francesca presumed.

Dark hair, vivid blue eyes, musculature she'd only seen in museum catalogs. He stood at the edge of the bed, wearing suit pants but completely bare from the waist up.

Tanned, golden skin gleamed like bronze over muscles that could have been carved by Michelangelo. She drank in the swell of his biceps, the expansive chest that narrowed to chiseled abdominal muscles. *My gosh,* she could count each one. A narrow trail of dark hair disappeared into his expensive-looking suit pants.

For goodness' sake, stop staring. Her teeth clinked when she closed her mouth.

Francesca twisted away from the much-too-attractive stranger and faced her wayward sister. Now that the shock ebbed, anger spiraled. "Get dressed. Now."

"Cessie." Isa scrambled off the bed. "How did you get in here?"

Francesca shook her phone in the air. "I tracked your location. What in the heck are you doing here?" She turned to the man at the side of the bed. "And *you*. What are you doing? She's a child. She just barely turned eighteen." She suffused the next sentence with all the disdain she felt for men like him. "What's wrong with you?" Her eyes snapped to Isa. "I said. Get. Dressed."

Nate, turning his back on her sister, strode toward her. His blue eyes flashed like desert lightning. "Who the hell are you? What game are you two playing?"

Francesca refused to back down. "You have my baby sister cornered in a sex club. We are not playing any game."

"First she accosts me and now you just happen to walk in at the right time?" His gaze flicked down her frame. "Who let you into Zohra dressed like an AARP model?"

Francesca glanced down at her grandmother's floral button-down. Anger heated her face. "I'm here to collect my sister. We'll be out of your hair. You can do whatever it is you want with anyone else here—the loud couple down the hall could use a third."

Shocked at her own words, she turned to go, expecting Isa to follow. Instead, strong hands closed around her shoulders. Nate flipped her, putting her within inches of his wrath-filled face. He puffed out air like a bull coming down with bovine respiratory disease. She hated liking the fresh mint on his breath, the wash of a crisp, citrusy cologne that rose from his skin.

"You're not going anywhere." He spied her phone. "What's this? You record us? You plan to blackmail me with this?"

His hand closed over the device, and he pulled it from her grasp. Her eyes welded to the jagged scar crisscrossing his knuckles. She was no stranger to scars, but had he punched something? Some*one*? Did a man with anger issues now hold her prized possession?

"Careful!" She reached for her phone. "Don't break it!"

She couldn't afford another. She and Isa had just gotten to Rome, spending the last of their meager savings on plane tickets. Her grandmother's pension wasn't enough to sustain all three of them. She hadn't been able to find a job yet—she had no education, little work experience, woeful Italian. That phone was irreplaceable to her.

He lifted it high above her head.

Gosh, he was tall. He towered over her. She couldn't even jump to grab the smartphone. Not that she would. She wouldn't give him the satisfaction of watching her squirm like a baited worm. She had dignity. Self-respect.

She raised her chin, meeting his angry gaze. "Give me my phone."

Turning away from her, he swiped through the apps. "Let's see here. Do you have photos of me? Recordings?"

"I don't have anything of you. *Please* be careful." That phone was her only connection to her littlest sister, the one they had to leave behind.

"It's already cracked," he pointed out.

"I bought it that way. Please don't break it."

Apparently satisfied that she held nothing featuring him in her images folder, he handed the cell phone back to her. The hot brush of his fingers against hers set off a misdirected spark of pleasure along her nerve endings.

His next statement set off nothing but annoyance. "Here. You should get the screen fixed."

"I'll get right on that," she sniped out. Checking to

make sure her phone was okay, she tucked it away in the back pocket of her jeans.

Isa, fully dressed now, gave them a wide berth as she headed for the door. "I'll see you outside, Cessie."

And she was gone.

Francesca turned to go.

Powerful fingers dug into her upper arms, and he twisted her around to face him again.

"Tell me what the plan was. What is this about?"

Confused, she blinked. "What plan?"

"I was supposed to meet a date in this room. Instead, a child shows up."

Irritation spiraled. "Didn't stop you from stripping down, did it?"

"I was already strip—you know what? It doesn't matter. Your sister interrupted my evening. You're lucky I don't have security escort you both out of here."

"Frankly, I'd invest in better security."

She turned to leave. He spun her around yet again. The pressure of his fingers against her skin sent awareness coursing through her most private parts. Her breasts felt heavy, the worn lining of her bra chafing her suddenly sensitive nipples.

"Will you stop that!" she demanded. "I'm getting vertigo. What more do you want from me?"

He didn't release her, surrounding her in his scent as he pulled her closer toward him. "Tell me how your sister got into the club."

"I don't know. The bozos out front let me in. I'm assuming they're the ones to blame for her entry too."

He cursed under his breath. "Who are you?"

"It doesn't matter. You'll never see me again. I'm not Zohra clientele. Trust me."

His gaze mined hers for the truth. When her tongue darted out to moisten her dry lips, he zeroed in on the movement. The fingers on her upper arms tightened—

Abruptly, he released her with another huff of frustration.

Time to go.

Instead of turning her back to him this time, she walked backward toward the door, keeping her eyes on him. He had planted his feet wide apart, his fingers clenched at his sides, as though he fought the urge to follow her.

His nostrils flared. "Stop."

She didn't know why, but she did. "What now?"

"You don't get to leave that easily. I know there's a story here. I want it. I don't need my face all over social media because your sister managed to snap a photo."

"Well, then hire better security." Francesca turned around and ran.

She made it as far as the hallway when he caught her, his arm locking around her waist.

Why does he have to smell this good? She inhaled hot male mixed with those summer citrus notes. Her whole body clenched, a pathetic attempt to hold on to his scent just a little longer. Her lady parts liked it. She didn't. She couldn't. She had a lot to do to extricate poor Sofia, and she couldn't derail her plans.

She puffed out his scent from her nostrils.

"What are you doing? Let me go." She tried to kick for his shin, but he evaded her. Opening the nearest door, he dragged her inside.

"Don't make a scene."

"*Don't make a scene?* You won't let me leave. That's illegal. That's… *kidnapping.*"

"It's not kidnapping."

When she tried to go to the door, he blocked her way, arms crossed like an angry goalie.

His throat worked as he swallowed. "What's your name?"

"None of your business."

"You're in my club. Tonight is a friends-only preview, restricted to lifetime or platinum members. Did you pay a quarter million euro to be here as a platinum member? Did your sister? You owe me half a million euro. I can call the police or you can tell me your name. Your choice."

She gawked at him. "Who in their right minds would pay that much to go to a sex party?"

"Everyone you saw here tonight. The lifetime membership starts at a million."

A headache pounded between her brows, and her gut knotted. He wasn't serious. He couldn't possibly hold her responsible for that much money. All she came here to do was get her sister. But when she glanced at him again, she realized he was incensed enough to try.

"My name is Francesca," she allowed.

"Last name."

"Why does it matter?"

"I deserve to know who my trespassers are."

"You're… Nate, right?"

His gaze narrowed. "You do know me."

"Isa—my sister—read about you in an article. She sort of… became a little infatuated. I think that's why she came here. It's very unlike her. She's usually very practical."

He raised a brow. "The naked girl from earlier?"

"We don't want any trouble. Our grandmother will be worried. She's out with her boyfriend tonight, but she always comes home by midnight. I need to be back before they are."

"Where does your grandmother live?"

"I'm not telling you that. I don't know you."

"All right, Francesca." He rolled her name across his tongue. "You may leave. But I want your number."

The declaration sent her stumbling back a step. "What? Why?"

"If anything is stolen here tonight, I'll know where to find your little sister."

"She wouldn't steal anything."

"If you're sure of that, give me your number."

Confused by what he wanted, but seeing no reason to deny the request, Francesca acquiesced. "Fine."

"I left my phone in the other room. Stay here."

Oh wow, even his back is pure muscle.

Francesca couldn't look away if her life depended on it.

Thankfully, he strode into the hallway and disappeared from view. She considered running for the exit, but he was fast. He'd catch her. Then he very well might call the police, and she couldn't afford that chance.

She wouldn't return to the Righteous Hearth.

When she and Isa had escaped their religious community, they knew their only refuge would be with Nonna. No one from the Righteous Hearth would find them here, in Italy. No one would ever suspect they'd have passports to travel internationally. Because Isa was eighteen, she was a grown adult, making it impossible for their parents to accuse Francesca of kidnapping their child. That was why they couldn't bring Sofia. Taking her *would* be kidnapping. But they'd return for her. As soon as Francesca found a job. Any job that would hire her.

"Fuck."

She recognized Nate's voice. Hurrying to meet him in the hallway, she faced him across the thick rug spanning the length of the corridor. The amorous couple nearby was still grunting away.

Reaching her, he snarled, "Your sister stole my phone."

"She'd do no such thing. Isa doesn't steal."

"Where is she?"

"Probably waiting for me outside."

His hand closed over hers, and he yanked her after him, towing her along as they navigated the stairs. She tried not to dwell on how pleasant his skin felt against hers. How… shivery his solid touch made her.

The partiers corralled around them.

"Nate!"

"Come join us!"

"The bartender is poppin' another bottle. Want a glass?"

"Be right back," Nate tossed over his shoulder as he tugged her along through the massive emerald doors, past the two bouncers, until they stood outside.

Isa was nowhere to be found on the cobblestones. Francesca scanned the length of the narrow street. *Nope, not here.* "Maybe she's around the back?"

He was already striding toward the other door; she had to run to keep up with his wide strides. Isa wasn't at the side entrance either.

"She must have gone home. She wouldn't have taken your phone. My sister doesn't steal."

Nate and the guard by the back door—Enzo?—exchanged a few heated words in Italian.

"He saw her leave down the back alley. Let's go."

"Go where?"

"Your grandmother's. I'm getting my phone back tonight or you're both going to jail."

Chapter 2

The trespasser lifted her chin. "I'm not taking you to my grandmother's. You're a stranger."

Fuck, she was pretty. Even dressed in… that. The too-large, garish floral print blouse looked like it was one tug away from falling off her shoulders, currently squared in mutiny.

Her brown hair had been drawn into a tight ponytail low on her nape. The sharp middle part would be unflattering on anyone else, but it sharpened the delicate contours of her features, amplified the clarity of her skin. She had thick, wild eyebrows above large blue eyes, almost lavender in the dim lighting, and blonde-tipped lashes.

The sleepless nights leading up to the Zohra pre-opening party tonight must have messed with his head, because his eyes zeroed in on her lips, found them lusciously plump. She wore no lipstick or gloss, and the satin surface looked delicate and sweet. He wanted to taste the pink softness, to feel her skin warm under his touch, to dip his tongue into her mouth and explore.

His just-healed knuckles burned. *Good.* An important reminder to stay the fuck away.

Francesca's lips flattened at his perusal. She crossed her arms.

He had to blink twice before he could focus on the conversation. "Fine. Call your sister. Have her bring back my phone."

Her face brightened at the prospect, and she reached for her cell with barely contained eagerness, dialed her sister, listened. Then hung up with a sigh. "She didn't answer."

"You were tracking her on your phone earlier. Track her now."

She looked like she wanted to argue, but shook her head as if telling herself that now wasn't the time. Pulling up her sister's location, she studied the map. "She's moving across Ponte Cavour."

"Where's she going?"

"I think to my grandmother's."

"I'll drive."

He stalked to his car ahead of her, still hard from the memory of having her in his arms. She'd smelled of lavender soap. Simple. Clean. Nothing exotic or lab-manufactured to arouse. Yet he had to restrain himself from pressing his nose into her neck, from inhaling deep.

Like an idiot who hadn't learned his lesson.

They stopped at the small, red Fiat he'd parked a block from Zohra.

"Aren't you going to make fun of it?" he asked when she said nothing.

She looked up at him, confused. "Make fun of what?"

"My car. I'm not staying here long, didn't need any-thing fancy."

She studied the Fiat, then glanced back at him. "It's

a nice car. I've never had one, so I have nothing to compare it to."

"Never had one? How old are you?"

"Twenty-five."

"You from Manhattan or something?"

She shook her head. "No."

When she didn't offer more, he held open the passenger-side door for her. He waited for her to settle herself, then came around to the driver's side, sliding across the tan leather.

"My brother Oliver almost tripped over his luggage laughing when he saw me pull up to get him at the airport a few months back. Won't let me live it down. But I like it. It's compact. Electric. Gets me from point A to point B."

She ran a slow finger across the console, her voice pensive. "It's beautiful."

"I wouldn't go that far," he snorted, starting the engine. "Navigate."

Francesca focused on her phone screen. "I think we can catch her along the route. Looks like she's walking."

He pulled out of the tight parking space and headed toward the Cavour Bridge.

"How'd you get to Zohra?" he asked, navigating the one-way streets.

"I walked."

"Alone? At night?" His chest tightened at the thought of her traipsing around in the dark. *Where the hell did this protective instinct toward an intruder come from?*

She glanced out the window. "It's not that late. Besides, I've never used public transportation before, so it makes me too nervous to try it here. And I can't afford a cab."

"You don't drive, but you've never used public

transportation? You have a driver or live in a small town?"

"Mmmm… small town."

"Where?" he prodded, fascinated despite himself.

"Doesn't matter." She turned to him and gave him a bland smile. "I don't live there anymore."

He'd always been a sucker for puzzles. "What brought you to Rome?"

"Visiting my grandmother," she answered as she would a customs agent. Practiced.

"You two close?"

"I'd like to be."

He slanted her a glance. "But you're not?"

"We lost touch after she had a falling-out with my parents. We're trying to rebuild our relationship." Her teeth sank into her lower lip for a tense pause before she continued. "It's odd. She's my grandmother, but we're strangers if you really think about it. I last saw her when I was five or six. She's never even met Isa before."

"Is that why you came out here? To see her?"

Her eyes scanned the road as he drove. They sharpened on someone a distance ahead. "That's Isa. Pull over."

She was opening the car door when he grabbed for her elbow. "Hold it. Let me get you closer."

He traversed the intersection and pulled off the road next to Isa, who marched along the sidewalk with a peppy spring to her step.

Francesca hopped out of the car. "What are you doing?"

Isa stopped, turned. Her eyes widened as she recognized her sister and, behind Francesca, him.

Her chin lifted. "Walking to Nonna's."

"Did you take his phone?" Irritation gathered in Francesca's voice.

Isa threw him an angry glance over her sister's shoulder. "I did."

"Give it back."

"I can't."

"Why not?"

"I sold it," she announced cheerfully.

"Why would you sell something that doesn't belong to you?" Francesca demanded before he could react to the statement.

"We needed the money. Pay was good." Isa's brown eyes pinned his. "Plus, he turned me down. Serves him right."

"Get his phone back."

The command sent a pang of surprise through him. He hadn't expected her to take his side.

Her sister shrugged. "Too late now."

"I don't even recognize you tonight," Francesca said. "Where's the money? Give it to him."

"It's not his. It's mine."

Francesca jerked her thumb toward him. "It was his phone."

"But *I* sold it."

Entertained by the exchange, Nate hung back to see what Francesca would do next.

"It wasn't your phone to sell," she pointed out.

Her sister pouted. "It's not like he can't buy himself a new one."

Irritated by Isa's callous response, he intervened. "I don't want a new phone. I want *my* phone. You either get it back now, or I'm taking you to the police."

"Do you want to speak to the police tonight?"

Francesca asked slowly, each word buzzing with an undercurrent Nate couldn't follow, but Isa clearly could.

Her gaze widened, her back straightened. She seemed to consider the question, then shook her head. "I don't."

"Can you get his phone back?"

Her sister's shoulders drooped. "I can't."

"*Isa.*" The word burst with disappointment.

"But I have the cash!" Isa said, apparently moved by the frustration in her sister's voice. She turned to Nate. "Will you take the money instead?"

"I don't want the money. I want the phone."

"She doesn't have the phone," Francesca said forlornly.

His headache returned, pounding at his temples. Francesca seemed to experience a similar ache. She rubbed deep circles between her brows. This close, he could see that the ends of her brow hairs curled at the outer wings. The shadows under her eyes seemed more pronounced under the glow of streetlamps above them. In this light, she looked deflated—as though she hadn't slept in weeks and today was the tipping point.

"Fine," he said, deciding to be the bigger person. "It is what it is. I won't call the cops. Just… never return to Zohra."

Francesca's features relaxed at his words. "I promise you, we won't set foot in there again."

"Can I keep the cash?" asked Isa.

"No," Francesca answered before he could. "You give that to him right now."

"But he doesn't need the money. We do."

"We don't steal, Isa. Give him the money. Now."

Isa twisted her face, but she reached into her purse

and extracted an envelope. "Here." She extended it to him.

Nate didn't reach for it.

"Why do you need the money?" he asked instead, though he knew better than to pry. He had enough problems.

Francesca looked drained. "Nate, you've been a trooper today, but you don't know us and we don't know you. Just take your cash, and we'll be on our way."

A sensible suggestion. He should take her up on it. But instinct insisted he question further. "Tell me why you need the cash."

Francesca pressed her full lips shut.

Isa glanced at her sister, and she too remained silent.

"Are you in trouble with the law?" he asked.

Francesca's eyes flashed. "Of course not."

"It's a fair assumption given what I've witnessed today."

"Trust me, this is very out of character for Isa. It won't happen again." She grabbed the envelope from her sister and thrust it into his hands. "Here."

His fingers brushed hers, sending a current of heat straight to his groin. She snatched her hand back, as though she'd felt the charge too.

He tightened his hold on the envelope, but didn't look inside. "It's late. I got to get back to Zohra. Get in the car. I'll take you to your grandmother."

Francesca shook her head. "It's close. We'll walk from here."

"Not up for discussion. I'm not letting you walk when my car is right here."

"Thank you, but no."

Isa grabbed her shoulder. "But I'm so tired and

hungry, Cessie. If he drives us, we can get home earlier. Maybe we'll even beat Nonna back."

At the mention of her grandmother, Francesca seemed to reconsider. "All right. Fine… Thank you."

He motioned to the car. While he held the front passenger door open for Francesca, Isa climbed into the back. He expected the teen to poke fun at his ride, but she didn't. She smoothed her hand across the leather, played with the buttons on the door, but stayed quiet.

"Tell me how to get to your grandmother's," Nate told Francesca, pulling away from the curb.

"Keep going straight." They drove in silence until she pointed to a five-story building. "We're just up there."

He slid the car into an empty parking space right in front. "I'll walk you up."

"You don't have to…" Francesca began, but Nate was already climbing out of the Fiat.

He followed Francesca into the vestibule, unable to keep his gaze from drifting to her pert ass outlined by the worn denim. Isa trailed behind them as they bypassed the old-fashioned elevator and took the stairs to the second floor.

Francesca pulled out her keys. "She's not back yet, I don't think. Thank you for taking us home. I'm sorry for… everything today."

Her wide blue gaze dried any semblance of a response in his throat.

"Isa? Don't you have anything to say?" prodded Francesca.

The teen crossed her arms, expression mulish as she regarded Nate. "You really missed out."

Francesca did not look amused. "Try again."

Isa sighed. "I'm sorry I sold your phone."

"And?" Nate prompted.

"And that I chased away your girlfriend."

Francesca's eyes darted to him.

"She wasn't my girlfriend." He had no idea why he bothered to explain, considering he'd never see Francesca or her sister again. "And?" he nudged, turning back to the teen.

Isa tilted her head. "I'm pretty sure that's it?"

"You made your sister walk through the city to get you in the middle of the night," Nate reminded her.

"Oh. Yes. I'm sorry, Cessie."

Francesca smiled at her little sister. "It's all right. Just don't do it again."

He waited for Francesca to open the door, but she loitered, protective of her space. He suspected that she wouldn't unlock it until he left. Which he needed to do. Immediately. Turn around and return to the Fiat. But his feet had fused to the ground.

Isa raised a dismissive brow. "Bye!"

Nate directed his next request solely to Francesca. "Give me your number."

She gave him a pointed look. "You don't even have a phone anymore."

"I'll buy another tomorrow."

"Why do you want her number?" asked Isa, eyes slitting.

"In case something was stolen at his club," Francesca explained.

Isa's pixie face morphed into outrage. "I didn't take anything but your phone."

"I'll see about that," he said, though that wasn't the reason he wanted Francesca's contact information.

Francesca No Last Name intrigued him. He'd had

more fun with her during the mad dash for her sticky-fingered sister than he'd had in a long while. Tonight's party at Zohra—and the explicit show the Lee twins had put on for the guests—seemed as exciting as the DMV in comparison to watching Francesca argue with her sister about his phone.

He wanted her number. He didn't know what he'd do with it, but he had to have it.

Francesca looked too tired to protest. She reached into her cloth tote and pulled out a black-and-white speckled notebook and a ballpoint pen. She scribbled a phone number on one of the pages, tore it out, and handed it to him.

He glanced at the digits, chest expanding on a full inhale. He hadn't realized he was holding his breath until then. His heart inexplicably pounded faster as he folded the page and tucked it into his pocket.

"Have a nice night, ladies." He turned to go.

Chapter 3

"What in the world were you thinking?" demanded Francesca, closing the door as Nate's steps faded. Their grandmother's modest apartment, as always, was too warm.

Instead of answering immediately, her sister hurried into the kitchen. Waiting for a response, Francesca followed.

Isa scoured the small fridge for a snack, pulling out a couple of tangerines. "I was thinking of Sofia."

"How does you going into a sex club to seduce its owner benefit Sofia?"

Isa chewed her lip. She swallowed nervously, hyper-focused on peeling the citrus. When she finally glanced up, her eyes reflected fathomless guilt. "A man paid me to do it."

Francesca's pulse lanced her ears. Needing to anchor herself, she grabbed the counter. "To do what exactly?"

With a sigh, Isa set down the fruit and dusted her hands. "Okay, don't get mad. I was online… checking for jobs. I put an ad on a site, saying that I can be hired to clean, or walk dogs, or help launder clothes. A man reached out. He needed someone to go to Zohra and take a few snaps of the owner."

Holy moly, Nate had been correct. Isa did take his photo.

"I came as his friend's guest…" Isa continued. "We stopped by a shop at the corner and he got me a dress. It didn't fit right, but whatever. It got me in. I followed Nate to his room. He wasn't even waiting for me, but for some blondie who was too busy flirting downstairs. I was about to take a photo, but then you interrupted. I had nothing to give to the man, so I gave him Nate's phone instead."

The tips of Francesca's fingers went numb from clutching the edge of the counter. "Who's this man, Isabella?"

"I don't know him. He was nice. Around sixty or so? He wasn't a perv or anything. I'm assuming he doesn't want a sex club on his block, so he needed something against the owner. I felt bad doing it. Nate Icefall is cute. Old, but cute."

"He's not old."

"He's over thirty."

A headache pounded at her temples. "I'm not even going to start on how dangerous it was for you to leave with a stranger, but you also gave someone's phone to that stranger—that can be really dangerous for you and Nate."

"But I got us cash! It would have helped us get Sofia out, but you gave it back."

"It's blood money, Isa."

Isa reached for the citrus again. "It was the only money we had—and now we don't even have that anymore."

She wasn't wrong. Could they really afford scruples when their baby sister was stuck in an increasingly unhinged cult? Yet she couldn't have kept Nate's cash. Not after learning someone had purposefully targeted him.

Keys jangled in the door.

"Nonna's back. Please, please, please don't say anything," Isa begged.

Francesca considered her sister's soulful expression. "All right. I won't. We don't want to be kicked out."

"Nonna would never kick us out. She loves us."

Their grandmother appeared in the small kitchen a few seconds later. She looked darn good for mid-seventies. Her dark hair and complexion allowed her to pull off bright colors that looked overwhelming on Francesca. For her date that evening, she had worn a fuchsia top and matching fuchsia slacks the same color as her nail polish and lipstick.

"You are still up," she said in English, brows drawing together. "A bit late for you, no?"

It amazed Francesca how easily her grandmother could toggle between the two languages, but she had worked as an English teacher at a local school before retiring, so it came naturally to her.

"We are about to go to bed," said Isa. "I was just hungry."

Nonna's boyfriend, Dante, paused in the kitchen doorway. Francesca had never asked for his age, but she suspected he was at least twenty years younger than her grandmother, with dark hair and olive skin and a lean, toned body. Although he was kind and courteous, he was also quiet. She didn't know whether his perpetual silence was part of a reserved personality or simply a result of him not speaking English and them not speaking Italian.

The kitchen was too small for the four of them, so Dante smiled a hello and went on to Nonna's bedroom.

"How was dinner?" Francesca asked.

Her grandmother craned her neck to ensure Dante was out of earshot before placing her purse on the counter and pulling out thick stacks of American dollars. She piled them next to the bag, one after the other. "Here. This is for you."

Isa and Francesca both gasped.

Nonna tsked. "Don't overreact."

Francesca studied the startling pile of notes. "Where did you get this money?"

"I withdrew it from my account. There's twenty-five thousand dollars in all. A start to bring your little sister here."

Isa reached for the crisp bills, thumbing through one of the stacks with awe.

Francesca herself had never seen so much cash before, and she knew her grandmother couldn't afford it.

She glanced around the small kitchen, which hadn't been updated since at least the '90s. The small, yellowed fridge in the corner rumbled loudly. Parts of the parquet floor had rotted through, and Nonna had tossed faded rugs to cover those spots. The wallpaper peeled at the top corners.

Out in the living room, the ancient windows had huge gaps between their frames. It made the apartment much too hot in the summer and, she assumed, winter would leave this place freezing. The ceilings were stained from a long-ago leak from the upstairs neighbor that had been fixed, but Nonna hadn't had the money to repaint. Giving them the last of her cash was unacceptable. If something went wrong, and they were pulled back into their parents' commune, Nonna would be left destitute.

"Out of the question," said Francesca. "We won't take your money. Besides, that's not enough to hire the kind of attorneys we need."

"Take it," Nonna insisted. "I'll get you twenty-five thousand more tomorrow. And more after that."

Francesca removed the cash from Isa's grip and slid it back across the countertop toward her grandmother. "We appreciate it. But you can't afford this. Isa and I will get jobs any day now."

Nonna's wise eyes met Francesca's. "You know I have this, and it's yours. I want Sofia out of that looney town."

"So do we. But Mom and Dad won't let us have her, so we have to fight. And that requires much more money than this. You allowing us to stay here is already helping. Once we have jobs, we can save up."

"Nonna, are you sure you are okay with us staying here?" asked Isa. "What if they come looking for us? Cessie's intended won't let her go easily. He may send someone here to look for her. We doubt they'd travel to Europe, but what if they do?"

"You let me deal with that," assured Nonna. "I've lost you girls once to that cult. I won't let it happen again. And I want my littlest grandbaby here too. You work on getting jobs, and I'll work on supplementing your cash supply when the time to hire attorneys comes."

Francesca didn't point out that her grandmother lived in a dilapidated hovel, even if the neighborhood was nice. She could put that cash toward home improvements.

Sofia was her and Isa's responsibility, and they themselves would get the money to get their baby sister to safety. If they couldn't, then they'd turn to Nonna. But it wasn't fair of them to dump this on her at her age. She lived on a fixed income—they couldn't burn through her savings. They needed jobs, and fast.

An hour later, long after Nonna, Dante, and Isa retired for the night, Francesca sat at the kitchen table and searched for employment opportunities on her grandmother's old, molasses-slow laptop. She'd had a dusting of work experience in the States, but it didn't really translate to much here in Rome. Her résumé was woefully lacking, as was her Italian.

She sent off two more applications to the local hotels

that were hiring, and decided to stop by in person tomorrow. So far, she'd been turned down from every front desk and room service staff role to which she'd applied due to her lack of Italian, but maybe she could convince them in person to hire her to change bedding and clean the rooms. She'd work the night shift if she had to, or clean two—even three—hotels if only they'd hire her. Her small savings were close to dry and getting Sofia away from the Righteous Hearth would require a lot of resources.

Closing her grandmother's ancient laptop, Francesca headed to the small bathroom to brush her teeth. Shedding her borrowed top, she stared at the barely healed welts across her forearms. They'd scar like the other injuries on her body had.

As she did every night since arriving at Nonna's, she reached for the tube of ointment. Used to the burn by now, she slathered the salve over the reminders of her whippings. At least they hadn't gotten infected like her past injuries did. Ignoring the scars crisscrossing her torso, she dragged on her sleepshirt and tiptoed the short distance to the room she shared with Isa.

Isa lay on her narrow bed set against one side of the minuscule room, fast asleep. Francesca got under the linens of her own bed against the opposite wall, reshuffling the musty pillow and hoping that sleep would come and take her away from her mounting troubles for just a few hours.

Closing her eyes, she tried to focus on things she should be grateful for—her grandmother, who'd taken them in even though they hadn't really known each other; Isa, who'd braved the unknown to escape with her; her best friend, Haley, who'd helped her set up a bank account and apply for passports; Mr. Orson, who'd hired her and Isa to help him tend the farm animals and had paid them in cash, which had allowed them to save up for their escape.

An image of shirtless Nate popped into her head… unbidden, unwanted, absorbing. He'd smelled like candied lemons that Haley used to make for Christmas, and she'd had to stop herself from pressing her nose against the powerful muscles in his chest and inhaling. His fingers had felt dangerously pleasant as they'd closed over her upper arms.

Remembering his touch flooded her with warmth. She shoved the linens down her body in an attempt to cool her skin. The old cotton shirt felt as rough against her breasts as the hair shirt the Righteous Hearth had made her wear—the one with the spikes. Shifting restlessly against the mounting agitation, Francesca focused on the cracked ceiling above her.

Even with the windows open, the room stifled her as she tried to calm her racing heart. She needed to dislodge Nate from her mind. She'd never see him again, and she had more important thoughts to prioritize. Like getting a job.

The longer she stayed unemployed, the longer it would take to rescue Sofia.

Climbing off the bed, Francesca kneeled next to it to retrieve the file she'd tucked under there for safekeeping.

Plan Z. The very last resort.

Opening the folder, she reread the contents one more time. Using the information she and Isa had taken with them would get their parents arrested. She never wanted that, but she'd do whatever it took to get Sofia out before the cult did something unspeakable—like marry her off to Miles Decker in Francesca's stead.

Chapter 4

Returning to Zohra after dropping off the thief and her sister, Nate Icefall bypassed the revelers and took the back stairs to his room. Alone. Irritated.

He'd envisioned tonight's pre-launch party to go in a different direction. Like him tumbling into bed with Lina or the Lee twins. Instead, he'd had scalding coffee spilled on his suit, the very sexy blonde he'd invited to his room never showed, some oddly dressed teen appeared instead and tried to get naked, and that teen stole his phone.

Moreover, her fuming sister had interrupted just as he was about to tell the teen to leave, and it undeniably looked like he was about to get down with someone not even of US legal drinking age.

And now here he sat, cancelling mobile pay credit cards, locking his SIM, ruing the day he failed to set up the find my phone feature, and praying that whoever had his phone wouldn't be able to figure out his passcode.

Not that he had dick pics on his phone. But… he *had* taken copious photos of the strange mole on his thigh and hadn't deleted them after the doctor assured him not to worry. He couldn't have those images out in the world.

The last thing he needed was a social media scandal centered around his thigh.

Not now of all times, when Rhyme, Ryan, & Shuster were about to announce his return to the firm. Not now, when Steven Douglass needed a respectable attorney.

His mentor had almost been killed protecting his students from the teen shooter. The state hadn't been able to shut Clary Guns down, but Nate would.

In the morning, after filing a police report and buying a new phone, he entered Zohra through the side door. The cleaners wouldn't arrive for another few hours to set the place to rights, and he enjoyed the beat of silence as he made his way to the commercial kitchen in the back. Setting his still-boxed phone down on the stainless-steel prep table, he turned on the espresso machine it had taken him a few tries to master last week and made a much-needed shot of caffeine.

Unexpected footsteps from the main club area cut through the silence.

Who was trespassing now? The place was closed to visitors. He followed the sound.

Irritation thrummed as he recognized the intruder. *Fucking not again.* Giorgio Moretti was like a gnat he couldn't swat away. "What the hell are you doing here?"

The Italian looked tanned and relaxed in his designer casuals. He raised Nate's stolen phone. "Found something of yours. Decided to do you a favor and bring it back."

He should have known. "You're the asshole who bought it off the girl."

"Girl brought it to me," said the Italian. "You want your shit or not?"

Nate took a step forward. "Couldn't figure out the passcode?"

"Passcode was easy. Seeing your hairy thigh at every angle? Revolting."

"You went through my photos?"

"Texted a couple to myself." The Italian tossed the phone to Nate. "Don't need this anymore."

Nate caught it midair. The device had retained the oily heat of Giorgio's skin. "What do you want, Giorgio?"

The man's face revealed no emotion. "I'm on your side. My brother, too. We are at your service, whatever you may need."

Nate set the phone down on a nearby table. He couldn't have the same conversation again. "I told you before. I don't need anything from you."

"That's not up to you. The sooner you figure that out, the better." Giorgio sniffed at the air. "Do I smell coffee?"

"Kitchen's closed."

The Italian shrugged. "Suit yourself. But don't let it be said the Moretti family never did you any favors."

Turning on his heel, he strolled out through the front door.

The teen worked for the Morettis.

Did her sister? It explained why she wouldn't share her last name or her hometown. Was the whole thing a setup? Bring two poorly dressed people into his establishment to steal his phone, and… what the hell else did they take? The security proved useless yesterday. He'd have to contract with another firm.

A frosty headache pounded in his temples. He should have never believed his half-brother. Zohra most definitely did not run itself.

His club manager had quit before she even started, he had hired a second-rate security company that allowed intruders, and his bartender had allowed guests to have whatever liquor they had wanted last night—far beyond the two-drink maximum. Unacceptable. Zohra had strict rules. It prohibited its members from being inebriated, and a two-drink maximum policy existed across all clubs. Consent and safety were as important to him as they were to Jackson. Booze messed with people's inhibitions—a recipe for disaster at a sex club.

He'd have to hire a new manager, new bartender, new security company… all before Zohra officially opened next week. Then he'd go home. His new job and his mentor's case required his immediate return. Playing sex club owner had worked out great for Jackson, but it wasn't for him. Today, he'd finalize his exit strategy.

But he had a bone to pick with Francesca No Name and her little sister first.

Nate debated calling her, but he doubted she gave him her real number. If she had lied about her link to the Morettis, what else had she lied about? Was that even her grandmother's apartment? Nate folded himself into his car and took off for Francesca's grandmother's neighborhood.

Pulling into a parking spot in front of the multistory structure, he climbed out of the Fiat. As he approached the building, an older man exited through the iron-latticed entrance, allowing Nate to slip through. He took the stairs two at a time, arriving in front of Francesca's grandmother's unit.

Impatient to get some answers, he rang the doorbell and knocked for good measure. When he heard the soft thump of approaching footsteps, anticipation that Francesca would answer crackled through him. The anticipation angered him. He wasn't excited to see her again. He was furious. She and her sister were in bed with the Morettis.

His heart thudded against his chest, and his skin burned. Maybe he was getting sick.

The door swung open—and he faced her.

Her eyes looked shadowed as they widened in recognition. She was dressed in the same jeans as last night, but wore a tight, white tank top. The high neckline didn't reveal even a shadow of cleavage, but the ribbed material molded to her slender frame like skin. His throat went dry. He struggled to swallow. It took every ounce of strength to drag his gaze back to her face.

Her hair, freshly washed and still wet, curled softly around her neck. A tiny drop of water from her tresses plopped onto her bare shoulder, clung precariously for one second, two, before sliding down her arm—her very injured arm.

Raw, angry slashes crisscrossed her skin from elbow to wrist as though she'd been whipped with something slim and mean. The welts had been slathered with some sort of balm; they looked to be healing, but still had a long way to go.

"What happened to you?"

She crossed her arms behind herself to hide the lesions and disregarded his question. "What are you doing here?"

Disturbed by the markings on her, he tried to remember why he was there. "You work for the Morettis."

Her nose scrunched up. "Who?"

"Don't play dumb. Giorgio just dropped off my phone. He saved a few photos."

"Who's Giorgio?"

So this was how she wanted to play it. "Where's your sister?"

"She's in the living room—wait!"

He ignored her outraged yelp as he strode past her.

Their grandmother's apartment was small, outdated. It could use a full-out demo. The old wood floor creaked under his weight as he found the living room. Worn furniture pressed up against one wall, facing a dinky TV across a muted rug. Windows, bordered by tulle curtains, had been flung wide open to let in the already too-hot morning breeze. The apartment was spotlessly clean, despite the fact that the furniture looked as though it hadn't been replaced in decades.

Isa glanced up at him from her spot on the couch, leaping to her feet as recognition hit. "What are you doing here?"

The teen annoyed him. He stopped in front of her, searched her face for telltale signs of lying. "You gave my phone to Giorgio Moretti. That's who paid you."

Her eyes darted away.

Guilty as charged.

"Is that true?" Francesca asked from behind him.

Isa glanced at her sister before meeting his gaze. "I don't know his name. He just paid me, okay?"

Frustration built at her lackadaisical response. "What did you think he'd want with my phone?"

"That wasn't any of my business."

The teen wasn't even sorry. The anger he'd kept at a simmer rose to a rolling boil.

He wanted to strangle the kid, but turned to face her sister instead. "I don't know how yet, but I will make you both pay for what you did."

Fear flooded Francesca's eyes as she stepped around him to join her sister.

Good. Let her be scared. He regretted hiring that useless security company for last night's party.

"You got nothing to say?" By now, he knew that Francesca always had something to say.

Mute, she shook her head.

He unclenched his jaw. "I have a lot going on right now. I have no club manager, no bartender, and now no security team. Dealing with the two of you on top of that—" He threw his hands up in the air.

Both women recoiled.

He froze.

What the hell?

He wasn't going to hit them. It was a gesture brought about by frustration.

Francesca regained her composure first. "Please leave."

"I didn't mean to scare you," he grumbled.

She motioned toward the door. "I think it's best you go."

"Wait," her sister exclaimed. "Did you say you have no manager or bartender? Hire us. We can do the job. How much do you pay?"

"Are you fucking insane?"

Francesca looked like she agreed with him. "Out of the question, Isa."

Isa ignored her sister. Her eyes, for once earnest, met his. "Look, I know we got off on the wrong foot. But Francesca would make a great manager. She's great with numbers. She's reliable, and she has a good work ethic. And I can learn to tend your bar! I've always wanted to mix drinks for a living."

His headache was back. He pressed his fingers to his temples. He needed to go.

"How much would it pay?" pressed Isa.

"I'm not hiring either one of you. You're lucky I didn't come back with an army of Carabinieri."

"Cessie, you know you can do this job easy," pleaded Isa, her eyes boring into her sister's.

Francesca looked torn, like a part of her wanted to send him on his way and never see him again, but a part found merit in her sister's idea. She glanced desperately between Isa and him.

"Well…" she began, as if realizing her sister was right, "if you are in need of a manager, I can do the job. I'll be real good at it, I promise. I can't find a job in town because I have very little work experience, and I don't speak Italian, and I have no degrees, but I am good with numbers and we really need the money."

"And I want to mix drinks," Isa piped up.

Francesca threw her sister a sidelong glance. "You're not bartending at a sex club."

"But you're okay with managing one?" he asked, curious. *Who were these two women? Why did they need funds so badly?* He studied their grandmother's place. Anyone who'd live here lacked the monetary ability to fix it up. Maybe that was why they were so desperate for jobs. Nate jerked his chin at Isa. "I'm not hiring her. But I'd be open to hiring you. You got a résumé?"

She shook her head. "Not an impressive one."

"You got ID?"

Her eyes lit up. "Yes! Yes, I do. Wait here." She rushed off down the hallway and disappeared through a door. She reappeared quickly, carrying a crisp American passport. "Here."

He took it from her. It looked so freshly printed, he expected the pages to still be warm. Her unsmiling face stared back at him. Her eyes in the photo looked anxious, startled, like it was the first passport photo she'd ever taken. His gaze lingered on her name. Francesca Brook.

"How much does a job like that pay?" she asked.

Detecting a quiver of uncertainty in her voice, he

glanced up at her from her passport. She needed the job, that was clear. Hope and apprehension mixed in her blue eyes, and her shoulders had risen all the way to her ears, like she was afraid he'd say no.

He dragged his eyes across the old apartment again, adding ten grand to the salary he'd offered his prior manager. Francesca looked like she could use the cash.

She drew in a sharp breath at hearing the amount. "However long the hours are, I'll do it."

"What about me?" asked Isa next to her.

"I don't want you anywhere near me or the club ever again," he told the teen. "In fact, that's a condition of your sister's employment."

"But… but… oh, all right! Fine. But you'll hire Cessie?"

He looked at Francesca. "Yes. You're hired."

She expelled all the air from her lungs on a whoosh. "I can start today."

"Good. We got a lot to do." He didn't let his gaze stray away from her face to rake over her body. Too dangerous. "Go change. I'll drive you in."

She didn't utter another word, just rushed back down the hall.

He didn't know what inspired him to offer her the job. He should haul them both to the local police station. Yet Francesca was a mystery that, since yesterday, had become like an itch to him. He needed to ferret out her little secrets, or he wouldn't rest.

Less than five minutes later, she emerged in a bright-orange dress that was ginormous on her. She had tied it up with a man's belt, but the belt was too big as well, and she had looped it around itself to hold it in place. Like yesterday's shirt, the sleeves hid her arms.

He wanted to drag her to her room, undo the belt, strip her of her oversized dress, and solve the puzzle she presented. Instead, he led the way to the front door, held it open for her. As she walked past him, his nose drew in the subtle lavender soap scent of her. His dick jumped. Maybe hiring her was a bad idea.

Chapter 5

Francesca tried to breathe through her nose as she sat next to Nate and he drove them back across the Tiber toward Zohra. In, out. Sloooowly. *Ignore how good he smells. That's not important.* Her heart raced regardless. He seemed so large and so male, taking up more than his share of the small car. It would be so easy to—

No. Not important. Focus on the priorities.

She had secured a job. She could hardly believe it. *Take that, Righteous Hearth!* Girls weren't allowed to study beyond the homeschool curriculum the Spiritual Leader deemed appropriate. Francesca had longed for school, but her parents had prohibited it. Now she had a job, and an income, and soon a way to get Sofia out of there.

Inside, doubts nibbled at her organs like caterpillars. What if Nate changed his mind? What if someone more qualified came along? What if she messed up and was fired before she could save up money to rescue Sofia?

He parked near Zohra, and she leaped out of the vehicle, ready to be the best club manager there ever was… even if she didn't quite know what the role entailed. Either way, she'd do everything she could to ensure he didn't regret hiring her. He'd offered her twice what any other job at her skill-level would, which would allow her to save the money twice as fast.

Nonna wouldn't have to use up her rainy-day savings on them. Now she herself would have an income. It seemed so surreal, she wanted to pinch herself.

"You know what a club manager does?" he asked as he walked alongside her to Zohra.

"I'm a fast learner."

He sighed, as though already regretting his decision. "First, you need to find a new security company. Zohra opens this Saturday, and the team last night won't cut it. Second, I'm going to interview a few new bartenders. I want your input. Zohra comes with strict rules, and I need someone who can stick to them."

"What kind of rules?"

"Two-drink maximum, for one. Not the rivers of champagne the guy yesterday was pouring." He flicked her a glance. "Other rules include condoms for any penetrative sex. All members undergo an extensive screening process, including background checks."

Panicked, she swallowed. If he ran a background check on her, would it notify her parents and the fiancé they forced on her to her whereabouts?

She must have stopped walking, because he paused and peered down at her. "Afraid I'll run a background check on you?"

Francesca didn't see the need to lie. "Yes."

"You on the lam or something?"

She opted for the truth. "I'd rather an ex doesn't track me here."

"Bad breakup?"

"He's… controlling. Won't take no for an answer."

"Is that who hurt you?" He indicated her covered arms with a jerk of his chin.

She shook her head. "No. And I'd rather not talk about that."

He looked like he was about to argue, then changed his mind. "Is your ex back in the States?"

"Yeah."

"He won't be able to access a secure background check."

"Just in case, I'd rather play it safe."

She could see the debate raging in his gaze.

"Fine. But I hire you legally. No under the table cash shit."

"That's fine."

He resumed his walk, letting her in through the side door. "You know how to use a computer?"

"I'm learning, but I've gotten pretty okay at it."

"Where the hell did you grow up? Who doesn't know how to use a computer?"

"My parents are… strict. We weren't allowed to use any technology."

He waved her through the now-familiar hallway toward what she assumed was his office. "I just bought a new laptop for the club manager who quit. You can use it. You hear of Microsoft Office?"

An instant rush of relief. "Oh yes, I've been watching YouTube videos about it on my phone."

Her response seemed to confuse him. "YouTube videos?"

"I… I don't own a computer to practice, and my grandmother's laptop is really old and doesn't have enough memory for Microsoft." She didn't add that Microsoft was an expense they couldn't afford right now.

"But I took real good notes from those videos, and I know it in theory." She hoped her voice sounded bright. Inside, she was dying of embarrassment.

He studied her closely, as if unsure whether she was serious. "Let's get the new laptop unpackaged. I'll show you some of the features. I'm not as good at Excel as my brother Hayes, but I'm much better than my brother Oliver."

Intrigued, she pried further. "How many brothers do you have?"

"Three. Jackson is the oldest. He's my half-brother—different dads. He's the one who founded Zohra. Has twelve clubs across seven countries—Zohra Rome is the thirteenth, and Italy is the eighth country."

"Are you the youngest?"

"No, that would be Oliver. He's an art historian. No need for Excel in his job. Is Isa your only sibling?"

A flash of panic scalded her. She couldn't lie to him about Sofia, but she didn't want to explain why they were in Italy without her. "Uh… I have a baby sister. She's ten. She's with my parents right now."

"Where at?"

"Back in the States."

It looked like he wanted to ask a follow-up but thought better of it.

He reached for a shiny white cardboard box that lay on top of the desk and pulled off the lid. Francesca studied his face as he focused on plucking the laptop from its moorings. No wonder Isa hadn't been able to stop looking at his photo in that magazine. He really was handsome, with chiseled cheeks and a sharp jaw. His eyes were a startling kind of blue—made more so by his raven-black hair and tan. She wished she had her charcoal and sketchpad with her. She'd like to map out the severe planes of his features, study how the curling locks of hair and sun-pinkened cheeks softened the angles of his face and made him look… approachable.

"Want to come over here?"

"Sure." And she stepped closer.

The citrus-fresh scent of him mixed with a male warmth she desperately liked. *It's just cologne. Nothing special.* She took an extra whiff regardless.

Nate pulled up a second chair to the desk, taking it while Francesca took the other. She tried to ignore his closeness as he showed her how to turn on the laptop, how to set and enter a password, and how to navigate the screen. He downloaded Microsoft Office and walked her through Word and Excel. Then he downloaded the platform Zohra used for tracking memberships, member dues, and member special requests, and they practiced creating and accessing records.

"Zohra employs offsite accounting, HR, and legal teams, so you don't need to know all that, though I do want you to have a contact at each department. I'll also connect you to the Zohra Paris manager, Noémie. She's good friends with Jackson and his wife, Evie, and is a good go-to for questions."

"All right," breathed Francesca, a little over-whelmed.

"Let me give you a tour now. Then we can email HR and ask them to get you into our system on Monday."

HR? Their system? That sounds traceable. "It's a secure database, right? No one will know I work here?"

Nate's face was sincere when he responded. "Absolutely. I wouldn't jeopardize your safety where your ex is concerned. Jackson had a crazy ex too—she did a lot of damage. I take that shit seriously."

She relaxed at his reassurance. "Thank you."

When Nate rose from his chair, her stomach gurgled. She had planned to hurry back to Nonna's apartment and eat lunch there, but lunch hour had long passed and she was starting to feel queasy. She'd have to spend what little cash she had left on a sandwich today, but that was okay. She had a job. A real job. A store-bought sandwich was the perfect way to celebrate.

"On second thought," said Nate, "let's go eat first. My treat."

"I can't allow that, I'm sorry."

His lips curved up in amusement. "You can't allow lunch?"

"For the lunch to be your treat," she clarified. Never again would she be indebted to someone.

"Why not? We're celebrating your first day."

"Be that as it may," she stood too, "I insist on paying for my own meal."

"As you wish. You like pasta? There's a local place nearby. A bit touristy, but the food's great. I usually have lunch there."

"I love pasta."

Francesca grabbed her bag and they walked the two blocks to the restaurant. The sweltering heat seemed to be multiplied by the buildings and cobblestones, and sweat beaded her temples by the time they arrived.

The café was tiny inside, but had plentiful outdoor seating that wrapped around the corner. They were shown to a shaded outdoor table set out on the cobbled street.

The waiter pulled out her chair. Sitting, Francesca drew the pristine white napkin onto her lap just as she'd read in the Emily Post book she'd gotten from the library, before Righteous Hearth had banned outside books. The waiter, who recognized Nate as a regular, slapped him heartily on the back and returned with a bottle of wine, pouring generous servings into both of their glasses before heading back inside the restaurant.

"His brother grows the grapes himself," said Nate. "It's pretty good. You like wine?"

Francesca hesitated. "I've only tried alcohol once."

"Really?" He looked intrigued. "Do tell."

"My friend, Haley, and I snuck some of the communion wine at church when we were fifteen or so. We had too much of it, then threw up behind the church building."

He chuckled. "What a rule breaker."

She picked up the glass by its stem, swirling around the garnet liquid. She brought it to her nose. A sharp, yeasty smell made her nose crinkle. She smelled it again, detecting the whiff of red berries. Before she could change her mind, she took a sip. A tangy-bitter taste hit her taste buds. "Oof," she said, her head retracting into her shoulders. "That was unexpected."

Nate, who watched her swallow the liquid with hot eyes, motioned for the waiter. "Can you bring her a glass of Lambrusco?"

"What's Lambrusco?" she asked, curious.

"It's a bubbly, sweet wine. Low alcohol. I think you'll like it better."

The waiter brought out a chilled glass of dark-purple wine that fizzed playfully at her as she sniffed it. She took a cautious sip. It didn't smell yeasty, and covered her tongue in effervescent sweetness. "Ooh," she said. "This is good. I like it."

"Better than altar wine?"

"Much." She took another sip. The bubbles unfurled

a gentle warmth through her chest and neck. She set down the glass. "What do you recommend for food?"

"They're known for their pasta. Get the four Roman pastas sampler. Try a bit of everything."

She peered at the menu. *Thirty euros?* That was much too extravagant. She scanned for the cheapest dish.

It was as though he'd read her mind. "Get the pasta. You'll like it. It's my treat to celebrate your first day at Zohra."

She didn't take handouts. She could afford her own lunch—granted, she couldn't afford a thirty-euro lunch, plus the wine—but she could pay her own way.

"I insist you take it out of my salary," she said.

"Don't be difficult. It's on me. What would you like to try?"

She couldn't help herself. She wanted to try the Roman pastas, but she'd pay for them herself. "I'll get the sampler."

Ordering such an expensive meal smarted, and she had to fight the panic that rose through her body as soon as the words left her mouth. *It's okay. You have a job now. You'll be paid a salary soon.* She'd figure it out, and she wouldn't let Nate pay. Keeping her independence meant more than all the money in the world combined.

Nate ordered the same. The waiter brought out the four pastas, presented in four perfect circles across a gleaming white plate, to each of them.

Amatriciana, cacio e pepe, carbonara, and gricia: she knew she should know the difference, but she only knew one. "What are they again?"

"Amatriciana is guanciale and tomato and cheese, cacio e pepe is cheese and black pepper, carbonara is basically cacio e pepe but they add egg and guanciale, and gricia is guanciale with black pepper and cheese."

Her mouth filled with saliva as she stared at the dishes. Isa and she had mostly been eating at home except for the occasional street-food treat. Nonna, when she was home, whipped up delicious dishes and Francesca was grateful for them, but nothing looked as good to her hungry stomach today as the four pastas in front of her.

She dug in.

***

Watching Francesca try the red wine for the first time had been more erotic than anything Nate had experienced in his life. Her single-minded focus on tasting it had sent every drop of blood straight to his dick. When she'd swallowed the liquid and then ran her tongue across her upper lip, he had to stop himself from leaping over the table to bite at her mouth.

She released a low moan of pleasure as she tried one of the pastas on her plate.

He almost bent the fork in his hand in half. *Where the fuck had this infatuation with her* eating *come from?* He stabbed his fork into his own pasta and swallowed it without tasting it.

After Padma left him, he only pursued double-jointed twins and double-D blondes. This strange, makeup-free creature in secondhand garb the color of waxed oranges didn't fit that pattern. She focused all her attention on her food, finishing everything on her plate. The strange craving he had for her had squeezed out his hunger for the al dente pasta.

He'd fallen hard for Padma—and almost destroyed his life. The reminder cooled him with the efficiency of a fire extinguisher.

He reached for his wallet and counted out the euros.

Seeing his intention to pay, she opened her tote. "I'm paying for myself."

Man, she is stubborn. "Put that away."

Her chin tilted up. "I appreciate you introducing me to this place, but I won't let you pay."

"It's just lunch."

"It's never just lunch." She pulled out a small wallet, counted out the correct bills, and set them on the table between them.

With a frustrated sigh, he tossed his own share on top of her euros.

"We should head back," he told her. "We have a lot to do. You have one week to get situated and then the club is yours to run. On Sunday, I leave for New York."

Chapter 6

The sun around them flashed even hotter.

"You go to New York on Sunday?"

How could she learn the ins and outs of club management in seven days? What if she messed up and ran it into the ground? She'd never find another job, and Sofia would be stuck.

Nate must have picked up on the panic that suffocated her. "Don't worry. You'll be fine. As Jackson once told me, Zohra practically runs itself."

She didn't believe that for a second. "Is that true?"

He chuckled. "No. But it does make one feel better, doesn't it? I fell hook, line, and sinker for that line."

He came around to pull out her chair. His sudden proximity heated her for a different reason.

"Why are you going to New York?" she asked as they weaved around the outdoor tables and returned to the cobblestoned path that would take them back to Zohra.

"I got my old job back—with a hefty promotion."

"What's your job?" The article Isa had found hadn't mentioned a profession.

"I'm a lawyer."

They passed a gurgling wall fountain; Zohra loomed just ahead.

Curious, Francesca glanced at him. "How does a lawyer from New York come to run a sex club in Rome?"

He met her curious gaze with a sardonic one. "Several unsound decisions."

After they returned to Zohra, Nate walked her through each layer of the database again until she felt comfortable navigating it herself. Once he was satisfied with her knowledge of the system, he took her on a prolonged building tour, ending at the base of the stairs.

"You did good today. Tomorrow, you focus on finding a new security company. I'll focus on the bartender. Divide and—" An incoming text message interrupted his train of thought. As he glanced down at the screen, a lock of dark hair fell over his tanned brow and he haphazardly swept it away.

Francesca's fingers twitched to sample the strands. She shook off the silly thought.

The flitting frown dissipated, and he returned his attention back to her. "Sorry, that was my brother Hayes. He's helping me look into something."

The man had a lot of siblings.

With a stabbing pain, she pictured Sofia's sweet face. How she missed her. Although she'd given Haley her phone number to share with Sofia for emergencies, she hadn't heard from her baby sibling. Maybe it was a good thing—maybe she was okay, and didn't need her and Isa yet. Maybe.

She glanced in the direction of the office, then back at him, itching to ask... *But what if he said no?* She couldn't risk coming off as unprofessional on her first day.

As though sensing her vacillate, he looked toward the office too. "What is it?"

Just ask him. "I don't want to come off as unprofessional…"

When she hesitated, he leaned closer. "Yes?"

Nope, can't do it. I can't ask him if I can bring the brand-new laptop home.

She shook her head. "What time should I be here tomorrow?" A much safer question.

He didn't seem to hear her at first.

"Nate?" she prodded.

He cleared his throat. "I'll pick you up at eight sharp."

Pick me up? "I'll get here by myself. The walk is only a half hour, and I like the scenery."

"Suit yourself. Be here by eight thirty. But I'm driving you home tonight. Wait here. I'll get you a copy of the keys, in case I'm not here when you arrive in the morning."

It was hard not to stare at his perfect posterior as he climbed the stairs.

Chapter 7

He was an idiot. For a moment, he had expected her to ask him to take her to the office and make some bad decisions together. Instead, she inquired about her work schedule. He had it bad, and he couldn't understand why.

Every time Francesca's intelligent eyes focused on him, all logical thoughts fled and images of taking her against any surface flooded his mind. Women tended to chase him, not the other way around. He'd chased Padma, though. From the moment he saw her in that restaurant, he'd wanted her. Charming, polished, pampered, she was beautiful arm candy he could show off at dinners with his firm's senior partners, but it became so much more.

Together with her little girl, they'd become a family. Until he came home to an empty apartment and one short note. She'd taken everything from him—the kid he loved as his own, the future he'd envisioned. Hell, she even took the cat.

He would never leave himself that open and stupid again.

After work, they drove back to Francesca's grandmother's in silence. She thanked him as she got out of the car, but refused his offer to walk her to the apartment. Gripping the wheel with enough pressure to yank it off, he forwent arguing with her, but his heart raced as he watched her disappear inside her nonna's building. He forced himself to drive away.

The sway of her hips had burned itself into his brain even as he navigated back over the Tiber, re-parked, and went to scout out a bar. Maybe meeting a woman would clear his head of the odd—and oddly tantalizing—Francesca Brook.

As he walked into the first bar he found, his phone rang. The screen reflected his half-brother's name.

"Yo," he answered, sliding onto a barstool. "How's Evie? She regret marrying you again yet?"

He could hear the smile in Jackson's voice. "She's doing great. How was the pre-launch party?"

Nate glanced around the bar. Because it was Sunday evening, the place looked abandoned. The bartender asked him for his order, and he pointed to a random beer on tap, shifting the phone to his other ear. "I can't wait to get back to my day job. How did you launch twelve clubs?"

"I was lonely and depressed and had nothing better to do."

The bartender brought him his beer. Nate curled his fingers around the cold pint and pulled it closer to himself. "I should have stuck to a vacation."

"Oh, I don't know," said Jackson. "Your dad's face when you told him about Zohra was pretty priceless."

"And karma bit me in the ass. The Moretti family keeps offering me their services."

Jackson cursed. "You're only telling me this now?"

"It gets worse. I cheapened out on the security team, and they let in some child who stole my phone and handed it off to the Morettis. Now Giorgio Moretti has pictures of my mole."

"You didn't delete those?"

"No," he bit out as Jackson sighed. "I didn't. I did hire a new club manager, though."

"What happened to Nicole?"

"She quit."

"Why?"

"Fuck if I know. She didn't tell me."

"Do you want me to fly in? I didn't think it would be this much trouble."

Jackson was in the middle of opening up his first nightclub in Vegas, a partnership with their brother Hayes. Nate wouldn't tear him away from that—or from his wife. "No. Zohra Rome is my responsibility. You have enough on your plate."

"Who's the new club manager? Where'd you find her?"

Nate took a long drag of the beer. Jackson wasn't going to like this. "The girl who stole my phone and gave it to the Morettis? It's her sister."

A pause. "I don't think I heard you correctly."

"No. You did."

"Are you out of your fucking mind?" Jackson's voice almost split his eardrum.

"Maybe."

"Fire her."

"I can't," said Nate, waiting for another explosion from Jackson.

His brother released a frustrated sigh. "Why not?"

"No one else will hire her, and she needs the money. She's pretty impressive. She doesn't own a computer, but she watched all these YouTube videos on how to use

Microsoft Office. She's actually pretty good from those videos alone. She watched them on her old, cracked phone." His brother didn't say anything for a long time. "Hello? You still there?"

"I'm still here."

"You're not saying anything."

"I've lost all words. Do me a favor. Send me her name. Let me run a background check on her."

"You can't do that. She has an ex she's avoiding. Doesn't want her location becoming public."

"I'll be discreet. I wouldn't endanger her that way."

Nate debated refusing, but deep down, he wanted to know all he could about his mysterious new hire. "I'm holding you to that. I gave her my word. Her name is Francesca Brook. I'll send you her Social as soon as she fills out the paperwork with HR on Monday."

"You hired her legally then?"

"I'm a rule follower, you know that."

Jackson chortled. "Yeah, a regular ole altar boy."

Nate took another sip of beer. "Did you know the only wine she's ever had was altar wine? She tried two different kinds at lunch today."

"Soooo, now you are dating her?"

"I'm not dating her. It was lunch between colleagues."

"She hot?"

Nate tried to keep his voice level even as his fingers on the pint glass tightened. "I didn't notice."

His brother knew him well enough to read between the lines. "She's hot."

"I'm gonna get back to my beer now."

"Don't make me come down there. Oliver told me about the car you drive. I won't get in a Fiat."

"It's eco-friendly and practical," ground out Nate.

"Just promise me one thing. Don't do anything stupid with your new club manager until I run her information."

"I wasn't going to do anything stupid with her in the first place."

***

"Cessie, come look!" Isa's voice reached her from the living room.

Francesca tore her gaze away from her phone, blinked to clear her dry eyes. She had been in her bedroom since Nate had dropped her off, working on a research project for Zohra. She set the cracked smartphone aside and rose from her narrow bed.

Her grandmother and Isa were sorting clothing items on the living room sofa. She had been so focused that she hadn't even heard Nonna return.

"What are these?" she asked, curious.

"Isa called me earlier and told me you got a job! I'm so proud of you. These are a gift—to celebrate," said Nonna. "You can't keep wearing my castoffs. Dante and I walked by a store that was going out of business and discounting everything, and I thought these might look good on you."

Francesca drank in the three professional summer dresses in white, gray, and navy, a couple of cotton button-downs, and tan slacks.

"I also found these there." Nonna pulled out a leather bag and sleek flats. "You can't wear your sneakers and bring that cloth tote with you to work."

"This is too much!" exclaimed Francesca, accepting the purse from her grandmother. "You shouldn't have. I'll pay you back."

"Don't be silly."

"And since you and I are pretty much the same size, I can borrow these dresses," added Isa.

"Any time you want," Francesca promised, stroking across the bag's supple leather. She turned to her grandmother. "Nonna, thank you. I love them."

"Go try them on," her grandmother encouraged.

When Francesca anxiously eyed the short sleeves on several of the dresses, her grandmother noticed.

"It's sweltering outside, Francesca. You can't keep covering up in this heat. Your tight sleeves are slowing the healing."

Wounds left scars. Francesca knew that better than anyone. The ones disfiguring her torso for so many years now would never go away.

The damage to her arms would never fully heal either, and she couldn't hide her arms forever. The Righteous Hearth had taken enough from her. This was her life. If she wanted to show her arms, she would.

"I'll go try them on," she said. "It really is hot in long sleeves out there."

Nonna smiled, pleased. "I'll go start dinner."

"We should make dinner," Francesca countered. "You do too much for us. Before Isa and I got here, you probably never cooked."

Nonna looked surprised. "What makes you say that? I cooked all the time."

"You barely recalled what herbs and spices you had." Isa laughed. "Remember? It took you forever to find a ladle that first night you made dinner for us. Cessie is right. We'll cook tonight. You go relax. We'll call you when the food is ready."

Nonna looked doubtful. "Don't burn down my kitchen."

Chapter 8

He woke thinking of her.

Of the way she danced in the office chair yesterday when she completed a successful Microsoft task or learned a new trick in the database. The easy way she'd grin, revealing slightly crooked teeth. Her delight at accomplishing even the most mundane tasks had warmed the room around them, and he'd wanted to take her in his arms and spin her around, to celebrate with her. Ridiculous.

At least Zohra would be in good hands with her. She was meticulous, intent on acquiring as much knowledge as possible to take over running the club next week. He could return to Manhattan without guilt, and focus on his mentor's case.

His morning alarm had yet to go off, yet he buzzed with curious energy. Francesca would be getting to the club in just a few hours—

Shit. He was anticipating spending another day with her. *Nip that in the bud, buddy.* He glanced down at the angry markings that puckered across his knuckles. A good reminder to not get attached to a woman ever again.

Vaulting off the bed, he jerked on his shorts and went for a run. Maybe he could sweat Francesca out.

He'd screwed over his life because of a woman once. He wouldn't make that mistake again.

This early, the tourists still slept in their hotel rooms, leaving the Roman streets quiet and empty. Locals walked their dogs, strolled to work, stopped at a panetteria. The air smelled fresh and clean, yet to be soiled by the car smog that would soon fill the streets. Right now, before rush hour, the fresh air and car-free silence reigned. He'd miss this memory of Rome when he was back in Manhattan and the clogging traffic there.

***

Francesca woke before sunrise, assembled a sandwich to take with her to work, pulled on her new navy dress, tried not to think about the ugly, exposed wounds on her arms, and speed-walked to Zohra as the climbing sun bathed the Eternal City in shimmering gold.

She had a good few hours before her shift at Zohra started, and she hoped to use the laptop until then. She hadn't felt comfortable asking Nate if she could take it home with her last night, but her grandmother's computer was a decade old and she could really use a newer version so she could a) compile a list of possible attorneys to help her fight for Sofia and b) continue studying for her GED.

Although she had found a list of free sites online that would allow her to practice for the test, they downloaded slow on her grandmother's laptop and her eyes burned if she stared at the small screen of her phone for too long. She hoped Nate wouldn't mind her arriving early to borrow the work computer for a few internet activities.

Inserting the key into the side door lock, she tiptoed to the office. Nate's room was on the floor above, and she didn't want to wake him this early in case he was a light sleeper.

She slid into the leather chair and opened the laptop, stifling a yawn. She'd catch up on sleep later, after she got Sofia out of the Righteous Hearth and herself and her sisters situated.

***

As Nate looped back to Zohra, he debated hitting the gym, but weightlifting could wait. He had a bartender to hire. Reaching the club, he pulled open the main door and jogged up the stairs to his room to shower.

As he stood under the pounding water, images of Francesca churned through him. He wondered what she was doing right now, probably all tousled and asleep in her bed. He saw her naked, lying across her mattress, her hair loose and tangled around her. He wanted her naked in *his* bed, her eyes glazed with need as he filled her. He fisted his dick in increasingly rough jerks, his scarred hand flying. His groan filled the glass-and-stone walls of the shower as he came thinking of her.

Drying off, he stomped to the sink and reached for a razor, disturbed by his odd fascination with Francesca. Too distracted to escape the shave unscathed, he pulled on his boxers and jogged downstairs to the kitchen.

The espresso machine hissed as it expressed his double shot.

He smelled lavender. Impossible. Now his mind was playing tricks on him. And yet the scent was there, faint but present, and stronger when he followed it to his office.

***

Having completed the social studies portion of the GED practice exam, Francesca jotted down topics she needed to learn into her notebook, frustrated with herself and her lacking education. Next, custody attorneys—

"What are you doing here so early?"

Nate's voice jolted her out of her chair.

Her eyes flew to his face… but didn't stay there.

He must have just taken a shower. His hair looked towel-dried, sticking up in every direction in damp spikes. He'd shaved, but nicked himself. A teeny, tiny piece of tissue clung to the sharp edge of his jaw, a little droplet of blood visible through it.

Oh boy, he was naked from the waist up again. It was official—she'd never seen such a collection of muscle on anyone before; they rippled under his tanned skin as he shifted. She followed the trail of dark hair from his belly button to his boxers. His erection was unavoidable. She gasped, her eyes flying back to his face.

"Sorry," he grumbled, voice strained, and sank into the chair in the corner of the room by the door. "Not immune to this kind of perusal."

"I didn't mean to—I—" Her face burned hot, and her tongue turned thick and lazy. Knees wobbly, she plopped back into the desk chair, and finally closed her mouth.

He studied her for a beat too long, his eyes predatorial as they skimmed down her face to the modest cut of her new dress. Her heart almost cracked open a rib at the intensity in his face.

Finally pausing his survey, he lifted his cup and took a sip before repeating his earlier question. "Why are you here so early?"

The coffee's drugging aroma mixed with the by-now familiar scent of him in the small space. Every inhale sent tension to her private parts. She wiggled in the chair.

"I came early to… to use the laptop. I hope that's okay."

"Of course." The rigidity in his face loosened and his gaze turned curious. "Whatcha using it for?"

He deserved to know. It was, after all, his laptop. "I took a practice GED test."

His brows drew together. "Why?"

She swallowed. Her cheeks burned again, but she shouldn't be embarrassed. It wasn't her fault her parents had restricted her studies.

"I want to go to college. And… the way I grew up, my parents homeschooled, and there were no grades, and it's hard to get into college without a high school diploma or transcripts. I can apply through admission by exception, but I also don't know anything, and I want to learn. I'll start at community college, but I want my GED before that, so I'm practicing."

She'd surprised him, that was clear. He looked like he had a treasure trove of questions bouncing around his brain.

"I didn't realize. That's very admirable."

Needing something to do with her hands, she reached for one of the bobby pins in her hair, tugged it out, twisted it between her fingers. Although she'd worn her hair down today, she still hadn't managed to stomach being without at least one bobby pin. His eyes followed the markings on her arms.

She held them up so they faced him. "You're curious."

"I'm disturbed—they look painful."

Resettling her arms in her lap, she met his fuming

gaze, wished to clear it of the anger and the pity. "They throb a little sometimes when I think about them too much, but they barely hurt anymore. I'd prefer if we don't discuss them. It's done, it's over. I'm free." The smile that began to tug at the corners grew, widened, as realization thrummed through her. She really *was* free. And soon, she'd free Sofia. "And I'm in Rome—and I have a job. I'd rather focus on all the good things."

The pity in his eyes lessened, but the anger remained. "Where's the person who hurt you?"

She tucked the bobby pin back into her hair where it belonged. "It doesn't matter, because I'm here." Her eyes strayed to his chest again. She forced them away from the span of sinewy muscle and concentrated on his face. "How did *you* find yourself in Italy?"

He rearranged himself in the chair. "Bad breakup. I needed a change, so I quit my job. I took Zohra on as a hobby—and as a little fuck-you to my father. Jackson said Zohra would occupy a couple of hours a week, tops. He was wrong." He drained the rest of his coffee. "I won't leave you stranded. I'll check in on you from New York—we'll hire more help, if you need, but I have to get back."

The guilt sidled in, slow but steady. Should she tell him that she couldn't stay in Italy long, that she had to return to Nevada for her sister as soon as she had the means to do so? Clearly, he needed the club off his shoulders. What if he replaced her with someone who could take Zohra off his plate forever? She couldn't chance that kind of setback.

"I don't believe you took this place on as a hobby," she said instead.

Nate's gaze fastened to hers, as if surprised by her

statement. "Jackson found his calling when he started Zohra over a decade ago. He was pretty lost and adrift then. I thought, just maybe, if I help launch an offshoot of it, I could find my bearings."

"Did it work?"

He laughed. "In a way. It was a break, and it reinforced that I like my day job." He stood, his face determined. "And I'm glad to be getting back to it. Someone very close to me got hurt. I intend to prevent what happened to Steven from happening to others in the future."

The anguish etched in his features gutted her. She swallowed the lump in her throat. "What happened?"

He stalked to the door, hovered there as he faced her. "I had a professor at community college years ago—he changed my life. Last year, when he was teaching a class, a student shot up the place. Steven stood between the gunman and his class, wouldn't let him through the door, and no one but him got hurt."

Her hand flew to her mouth. "Nate, that's horrifying. Is he okay?"

"He recovered—almost fully. But I will make Clary Guns fold. They marketed their weapons illegally, and I can prove it. Steven had his pick of attorneys, but he chose me. He won't regret it."

The constriction in her throat eased. "He's lucky to have you. Do you want to leave before the official launch?"

"I'll stay here for the launch. I promised Jackson, and I'll see it through." He looked like he wanted to say more. She could see his thoughts flying, but his face was set. "I won't let Zohra Rome fail, but I have to get back to New York."

"I understand. I admire it." But the reminder that she'd soon run the club by herself sent a stitch of anxiety through her. If she had limited time with him, they better make the most of it. "What's on our schedule today? Since I'm here early and you've had your coffee, we might as well get started."

Nate answered her question with one of his own. "You eat yet?"

"I brought a sandwich with me."

"I'm starving. You stay here and study. I'll make breakfast."

Her eyes glued to his butt as he walked away. Catching herself, she dropped her head into her hands and sighed. She could not be lusting after Nate Icefall. He'd be gone next week, and she had more pressing matters to consider—like getting Sofia away from the Righteous Hearth.

***

Nate went upstairs to layer up. Her slow perusal of him had sent every drop of blood to his dick, and kept it there. As much as he enjoyed the feel of Francesca's hungry gaze on him, walking around with a throbbing erection would not be professional.

Angry at himself for his reaction to her, when his every focus needed to be on moving Zohra from his plate to hers this week, Nate returned to the kitchen and reached for a metal bowl.

He cracked eggs into it one after the other, chipping away at the unbridled frustration churning inside. Francesca Brook was a distraction—one he couldn't indulge. He had no room for her in his life—the life he missed, the one he'd struggled to achieve. The one he'd almost destroyed.

He reached for a knife, plucked an onion from the small stash he'd bought for his own personal use. Peeling away its red skin, he slid the blade through its pink-white flesh, splitting it in half, then took to mincing the pieces.

As though his whole body had become attuned to her every move, he felt her approach before he heard her footfall. She stepped inside the kitchen, her gait uncertain. The navy dress skimmed just above her knees, but man, she had hot knees. Her legs were smooth and muscular, and he wanted to lift the modest skirt and put his head between them. The sharp sting of the knife scored his finger.

"Ow. Fuck." He glanced away from Francesca's knees to stare at the blood that dripped from his hand, splattering the onions.

She hurried toward him. "Are you okay?" Cutting right between him and the metal counter, she grasped his hand in hers. "Let me see."

He fought her sudden proximity. He didn't want to see the Mediterranean play in her eyes, to smell the lavender on her skin. The blood continued to spurt.

"Oof, it's deep," she said. "Rinse it under the tap, so we can see what we're dealing with. You may need stitches."

"I'm not getting stitches. It's just a scratch."

"A scratch? Any deeper and you'd have sliced off your finger. Go wash it. And use soap."

He trudged to the sink. The cut stung as the water hit it, more so when he lathered it with soap. Francesca studied the wound over his elbow, keeping enough of a distance to not touch any inch of him. Perversely, he wanted to step into her, to feel her against him. He rooted himself in place. "See? It's nothing."

"Here." She gently took his sliced hand into hers.

The blood continued to gush, but the water had cleared it enough for them to see that the wound wasn't deep enough for stitches.

Stepping away, she pulled a clean kitchen towel off a rack and brought it to him. "Use this. I'll go get Band-Aids."

"They're in the office. Bottom desk drawer."

When she hurried away, he released the breath he was holding, his heart pounding at the brief contact of her hand on his. This sealed it. He needed to get laid. He'd get to it tonight. Maybe he'd call the Lee twins. Double the fun. Anything to work this craving for Francesca out of his system.

She returned quickly, a small box of bandages in hand.

He reached for the box. "I got it."

"You can't bandage yourself one-handed." She kept the box securely in her grasp.

"Of course I can. Did it my whole life."

"Well, not today. Untwist the towel. Let me see if the bleeding slowed."

"It has. It's fine." He didn't know why he sounded grumpy. All she was trying to do was help, but he couldn't handle her nearness. She was all soft and sweet-smelling and he wanted to tangle his fingers in her hair and kiss her. Unacceptable.

"We don't have all day, Nate. Don't be a difficult patient."

He huffed out a reluctant breath but gave her his towel-wrapped hand. She unpeeled the towel with nimble fingers.

His bleeding had tapered by the time she revealed the cut. She studied the wound from every angle, her entire body focused on the slash. He liked her single-minded attention. His dick hardened at having her so close. His fingers curled to keep himself from reaching for her.

"Easy, relax your hand," she chided. "Hold it like that, and I'll apply the Band-Aid."

She tugged one out of the box and attached it securely to his finger. After another inspection, she reached for a second one.

"In case you bleed through." Satisfied with her work, she stepped away from him.

Nate fought to swallow. His throat didn't seem to be working; it felt all thick and scratchy.

"Thanks," he managed.

She glanced at the blood-speckled onions. "Let me clean that up. Go sit at the bar in the ballroom. I'll bring breakfast to you."

There was no place to sit in the kitchen, and he wasn't ready to leave her presence yet. He leaned his hip against the metal countertop. "I can help."

"I don't need your DNA all over my food."

He could think of a few places on her where he'd like to leave his DNA. His erection became painful. He turned away, reaching for the ruined onions.

"I got it." She settled her hand on his arm, and they both froze at the contact. He counted three beats before she dropped her hand. "If you don't want to sit, go stand over there while I finish breakfast."

He didn't argue, distracted by the warmth of her touch that had branded his skin.

When he took a few steps back to give her room to move, she made quick work of cleaning up his mess.

Grabbing a fresh onion, knife, and chopping board, she turned to him. "What do you want in your eggs?"

He struggled to focus. "Your choice."

Her eyes lit up.

God, she was beautiful.

"How about onions and mushrooms? Where're the mushrooms?"

"I'll get them," he offered, bringing them to her from the fridge.

Picking up the onion, she started peeling. "What's it like living here? It's such a large building. Is it ever unnerving?"

He leaned back against the metal surface of the counter. "Not really. It's spacious and quiet. Gave me some space to think."

Expertly, she heated the pan on the stove, added olive oil, and tossed in the chopped onions, mushrooms, and spices, then added the eggs. He watched her work, fascinated by the way she moved, graceful like a wild cat. A tiny trail of freckles ran up the back of her thigh, disappearing under her skirt. *How far up did the trail lead?* He fought the urge to kneel behind her, lift her skirt, and run his lips along the freckles.

He couldn't remember the last time he wanted a woman this badly. Maybe it was his impending return to Manhattan, to the apartment he'd once tried to make a home.

Whatever it was, he couldn't act on it. Francesca would never be okay with a hookup, and he didn't want anything but. He was still picking up the pieces from his last relationship.

Tearing his gaze away from her legs, he took a step to his favorite purchase—the espresso machine.

"Want coffee?" He hoped she couldn't tell that his voice had thickened to mud.

"Please." Ever polite.

He busied himself with the espresso maker. The steam hissed as it expressed the coffee, and the sweet, nutty scent filled the sterile space.

"I've never been to Manhattan," she offered as the silence stretched. "But it's on my list of places to see."

Who was *this girl?* The urge to unscramble her like a jigsaw puzzle whirred within him. "Where'd you grow up?"

She studied the omelet with more interest than it warranted. "Near a small town in Nevada called Rose Falls. It's not much. Very remote."

It was more than she'd revealed to him before. "Your parents and little sister are there now?"

Her face shuttered. "I think so."

Refusing to see her as anything more than his club manager, he moved the subject to safer grounds. "What other places are on your list?"

"In the States or here?"

When her gaze met his, he got lost in the lavender shift just beneath the blue.

Belatedly, he replied, "Both."

"Manhattan, Los Angeles, and Chicago in the States. In no particular order." A hopeful smile broke across her face. "Maybe I'll even move to one of those someday."

"You've never been to LA? It's close to Nevada."

She shook her head. "Never."

"My brothers and sister-in-law live in Nevada, and they drive over to LA when they need a break from the heat for a weekend."

Her face turned wary. "You have family in Nevada?"

"Yep. In Henderson, near Vegas."

"Henderson is about an hour from Rose Falls, but I've never been." She reached for a spatula. "Eggs are ready. Want to eat at the bar?"

He wanted to eat her. It would be so easy to step into her personal space, lift her to the countertop and—

"Nate?" she prodded.

What did she just ask him? Oh, right. "Yes, let's eat at the bar. Here, I'll take the plates over."

After she portioned out the eggs, he took the dishes to the solid oak bar-top in the ballroom while she brought the cutlery.

"I'll go grab our coffee. What do you want in yours?" he asked.

"Milk, please."

He assembled their coffees, splashing steamed milk into both their cups. Maybe the caffeine from his second coffee of the day would take his mind off Francesca.

When he returned, she stood by the bar, waiting for him. The neckline of her dress didn't dip low, but he yearned to trace along the edge, to feel the weight of her breasts. Placing the coffee on the polished surface, he slid her cup over to her, careful to keep his distance.

She took her food and coffee to the farthest chair at the bar, far away from him.

Good. He didn't want to sit close enough to smell the lavender soap on her skin.

She'd left her hair loose today, and it curled around her neck, teasing her shoulders, highlighting the perfect cut of her jaw. The strands looked silky soft, shot through with gold where the sun grazed them most often. He fought the compulsion to run his fingers through the loose curls and feel them wash over him, to bury his nose in her hair and see whether it smelled of lavender too.

Her eyes fastened on his right knuckles. It took several beats before she asked the question. "How'd you get the scar?"

The tight tissue pulled as he stretched out his hand. "Punched a mirror."

Her face blanched at his curt answer, perhaps at the mention of violence. Someone had hurt her in the past—had made her sensitive to sudden movements and talk of hitting.

Despite wishing to keep the story private, he hastened to explain. "I was alone at my apartment. I was angry, and I punched a mirror."

"Do you get angry enough to punch something often?" She set aside her fork, scooting a smidge farther away.

"That was the one and only time."

Her wary eyes met his. "Someone must have made you really mad."

Fuck. He didn't want to get into the details, but she looked terrified of him now, and he didn't like it. "I was mad at myself."

"Did it have something to do with your breakup?"

"It had everything to do with it."

"What happened?"

He wanted to offer a shallow rejoinder, but the violent visual had alarmed her, and he had to dispel the conclusions she'd reached.

"I dated Padma for two years. She had a little girl, Sammy—the coolest kid. Sammy was three when I started seeing her mother. She and Padma moved in with me. I figured I'd propose eventually, and we'd get married."

"Did she end it?"

That was one way to put it. "Yeah. She did. Really took me aback. I worked a lot—I had a goal of making partner within seven years of starting at the firm, and I did. Just before Sammy turned five. I was in the middle of a big case—long hours, little sleep—but it was Sammy's fifth birthday the following week, and I planned to take a few days off around then to take them on an adventure, so I frontloaded the work."

Unsure whether or not to continue when he hadn't provided the details of his breakup even to his brothers, he stopped. Francesca didn't rush him, just watched him with wide, compassionate eyes.

"That was thoughtful of you," she encouraged as the silence stretched.

Padma would disagree. Taking a deep breath, he told her the rest. "I came home late one evening a few days before her birthday, and they were gone. Padma scribbled one sentence on a Post-it, telling me we were over. I tried to call, text. Hell, I even downloaded social media to message her. She blocked me everywhere. Cut me out without an explanation."

Her gorgeous eyes rounded as horror dawned. "That's awful."

"So yes, I was angry. Shocked. Sleep-deprived. I loved her, and she left me without a conversation—and took the kid I began to think of as my own with her. I never saw it coming. So I punched out my hall mirror."

Their relationship was a chimera. A mirage. She'd moved in with some real estate asshole several months later, he'd learned. He'd been an idiot to believe she ever loved him.

God, he missed Sammy, though. Did she ever ask

about him? Did she wonder why he wasn't there to keep her safe during the thunderstorms she hated? Who carved her apples into flowers now? It was the only way she'd eat them.

The memory of her slashed through him, drew fresh blood, fresh pain. Reaching for his coffee, he let the warmth seep through his chilled body.

Climbing off her barstool, Francesca crossed to him, but he couldn't handle being touched right now. Especially by her. He put up his hand. "I don't need a hug." The phrase came out brusquer than he had intended.

She swallowed and hurried back to her seat. "I'm sorry, Nate. I'd have punched a mirror too."

He didn't know what prompted him to continue, to share more with her than he had with anyone else. "I didn't get out of bed for days. I was depressed, couldn't focus on work. My clients deserved better. So I quit. Figured I'd go to Italy or something. My father called me a loser."

Sympathy softened her features. "Whoa, that is *rotten*."

"Eh, that's Dad. But I wasn't in the mood. He's always had issues with Jackson—a reminder to him that my mother was married before. So, I decided to help the stepson who irritates him launch a sex club in Rome. Call it childish, but I found it amusing at the time." He tore his gaze away from her, dug into his omelet. He didn't have it in him to continue the conversation. "You need a few more hours to study?"

She reached for her coffee, letting him change the subject. "I'm done for the morning. Thank you for letting me use the laptop."

"Take it home tonight, so you're not walking the streets at the butt crack of dawn just to use it here."

Her face exploded in a smile. "Really? Thanks! That is so nice of you to offer. It would really help me if I could study in the evenings, after work."

"I can research security companies this morning to take that off your plate."

She hopped down from the barstool and disappeared in the direction of the office. Returning with her notebook, she flipped it open and set it in front of him. "I did the research last night. These are the top three security companies that I found most reputable and recommended. I think we should go with this one. It's smaller, woman-owned, in business fifteen years, and has testimonials from real clients. I verified."

He pulled the notebook closer. "You researched last night?"

"Yeah. On my phone. I've reached out to all three companies just in case, and received quotes from two already, including the one I think we should go with."

Did she never sleep? He studied her thorough notes. "Impressive. We'll go with your top choice."

Her face turned serious. "I don't really know how to look for bartenders though."

"I listed the position last night. Already got a few applications, but not what I'm looking for."

Taking back her notebook, she hugged it close to her chest as she contemplated his statement. "Maybe more will apply."

"There's a mixology lounge I've been hearing buzz about." He popped a slice of mushroom into his mouth. "I'm going to check it out tonight, see if I like the drinks. Maybe I can convince the bartender to come work here."

"That sounds like a good plan."

Yes, yes, it was. He'd use the opportunity to go pick

up a woman. This craving for Francesca had to stop. "I have a call with marketing in a half hour. Want to join it?"

"Sure," she responded brightly. "I've never been a part of a business call before."

He wondered what else she hadn't done before. Dark, lustful thoughts surged through him as he watched her drain her coffee. His fingers twitched to expose her to all the things she hadn't tried yet.

"You'll have a few today," he managed to squeeze out. "HR is next, then Memberships."

And then he'd go get himself laid.

Chapter 9

After their call with Memberships concluded, Francesca stayed in the office to review her notes and map out her work plan for the week. Because many Zohra members were in Europe for vacation, the upcoming opening night had already reached full capacity. It was up to her to memorize each member's likings so Zohra Rome could deliver a good experience for them. She logged into the database to learn more about the registrants when Nate popped his head into the office.

"Delivery is here," he said, an undertone of challenge in his gaze. "Come see this."

Intrigued, she followed him to the side door to find four columns of boxes, taller than even Nate, piled against the wall.

"What'd you order?"

He lifted the top box from the stack nearest him. "I can show you, but you'll blush."

She took a step closer anyway.

Plunking himself down on the stone floor, he tore open the box to reveal neatly stacked packages of... handcuffs?

"Adult toys," he explained, glancing up at her with

80

a grin. "They were supposed to arrive by last Saturday but got held up in customs. We got handcuffs, vibrators, lube… all sorts of goodies. Merry Christmas, Zohra."

He was right. She was blushing. She didn't know what drew her to ask, "Have you tried any of these?"

His voice dropped to a suggestive rumble. "Want me to show you my favorites?"

Imprudently, she did. Images of Nate using the items he'd mentioned on her flashed through her mind in scorching detail. She shifted against the deluge of heat between her legs, struggled to slow her breath.

Once she trusted herself to speak, she changed the subject. "I'll help you get these unpacked and organized. Where do you want them?"

His eyes turned feverish and glassy as he watched her, and he didn't answer. When she repeated the question, he leaped to his feet. "I got it."

"No, there are a ton of boxes. I'll help." Taking a step closer to him made him take two steps back. Halting, she motioned to the boxes around them. "We should inventory them, so we know when we run low."

His exhale sounded pained. "Stay over there."

Moving to the box farthest away from her, he tore it open.

Francesca, who'd never even seen a sex toy before, found herself handling and organizing an array of items: colorful vibrators of all shapes and sizes, a selection of lubricants, silk blindfolds, masks, feather-tipped rods that Nate had called ticklers, and linked silicone beads Nate refused to explain.

He'd become very quiet as they sorted the items. Never once did he look at her. When she asked him questions, he answered in as few strangled words as possible.

After they sorted and distributed the toys to the rooms, Nate flattened the boxes and set them by the side entrance. She forced herself to look away from the play of muscles under his shirt as he set the last cardboard against the wall.

Only then did he face her. "I'm going to lunch."

But when she passed by him on her way to their office, he caught her hand.

Her heartbeats scattered. His skin felt warm and smooth against hers, the gentle hold sending tiny electric shocks to activate her nerve endings.

He had beautiful eyes, light turquoise surrounded by a dark blue-gray, framed by long, dark lashes. This close to him, she could see little flecks of gold just around his pupils. Her lungs struggled to work. Suddenly light-headed, she concentrated on the wall beyond him.

As if feeling the same electric hum, he dropped her hand and gave her a wide berth as he slipped out the side door.

Hours later, eyes burning from staring at the laptop, Francesca checked the time at the corner of the screen. Almost dinnertime. She needed to get home. Nonna would have made something hearty and tasty, and her stomach clenched in anticipation.

Leaning away from the desk, she closed the computer just as Nate strolled through the open door. He'd been avoiding her since they'd organized the plethora of sex toys earlier and he'd gone out for lunch. She didn't even know how long he'd been back.

"I stopped by the mixology lounge after lunch." He halted in front of the desk. "Bartender was great and is interested in coming to work at Zohra. Want to join me and check him out? He said he'd prepare a few sample drinks for us to try."

For us to try?

"You want me to go with you?" she clarified, in case she'd misunderstood.

"I'd appreciate your opinion. I'm a beer and wine guy. Not a cocktail fan. Figured you can tell me if you like them."

"I don't really drink, remember?"

He shrugged, as though it was no big deal, but the anticipation in his gaze disputed his tepid appearance. "We'll have him make nonalcoholic ones."

Nevertheless, she hesitated. "When would you want to go?"

"How about now?"

She craved to accept, to go with him and try fun drinks and spend a little more time in his company. He drew her to him like an exceptionally vibrant flower drew a bee, but she couldn't take him up on his offer. She had to cut through the imprudent undercurrent vibrating between them. Maybe the tension was a figment of her imagination, a chemistry she spun solely in her head, but she needed to make it stop.

"I can't. My grandmother made dinner."

She must have imagined the disappointment in his face. Wishful thinking.

"What about after dinner?"

Her tongue wouldn't form the word *no*, though it would have been a wiser answer. "That would work."

His slow smile held a predatory edge. "I'll drive you to your grandmother's."

Uncomfortable with the excitement his offer propelled through her, she shook her head. "No, thank you. It's a nice day and I've been indoors all day. I'll walk."

He looked like he wanted to offer to walk with her, but held off. "I'll pick you up at eight."

***

Nate watched her slip out the side door. Did he just ask her out? What in the hell was he thinking?

He had to return to Manhattan, not start an affair with an employee. That's what she was, for all intents and purposes. Making anything more of it was a legal disaster waiting to happen. Yet when he'd gone to the mixology lounge a few hours earlier, all he could focus on was how much Francesca would love the view from there, and how much he longed to share it with her.

He'd gotten used to a certain lifestyle—being a partner at a big law firm had afforded him access to expensive restaurants and exclusive clubs, and Padma wouldn't settle for anything less. They were places to be seen, and she liked showing off.

But the experiences he'd started to overlook captivated Francesca. He liked seeing the world through her eyes. It brought back a spark of something he'd lost a long time ago.

His phone buzzed with a text from Jackson asking Nate to call him. Before Nate could dial his brother, an echo of footsteps from the ballroom had him turning his head. Slipping the phone into his pocket, he strode down the hall to see who the hell was at Zohra now.

He encountered the back of a well-dressed stranger.

The uninvited guest ran his finger along the velvet nap of a nearby sofa before he turned and faced Nate. His closely shorn white hair clung to a receding hairline and clashed with his dark, bushy brows. The dark-blue blazer he wore looked bespoke, made of fabric the exact color of his bow tie. The creases in his tanned skin deepened as he smiled.

"We're closed," Nate said in Italian.

"I know," the man replied in English. "You'd be closed a lot longer if Frascati didn't step in. Got your items released from customs. Stopped that inquisition into your liquor license."

"There was no inquisition into my liquor license."

"Because Frascati took care of it."

Nate narrowed his eyes. "You linked to the Morettis?"

"Those coke pushers?" The older man chuckled. "No, most decidedly not. You need anything, you holler."

"I won't need anything."

"You will. The Morettis are rabid dogs. Frascati can send them to the pound for you. I left my number on the bar. Call me when their mouths get all"—he motioned with his fingers in front of his face—"foamy." The man cast another glance at the couch. "Who designed the sofas? Been looking for something similar."

"I don't recall. You need to go."

The stranger didn't argue. "I'm late for dinner as it is. You remember the designer, you text me."

I've got to start locking the front door.

When the Italian left, Nate pulled out his phone and called Jackson in a belated response to his brother's earlier text.

His brother didn't bother with pleasantries. "You sitting down?"

Nate groaned. "What now?"

"I'm going to email you what I got back on your new club manager."

"Shit. Tell me."

"Read the report. Then call me back." His brother promptly hung up.

Nate downloaded the file, sinking onto the couch as it opened on his phone. His eyes skimmed down the copious paragraphs.

"Fuck." He dialed Jackson back. "What the hell kind of mess did I get myself into?"

Chapter 10

Although ten minutes still remained until eight o'clock, Francesca came downstairs early to wait for Nate in front of her grandmother's building. The sun had yet to set, and the evening gleamed warm and bright around her as she waited for Nate's Fiat. He seemed like the punctual type, and she didn't want him meeting her at Nonna's apartment.

Nonna had already asked too many questions, wondering why Francesca had to work late, how getting drinks at a lounge counted as work, and why Francesca hadn't invited Nate Icefall to dinner, as she'd made plenty of food. The last thing Francesca needed was for Nate to show up at Nonna's door, all tall and handsome. Her grandmother would immediately suspect it was more than work. And it wasn't. It couldn't be. This job was too important to her to get distracted.

Francesca had momentarily debated swapping out her simple navy dress for one more suited to a lounge, but she'd opted not to. It was a business excursion, nothing that necessitated her to gussy up. She did wrap a light shawl she'd borrowed from Nonna around her arms—unsure whether or not her wounds would be seemly at a mixology lounge, she'd erred on the side of caution.

A smudge of red appeared in the distance. As she had expected, he was early.

He pulled over at the curb right next to her, and she climbed inside before he could jump out.

I always forget how good he smells.

He waited for her to buckle up. "Ready?"

She nodded because the familiar scent of him curled through her, making it difficult to answer.

The small space seemed consumed with his large frame, and Francesca knew that she should press herself as far into her door as she could to avoid accidentally grazing him. Instead, she found herself shifting closer until her elbow brushed his on the center console between them. She let it rest there, expecting him to readjust, but he didn't. They both stayed that way, their arms touching, her heart hammering.

Even through the layer of cotton his button-down provided, the feel of him sent a flash flood of desire through her. How could he continue to have this effect on her, when she knew so much better?

Nate kept his gaze locked on the road as he navigated the Roman streets. When he turned at the Colosseum, Francesca stared. Even though she'd never been inside the Colosseum, she had circled it on foot with her sister during their first few days in Rome, when they had explored the city. Now, in the setting sun, its glow seemed ethereal, as though lit by the magic of Roman gods.

Nate pulled up to the front entrance of a five-story hotel just across the street from the historic amphitheater.

Francesca, hungrily drinking in the Colosseum's magical lines, didn't notice that Nate had jogged around to her side of the car until he opened her door and offered his hand.

Despite her better judgment, she took it, letting his warmth engulf her.

He didn't let go of her hand as he directed them toward the hotel, making it hard to focus on anything else but him.

"It's in here?" she asked as they reached the main entrance, surprised that her voice remained steady.

He nodded, his fingers tightening on hers as he encouraged her to precede him inside. "On the top floor."

They took the elevator to the rooftop restaurant. As the doors pinged open, they stepped into the excited chatter of voices and din of silverware. The place was packed, especially for a Monday night. Across the crowds, through the crystal-clear windows, the Colosseum drew her attention.

"Look at this view," she breathed, enchanted.

Nate moved close behind her; one deep inhale and her back would brush his chest. She straightened her spine and struggled to take shallow breaths. *Don't graze him.* This job—and saving up to rescue Sofia—was too important to let her hormones run wild.

A pretty maître d' in a tight black dress that dipped dangerously low in the neckline appeared at their side. She skipped over Francesca and glued herself to Nate, her gold jewelry gleaming in the dim lighting. "Welcome back, Signore Icefall. I have your table ready."

Nate introduced the woman as Allegra. "Lead the way," he told the maître d'. Settling his hand on Francesca's back, he leaned in close to her ear. "I asked for a table out on the deck."

Allegra's hips took on an exaggerated sway as she walked ahead of them while twisting her head to ogle Nate every few steps.

Hope she trips, thought Francesca, surprised by the vehemence of the wish.

She led them to the roof deck, past well-dressed couples seated at cozy tables, until she stopped at a table at the far edge of the deck. The Colosseum, just a glass partition and a street away, seemed close enough to touch.

Nate pulled out her chair, and she sank into the cushioned surface, turning away from the amphitheater to catch Allegra slide her hand along Nate's bicep as he sat.

"Giacomo made it clear you're his special guests tonight," said Allegra. "He'll be here to take your drink orders himself." She handed Nate a menu with infinite care, then thrust the other menu into Francesca's hands before sashaying away.

"Charming," said Francesca.

Nate looked confused. "What?"

Disgruntled, she shook her head. "Nothing, never mind. I already ate dinner, so I'm not hungry, but if you want to eat here, don't let me stop you."

"How about dessert?"

Francesca, whose strong sweet tooth had been woefully denied after the Righteous Hearth had banned sugar, felt a delicious tendril of anticipation. "I'd like that."

A tall, skinny guy in a charcoal vest and a button-down shirt stopped at their table. He couldn't have been much older than Isa. "You made it. Remember, no one can know why you're here."

Nate turned to Francesca. "We're on a clandestine mission to lure Giacomo away from here."

"Understood," she said, lips twitching.

Giacomo lowered his voice further. "I put together a tasting menu of cocktails for you two. I'll bring them out now."

He returned quickly with a tray for each of them. Each platter contained three drinks: a pale-purple one in an antique coupe, one that looked like coffee and cream in a delicate double-walled glass, and a lemon-bright fizzing one in a crystal flute. "I call these… tastes of Italy. The middle one has alcohol, but the others are virgin." His gaze slid around the room, as if verifying he wasn't being watched. "I'll be back later." He hurried back inside the restaurant.

"I feel like a spy," said Nate.

"Sneaking around trying not to get caught is not all it's cracked up to be," Francesca murmured.

His eyes searched hers. "Care to tell me more?"

Realizing she'd said more than she had intended, she shook her head. "I don't know about you, but I'm trying this purple one first." Picking up the drink, she took a restrained sip. It tasted like the most delicate of candies: sweet but light, refreshingly cool in the warm evening. She let the flavors wash over her. "I don't think I've ever tried anything better."

He looked at her mouth for an unnervingly long moment. As she darted out her tongue to check for any stray droplets of the purple drink, he moved his attention sharply to the skyline, reached for his own drink, and took a long swallow.

Francesca leaned against the back of her chair, letting her gaze settle on the Colosseum again. The street below them hummed with cars. From somewhere in the distance, she could hear rowdy shouts, but up here, it seemed like it was just the two of them, despite the full tables around them.

When the waiter approached them, Nate ordered every dessert on the menu for them to share.

"Should we try the coffee one next?" she asked once they were alone again.

"Let's do it."

Francesca took a sip. Coffee and cream mixed with heady sugar, warming spices, and a slow-burn liquor she couldn't identify.

"I don't think I've ever tried anything better than *this*," said Nate.

"I'll duke it out with you. I still prefer the first drink, but this one is delicious."

They both reached for the third glass. Bubbles teased her nose as she sampled it. The lemon was vibrant, warmed by a floral syrup and cooled by the fizz of the sparkling water.

"I could drink this by the gallon," Nate said.

"We need him at Zohra. Pay him whatever he wants."

The waiter returned with a platter of desserts: a perfectly round sponge cake layered with cream and berries, a crystal vase of tiramisu, little cookies speckled with rose petals and gold leaf, and pistachio cream-filled castagnole dusted with sugar.

Francesca reached for one of the castagnole, and sampled the escaping pistachio cream with her tongue. "Who's their pastry chef? Let's take them too."

Nate watched her with an expression she couldn't decipher. *Maybe I have sugar on my lip?* She tried to dust it away with her napkin.

Allegra, having led another couple to a table at the other end of the deck, approached them again.

Francesca smelled her cloying perfume before she even neared. She must have gone to the restroom and doused herself with it. The closer Allegra got, the stronger her perfume burned Francesca's nostrils.

The maître d' laid a red-manicured hand on Nate's shoulder, leaning low enough for her breasts to almost pop out of her dress. "How are you liking our dessert?"

Allegra waited for Nate to respond, but he remained distracted. His gaze, which had welded to whichever stray sugar crystal he must have found on her lip earlier, stayed squarely on Francesca.

"We haven't really tried them yet," Francesca pointed out when Nate hadn't spoken.

Nate glanced at the maître d' and, as if just realizing how close she'd gotten, slid his chair away from her free-range breasts.

Allegra slanted into him, following his movement. "Well, let me know if you need anything at all."

He leaned farther away. "We're fine."

"Should I leave?"

Allegra didn't seem embarrassed. "We like to make our guests feel as welcomed as possible. I'll be over there. Just call out." And she strutted away.

"You want to get her number?" Francesca, gripped by the steely claws of inexplicable jealousy, tried to affect a cool tone.

"I have her number," said Nate. "She slid it into my pocket when I was here earlier."

Francesca blinked. "Oh. Then why did you bring me? I'm sure she'd have sampled your… drinks."

"I don't want her sampling anything. I wanted your opinion on the cocktails. You liked them. We'll hire Giacomo."

"She's all over you like a cattle fever tick."

"Really?" His eyes gleamed in the setting sun. "I didn't notice. Her breasts were in the way."

She almost lobbed the pistachio-filled dough ball at him.

He reached for a dessert spoon. "Don't know about you, but I'm digging into this tiramisu."

Before Francesca could respond, Giacomo appeared at her elbow, his feet dancing from side to side as he waited for them to look up. "What did you think?"

"The job is yours," said Nate. "And I want these exact cocktails on the menu on Saturday."

Giacomo exhaled, his shoulders falling clear to the floor with relief as a wide grin cracked open his tanned face. "I can't wait to get started."

When he gamboled away, Francesca popped a cookie into her mouth. Recognizing the feeling of being watched, she raised her head to find Allegra staring from across the deck. Inexplicably irritated, she dragged the napkin from her lap and tossed it on the table. "I should get going. I'll leave you to your… adventures for the evening."

Nate leaned across the table. "If I wanted to pursue that adventure, I wouldn't have brought you with me tonight. Will you stop fuming? Enjoy our dessert."

"I'm not fuming."

He gave her a look that said otherwise.

"I just find her highly inappropriate is all. And rude. She doesn't know I'm not your date. She's hitting on you right in front of me." Her gaze narrowed. "You asked for her number when you were here earlier today. That's why she's all over you."

"I didn't ask for her number." He paused for a beat before grinning. "She gave it to me."

"I think it's rude she's pursuing you when you might be out with your girlfriend."

"So we shouldn't offer her a job at Zohra?" The corners of his eye crinkled.

Francesca, charmed by him despite herself, relaxed against her seat and reached for a bite of the sponge cake. "No, but I stand firm on the pastry chef."

***

Francesca was jealous. Seeing her discombobulated appealed.

When he had arrived at the mixology lounge alone earlier that day, his plan had been simple—scout out the scene, meet the bartender, pick up a woman. Allegra had homed in on him as soon as he'd walked in, rubbing herself against him as she pulled out his chair, bringing him appetizers he hadn't requested, slipping her number into his pocket with a dirty whisper. It would have been so simple to call her that evening, take her to Zohra, and fuck her in one of the rooms.

Yet none of that had enticed. From the moment he had stepped into the lounge and saw the Colosseum a spitball away, all he could focus on was how much Francesca would love the view. He knew she hadn't had the time to explore Rome, and he wanted to be the one to show it to her, to share the moment with her, to feel some of the same awe too.

Her delighted gasps at the view, the cocktails, the dessert, had made him feel more alive than he'd felt in months. Unexpectedly, seeing her get all riled up because of Allegra was the crema on his espresso.

Allegra was hot, and yet he found Francesca in her prim navy dress and orange shawl more stimulating than all the women in the restaurant combined. When she had licked the filling in one of the castagnole earlier, he had almost dragged her across the table and tasted the cream on her tongue. He wanted to watch her sample other things that way—images of her lips around his cock, her tongue exploring, filled his head, and he had to readjust in his chair.

He shouldn't indulge this weird obsession with Francesca. Better to take her back to her grandmother's, call up Allegra, and continue with his night. Instead, he searched for ways to prolong the evening, to spend more time with the woman who had so abruptly appeared in his club.

Motioning the waiter for their bill, he paid in cash and stood, walking over to Francesca's side of the table and pulling out her chair.

"Want to take a stroll?" he asked her as she rose from the table.

"You should take Allegra. She's sprinting over here now."

Nate followed her gaze. Sure enough, the maître d' had set a determined course for them. "We better hurry then."

Before they could escape, Allegra stopped in front of them, keeping her attention on Nate. "I get off in an hour," she told him. "If you'd like to grab a drink?"

He deliberately slid his hand into Francesca's, interlacing their fingers. "My girlfriend and I have plans."

Allegra threw a dismissive glance at Francesca. "Come find me later then." She flounced away.

He could feel Francesca fuming. "Told you. She didn't even care when you said I'm your girlfriend. I don't have much experience with relationships, but I don't appreciate that."

He took a deliberate step closer, making her face him. "I think you want to teach her a lesson."

She had to tilt her head back to meet his eyes; hers looked confused. "What kind of lesson?"

Staring down into her beautiful face, his deepest wish kicked to the surface in the form of an order. "Kiss me."

She blinked at him like a befuddled owl. "What?"

Keeping his fingers intertwined with hers, he lifted his free hand to her face, loving how her eyes went soft and blurry.

"Wh—what are you doing?" she asked in an alarmed voice.

"You know you want to."

"I do not," came her prompt response, but her gaze had glued to his lips.

"To teach her a lesson," he added. A belated clarification.

"Oh." Her brows drew together. "I thought you meant to kiss you."

He traced her pinkening cheek with his fingers. "You want that too, but your desire for revenge is greater."

She finally met his eyes. "You don't know that."

His thumb learned the dip of her lower lip. "Tell me I'm wrong."

"I'm not going to kiss you." But her quickening pulse belied the certainty in her words. He could almost see it through the delicate skin of her neck.

"I'd do it now. While she's watching," he suggested, enjoying their interaction more than he knew was advisable.

Her gaze darted to Allegra. "How do you know she's watching?"

He huffed out a laugh. "Man, you're stubborn."

Just when he thought she'd pull out of his hold, Francesca rose to her tiptoes and planted her lips on his.

The move was so sudden, he expected her to move away immediately, but she didn't.

Keeping her lids tightly shut, she lingered on his lower lip before exploring his top one. The feel of her against him felt like coming home, like the effervescent joy of Christmas morning or the anticipative hope of New Year's Day, comforting and celebratory, exulting and calming all at once. Her fingers squeezed his as her free hand moved to his upper arm for balance.

He had wanted to give her control, to let her lead, but the intention fled. Tracing the seam of her lips with his tongue, he delved inside.

She tasted of sweet dessert, of roses, of the brandied coffee they'd tasted earlier, of happiness. The merest taste of her imprinted her into his DNA.

She froze against him, pulled back.

He had taken it too far.

Stepping away, she let go of his hand. He felt the loss in every inch of his body.

Not making eye contact, she turned away from him. "We should go."

He grasped for any excuse to keep her with him longer. "Do you want to take a closer look at the view?"

She debated his question for a long moment before giving in with a nod.

The rooftop deck offered unencumbered views of Rome beyond. Taking her hand once more, he pulled her away from the tables and toward a quiet corner. Another couple chatted nearby but moved along when they approached, leaving them in relative privacy.

The gentle evening breeze sent Francesca's soft

curls to dance around her face as she spoke. "It's so beautiful at night, with all of the buildings glowing."

He didn't miss the slight tremor in her voice. He knew she was steering them to safer grounds, but the rough rise and fall of her breasts and the cherry flush staining her cheeks told him their kiss had affected her too.

As if feeling the weight of his stare, she averted her face farther away from him, until her neck strained with the effort.

Desperate to taste her again, he let his hand trace the tight tendon in her neck. Although she didn't look at him, her shoulders relaxed under his touch.

"Did I scare you?"

The question made her twist her head back to face him. She tucked a dancing tendril of hair behind her ear. "Of course not."

His heartbeat drowned out all sound around them as he closed the distance between them. Although her eyes widened at his sudden nearness, she stayed put, tilting her head farther back to maintain eye contact.

"Nate…" Her eyes fastened to his lips.

Blind with need, careless to where they were, and what they should or should not be doing, he caught her mouth with his.

She produced a small mewl of approval, sending heat to harpoon him, and her arms slid to his shoulders. As she opened to him, her tongue eagerly meeting his, exuberance flashed. Locking his hands low on her back, he pulled her in even tighter, kissing her under the just-waking stars and the moon and the lavender sky, the soft glow of Rome beyond them.

He teased her with playful strokes, encouraged as

she pressed even closer, her tongue learning his. The sweet exploration could have lasted a minute or an hour; he wanted it to go on forever. When she finally pulled back, he let her go, but she lingered near, her breasts brushing against his shirt on every fragmented inhale.

Her eyes looked passion-glazed and vulnerable and confused as they met his, searched. He wasn't sure what she was looking for, but she must have found it because, on a sigh of relief, she stood on her tiptoes and pressed a kiss to his cheek.

Before she could move away, he turned his head and found her lips again because it hadn't been enough. As her hands twined around his neck and she kissed him with a corresponding hunger, he wondered whether it would ever be enough.

He needed to stop, but his fingers wouldn't uncurl, his hands wouldn't release. His body had claimed her as his, and refused to let go.

She broke the kiss again and took a heedful step away from him, giving them both space to recover. The soft, summer night wrapped around them, reminding him of where they were. He traced her upturned face with his gaze.

"I overstepped." He fought the urge to take her mouth once more.

"No. I mean, yes, but so did I. I should go home."

He wanted to take her to Zohra, to his room, strip her—

"Nate?" she asked as his eyes lost focus.

Shaking off the mental images, he reached for her hand. "Come on, I'll drive you home."

She took another step away from him. "No. We both need some space."

Frustrated at her response, he motioned around them. "How do you propose to get home from here?"

"I'll… find a bus."

"You don't use public transportation."

She raised her chin, crossing her arms. "I'll figure it out. I don't want a ride."

"Why not? If I scared you—"

"You didn't." Her cheeks burned red and her eyes looked bright and glittery, as though she had started to run a fever. She strode past him. "Good night, Nate."

He didn't let her go far, snagging her elbow to stop her progress. "Fine. If you want to take the bus, take the bus, but text me when you get home."

Her hair swept her jaw as she shook her head. "I won't. My whole life, everyone's always kept tabs on me. I can get home without supervision."

"That's not what I—"

"You can't outargue me."

"I can try." She didn't look amused at his statement. He tried another tack. "I'll grab you a taxi through my app. You don't know this city. I don't want you on a bus this late at night."

"I don't need to be manhandled."

He let out a long breath, trying to harness his irritation at her about-face. "You have three choices. I drive you. I call you a cab. Or I take the bus with you. I'd prefer to avoid option C because I don't know the bus route either, and then you'll have to take the bus back here to my car with me and then we'll just go back and forth until the sun comes up, like we're on some haunted nightmare of a carousel."

A burst of laughter escaped her, and her lips curved.

Unable to help himself, he swooped down and tasted

her reluctant smile. "Let me drive you. Please?"

She pulled back to search his eyes. It was a good minute before she responded. "Okay."

He hadn't realized he'd leaned forward to kiss her again until she took a hurried step back. *Fuck. This has to stop.* Straightening, he waved her forward to precede him as they retraced their steps to the elevator.

As they passed their former table, he reached into his pocket, pulled out the crumpled napkin with Allegra's number, and tossed it next to their half-eaten dessert.

Chapter 11

Nate had kissed her. Nate had kissed her as Rome sparkled and breathed around them.

The car ride to Nonna's was quiet, as neither one wished to address what happened. He parked in front of her grandmother's building. Even though she insisted she could go upstairs by herself, he ignored her, getting out of the car and opening her door. He didn't touch her as they scaled the steps, but he walked closer than the wide stairs warranted.

As they reached the apartment and she pulled the keys out of her purse, he watched her with an intensity she found both exciting and unnerving. Slowly, as if giving her every opportunity to decline, he brushed a maddeningly soft kiss across her lips before stepping away.

Francesca restrained herself from tugging him closer.

Without another word, he left her. The thud of her racing pulse echoed the sound of his retreating footsteps.

A half hour later, teeth brushed, face washed, and lacerations slathered, Francesca changed into her sleepshirt and climbed into her narrow bed in the too-warm room she shared with Isa.

Sudden memories engulfed her—the feel of Nate's lips on hers, the way his tongue had teased her, the press of his hard body against her breasts. Their kiss made her feel as brilliant and vivid as the lit Colosseum.

She had foolishly gotten lost in the evening, in the romance of the setting and the ancient ruins that surrounded them. The sweetness of the dessert, the heady brightness of the drinks, the tempting scent of Nate had muddled her senses.

Tomorrow, he better pretend like nothing happened.

She had a plan for her life, and she wouldn't let Nate derail it. She needed the Zohra job, and continuing down this path would only lead to heartbreak and unemployment. She had to stay focused for Isa and for Sofia and for herself.

The last time she'd given in to passion, to desire, to love, she'd been humiliated, maimed. If her parents hadn't gotten her to the doctor in time, she'd be dead. She'd survived, barely, and now she carried the reminders of Miles Decker incised into her body.

***

Nate parked the Fiat next to Zohra and tried to wipe the taste of Francesca from his mind. He never should have kissed her, and he certainly shouldn't have done it more than once. Now that he'd sampled her, memorized the contours and textures of her mouth, he clamored to do it again… and again—

It had to stop. First thing tomorrow, he'd make it clear that kissing her had been a mistake.

Getting out of the car, he ignored the warmth of the summer evening, the pulse of history around him, and stomped to Zohra.

He smelled the carcass first—a tang of fresh meat. It must not have been there long; lying out in the evening heat would have spoiled it otherwise. Gangly, dead, the skinned goat lay at his doorstep, a blown-up photo of his thigh—more specifically, *his mole*—stabbed through its leg with a switchblade.

Sitting on his haunches, he studied the barely thawed dead animal. Something one could buy whole from a butcher easily, but it was a message, nevertheless.

Moretti wanted to scare him, did he? The man paled in comparison to the brutes Nate had worked with at Rhyme, Ryan, & Shuster—Mrs. Klein made grown men weep. Hell, one executive had wet himself after a minute in a room with her. God, he missed the woman. Getting her back as his secretary had been a nonnegotiable for him when he'd worked out his reemployment contract.

Making a mental note to bring Mrs. Klein a souvenir from Rome, Nate dragged the animal inside. He reviewed the security footage first, but the soldato who'd dropped off the missive knew how to avoid getting caught. After plucking out the photo, he slogged the goat to the kitchen, took a butcher knife from the wall, and started hacking.

Tomorrow, this street would have a barbecue the likes of which they'd never seen before.

Chapter 12

Having hyperventilated the entire night in anticipation of facing Nate, the last thing Francesca could have predicted was for Nonna to hand over a plate of freshly baked sfogliatelle the next morning and insist she bring them to him.

What if he assumed the pastries were some sort of odd attempt to woo him?

Francesca tried to refuse her grandmother, but Nonna was unrelenting.

"Dante will drive you so you don't have to walk with the plate."

"Nonna—" The ringing of her phone interrupted her. Seeing Nate's name, she answered. "I'm still at my grandmother's. Can—"

"I'm downstairs."

"What do you mean you're downstairs?" She crossed to the window to confirm. Sure enough, he was there leaning against his red car.

"I'm driving you to Zohra today."

Hanging up, Francesca looked between Dante and Nonna. "Dante, you're off the hook. Nate will drive me to work."

Her anxiety skyrocketed as she stepped out of Nonna's building. She had banked on having at least another half hour before she faced him, and now she didn't know quite what to do. Aviators obscured his electric-blue eyes, but he pulled them off when she reached him.

Bracing herself for an awkward car ride, she handed him the kitchen towel-covered plate of pastries. "Nonna made you sfogliatelle. They're filled with apricot jam."

Nate blinked, as though processing the sudden turn of events. "She didn't have to do that."

Francesca took several steps away from him, wiped her sweaty palms against her gray linen dress. "She insisted. Especially after you declined her invitation to come to dinner tonight."

Nate frowned. "I never declined her invitation."

"I declined on your behalf. Didn't think you'd want to be subjected to innumerable questions from Nonna and Isa."

He appeared to think about it. "Depends. What is she making?"

Francesca ignored his question. "Why're you here?"

"I'll explain later." He opened the door for her, waited for her to get settled before coming around to the driver's side.

She took the plate from him as he slid into his seat. "We should talk about last night. It should have never happened."

He faced her across the console. Relief—clear, *annoying*—suffused his face. What had she expected? A protest?

"No, it shouldn't have."

She fought the glumness his words brought her. It

was a good thing they were on the same page. Why did his ready agreement irritate her?

"It can't ever happen again," she said, more to herself than to him.

Something flashed across his eyes just before he put the aviators back on. "No, it can't ever happen again."

Turning away, she lowered her window before she did something stupid, like toss the pastries aside, clamber across the console, and kiss him silly.

"Francesca," he said in a voice that had her turning to face him again. "There was an incident at Zohra last night."

Blood rushed through her ears like the Colorado River. "What kind of incident?"

"Giorgio Moretti again."

Moretti... For a terrified second, she thought he'd say the Righteous Hearth.

"The guy who sent Isa into your club. What did he do now?" she asked, tension easing.

"Giorgio is part of the Moretti crime family. They want a piece of Zohra Rome. They left me a goat carcass last night at the front door."

The fear returned. She reached for him because she needed to touch him, to feel him safe and solid next to her. "Are you okay?"

"A scare tactic, nothing more, but I didn't want you walking alone today."

That's why he came to get me. It had nothing to do with the kiss last night.

He laid his hand over hers on his arm. "The cameras caught a guy with his face covered. No license plate. The Morettis having a tiff."

"That sounds like more than a tiff," she pointed out.

"They've been a pest. I'm not worried but didn't want to chance it with your safety. If you'd rather bow out—"

"I'm not quitting."

"Well, if you'd rather work from your grandmother's apartment today—"

"No. I've had enough of bullies to last me the next three lifetimes. I'm going in to work, Nate. Not even the Mafia will stop me."

He surprised her by planting a kiss to her lips.

"Hey." She leaned away from him. "We said no more kissing."

"Sorry." But he didn't look it. "You impress me is all."

As soon as they arrived at Zohra, Francesca turned for the office, but Nate redirected her into the kitchen instead. "We have one thing to do today, and it'll be spectacular."

When he swung open the doors of the commercial fridge, Francesca wasn't prepared for what she saw. Meat—lots and lots of it—slathered in some sort of dry rub filled each shelf.

"Are you… are you cooking the goat?"

"Barbecuing it. I prepped it last night. The restaurant next door is letting me borrow their charcoal grill. There's a courtyard in the back of the club—we're making barbecued goat today and selling it for donations to anyone interested."

"Donations to what?" She tore her gaze away from the meat to look at him.

Nate grinned. "Every cento is going toward Libera. It's an anti-Mafia nonprofit here."

Francesca laughed despite herself. "You're crazy."

He looked infinitely pleased with his plan. "Want to help me grill?"

"Oh yeah, I'm in," she said, not hiding her eagerness. This was going to be an interesting workday.

It really was a spectacular barbecue, with plates of cooked goat being given out in exchange for donations to the nonprofit. The line of customers—who, Francesca guessed, were mostly there to sneak a peek inside Zohra—snaked through the club's ballroom to the courtyard, where Francesca gave out the to-go plates while Nate cooked the meat.

She'd worn a long-sleeved dress today. Though she'd been thankful it helped hide her arms and escape the aghast glances from the customers, the summer warmth—mixed with the heat of the grill—left her body beaded with sweat, the skin of her arms irritated.

After the last customer departed, while Nate stayed in the small courtyard to scrub the grill, Francesca went into the kitchen for a glass of water. Chugging the cold liquid, she glanced down at her dress, its front stained with stray juice of cooked goat. Darn. She'd better get the oily spots out of the linen fabric—it's not like she had clothes to waste.

Ducking into the nearest downstairs bathroom, she wiggled out of the dress and studied the stains. A little soap and hot water should get those right out. Reaching for the Zohra-branded soap bar, she worked it into the fabric, then rinsed it with water so hot it burned her hands. The method appeared to work, though the dress would have to dry before she'd know whether the stains were gone for certain.

Crap. The entire front of the dress was now thoroughly wet, but it's not like she could prance around in her underwear. She pulled the dress back on, watched the wet fabric plaster to her bra and saturate it fully. The linen had been thin, but not as thin as her worn bra. It made her appear almost naked. Not a look she'd been going for, but maybe it would dry before Nate was done with cleaning the grill.

Just as she'd thought of him, he called her name. "Hey, Francesca? Where'd you go?"

Bad, bad timing. She considered locking the bathroom door and hanging inside the small space until her dress dried. But how long would that take? She couldn't stay in his bathroom for a half hour or longer.

Realizing she had to face him, she crossed her arms over her soaked chest and exited the bathroom. "I'm here."

His footsteps got louder. "I have to return the grill—"

Whatever he was about to say after that wafted away and he came to such a sudden halt in front of her that she worried he'd topple forward.

She tried to appear nonchalant. Maybe he wouldn't notice the very wet, very thin fabric plastered to her very erect nipples if she acted casual. "You should go and do that."

His eyes fixed in the vicinity of her chest. "Um…"

Clearly, he'd lost his train of thought.

"Nate? The grill?"

"Um… The grill?"

"You were about to return it."

Finally, Nate seemed to remember where he was and what he was supposed to do. "Yes. I have to return it. Come with me."

She shook her head. "Not like this. I should let this dry."

Tightening her arms in front of her to cover as much of the wet linen as she could, she attempted to go past him, but he'd rooted himself to the floor. Reflexively, her eyes rose to his.

"This can't happen again," he said, repeating their decision from the car.

The reminder—to her, to himself?—didn't work, because in the next breath, his hands enveloped her shoulders.

She caught a glimpse of incredulity and desperation in his gaze before he hauled her against him and claimed her mouth with his.

Incited by the familiar taste of him, she wiggled to get closer, to let his heat scald her wet breasts. How she wanted to stay here… to kiss him and forget the insanity of the last few months just for a little while.

But they couldn't let this continue.

He must have felt her hesitation—or maybe he'd come to the same realization on his own.

Releasing her, he took several precautionary steps back and focused on his toes.

"Shit. Sorry." Without lifting his gaze, he fled.

So hot she burned, Francesca glanced down at her chest, surprised not to see drifts of steam rising from the fabric.

***

Nate ran.

He ran upstairs to change into his workout clothes, he ran out the front door to avoid Francesca, and he ran outside.

He ran for hours, around the Villa Borghese, to the Trevi Fountain, along the Colosseum and the Roman Forum

112

to the Pantheon, then to Piazza Navona, and across the Tiber to Vatican City. He ran to get the feel of Francesca's nipples straining against him out of his mind, to forget the excited rush of her breath just before he kissed her.

The temperature hovered in the mid-eighties but felt infinitely hotter. He'd shed his shirt a long time ago, letting the sun burn the sweat off his skin.

By the time he returned to Zohra, he hoped Francesca would be on her way to her house, but he wasn't that lucky. She sat at the bar, working on her laptop.

She turned to face him, and her eyes widened. "Oh my gosh," she exclaimed. "Look at you."

Confused by her reaction, he froze. "What?"

She hopped off the barstool. "You're burned to a crisp."

"It's nothing. Just hot." He couldn't meet her eyes. If he did, he'd flip her over the bar and take her right there.

"Where the heck were you? It's been hours. Were you outside this whole time? You could have gotten heatstroke."

"I'm going to take a shower." Ducking his head, he retreated to his room.

When he faced his reflection in his bathroom mirror, he understood why Francesca had looked shocked. He was as red as a tomato, his skin close to welting. His chest, arms, shoulders, back had been scorched raw by the hot Roman sun.

"That's going to hurt tomorrow," he mumbled.

Her approaching footsteps made him groan. He had already tried to escape her by running outside, now hiding in his room. How far would he have to go to free himself of this pull she held on him?

"I brought you water." She extended a glass his way.

Horror flickered in her gaze. "You look so burned. What were you thinking?"

Taking the water, he closed his eyes against the sight of her. "I need a moment."

She ignored him. "Do you have aloe vera?"

"Somewhere."

Stepping farther into his bathroom, she opened the mirror cabinet and found the bottle. "Go take a shower. I'll help you apply it."

He tried to snag it from her. "Can do it myself."

"You can't reach your back." She pulled the bottle closer to herself. "My goodness, you're really burned."

"Go. Away," he ground out, setting the glass of water on the counter. "Or that thing we said was never to repeat is going to repeat."

"Is that why you're so surly?"

"I'm not surly. I want to take a shower. Unless you'd like to take one with me, I suggest you remove yourself."

"I'll wait until you're done and help you apply the—mmmph!"

He didn't let her finish the sentence. Heedful of the welts on her forearm, he manacled her wrist, pulled her into his body and kissed her. The bottle of aloe vera clattered to the ground.

The feel of her against his burned chest should have hurt. Instead, it felt like finding a cool stream after wandering lost across the Atacama Desert. Drinking in the familiar taste of her, he let the coolness of her touch sweep over him.

Her hands moved up his biceps until they found the base of his skull, held on as he pillaged her mouth. She didn't seem to want to escape his rough kiss. Instead, she sought to deepen it.

He had to put an end to the insanity.

Step away, take an icy shower, and cool the fuck down.

Instead, he cupped her ass, lifted her to the travertine counter and stepped deeper between her thighs.

"Wait," she gasped, pushing away from him.

He barely felt the pressure of her palms against his singed skin. He reached out to help her get down, but she shoved at his hands as she leaped off the counter.

"We can't. We said we wouldn't. Go shower. I—I—I have to go."

It was Francesca's turn to run away.

***

Francesca ran down the stairs and sank onto the last stone step, dropping her face into her palms. Why did she keep doing this? What about him made her so off-kilter?

She'd think the torture she'd faced after giving in to her desire for Miles would clear all lustful thoughts forever from her brain. Guess it hadn't worked.

At first, she thought she imagined the sound of the front door opening, but when the sun flooded the entryway and a man stepped inside, Francesca jumped to her feet. She had locked that door herself after Nate had returned.

"We're closed until Saturday," she informed the stranger, approaching him with quick steps. "How do you have our key?"

The man had to be in his sixties, his salt-and-pepper hair slicked back, his skin richly tanned. Dressed casually in light shorts and a watermelon-colored polo, sunglasses tucked into the collar of his shirt, he walked toward her in suede espadrilles. Something about him unsettled her, like coming in proximity to a snake. Her body instinctively knew he was dangerous.

He spoke in Italian-accented English. "You must be the new girl."

Francesca didn't feel comfortable giving a stranger her name.

"Are you a Zohra member?" she asked, unsure of what to do with this intruder in the club.

His lips curved in an amused smile, though his eyes remained reptilian-cold as they slid up her body. "Not yet."

She crossed her arms against his oily inspection. "Then you should go."

"Where is Signore Icefall?"

"He's busy."

He trapped her with constricted eyes. The probing focus unnerved her. It felt as though he was waiting for a tell, to catch her in a lie. "What's your role here?"

"How do you know Nate?" she deflected.

"We go way back." His lips curved up. "I can pick his inner thigh out of a lineup. A little hurt I didn't get invited to the barbecue."

Nate appeared on the landing, already moving toward them. "The fuck you doing back, Giorgio?"

He placed himself—and his red and bare chest—squarely between her and the unwelcome visitor.

Giorgio gave him a disgusted look. "What happened to you? You fall asleep on the grill?"

"Don't make me throw you out of here."

Giorgio's gaze bounced between Nate and Francesca once, twice, before he spoke. "I see someone's trying to impress his lady. Have you had time to consider my offer?"

"The answer remains no. Get the fuck out. Now." Nate moved toward him.

Giorgio backstepped, arms outstretched. "I'd rethink that if I were you."

Nate grabbed the older man by the collar of his expensive-looking polo and dragged him to the exit. "Leave all the fucking goat meat you want, but you walk in here again, your brother will be carrying you out."

He slammed the door shut in Giorgio's face.

"That was Moretti?"

Turning to face her, he scanned her from head to toe, his hand still grasping the antique door handle. "You okay?"

"I'm fine."

"He say anything to make you uncomfortable?"

When she shook her head, Nate released the doorknob.

"He has a key to Zohra, Nate. What does he want from you?"

"Part of the profit in exchange for Moretti protection."

Realization sank in. "They really are the Mafia."

"A small-potatoes crime family finding the lowest-hanging fruit."

He didn't sound small potatoes. "Aren't you scared of what he'll do? You tossed him out of here. He could be dangerous."

"No one talks to you that way."

"He didn't say anything bad."

"Fine. Then, no one talks to you. Period."

The ridiculousness of his statement charmed her. She fought the smile that threatened at the corners of her mouth. "You're being silly."

Without breaking eye contact, he approached, stopping only a few inches away. She tilted her head back to watch him, uncertain of what he intended to do.

Warmth grazed her cheek as he brushed a lock of hair from her face. When he tucked it behind her ear, his fingers lingered, setting off sparklers as he traced her jaw.

His eyes darkened to a desert night as he watched her.

Francesca swallowed. She tried to make herself step away, but her body refused to budge. Not giving herself time to reconsider, she dove.

He froze at the kiss, his lips unmoving beneath hers.

Confused, she pulled back, tried to read the emotions reflected in his eyes. He didn't let her go far. With a feral snarl, he took her mouth in a spiraling kiss that left her knees wobbly. In an attempt to steady herself, she curved her fingers into the hot skin of his arms.

A groan reverberated deep from within him.

She dropped her hands. "Did I hurt you? You're so sunburned—"

He interrupted her mid-sentence, pulling her tighter against him. His lips moved to investigate the corner of her mouth, her cheek, the sensitive spot just below her ear. The hard press of his body against hers left no question to the things he wanted to do to her. She wanted those things too, but she couldn't let this—them—continue. Before she lost all willpower, she turned her head away. "Wait. We should do something about your burn."

"I want to do something about it," he growled, biting her neck.

"Let's take care of your *sun*burn first."

When she extricated herself, he reached for her again. "Come upstairs while I shower. I don't want you down here alone."

She smiled as she backed away. "I'm not falling for that. But I'll meet you in your room to help apply some aloe."

***

He never wanted to see Moretti that close to Francesca again.

The very image of the Italian talking to her—*breathing the same air as her*—swamped him with raging possessiveness, and he couldn't kick free of the unwelcome emotion. Moretti had gotten near enough to smell the lavender on her skin—*no one* was allowed that close to her.

Rattled by the surge of idiotic protectiveness, he cursed himself all the way to the shower.

He had someone else he had to protect too, and Steven Douglass took priority.

The icy shower burned. His skin was already blistering, and he expected it to get much worse overnight. Although he regretted his run, he regretted kissing Francesca more. The instinctive urge to claim her as his own made it imperative he keep his distance. He'd finally gotten his life back on track, and he'd allow no one to interfere.

Throwing a towel around his hips, he stepped out of the shower and into his bedroom, stopping short when he found Francesca perched on top of his comforter.

His heart stopped beating. She looked so soft and beautiful and vulnerable sitting on his large bed. The tall frame made her legs dangle as she waited.

Her eyes ran over his body in a perusal filled with pure female interest. He didn't know whether Francesca was aware of the desire clear in her features, but he reveled in seeing her reaction to him. It made him want to flex every muscle, puff out his chest, and watch her need grow.

Her gaze fell to the erection escaping through the opening in the hastily tied towel.

"Ummm," she said in a thick, unsure voice. "Come sit on the bed. I'll put the aloe vera on you."

He closed his eyes at the need that spiked through him. "I can't handle you touching me. You should go."

He turned away and waited for her retreating footsteps, but they never came.

"I want to stay," she murmured.

He didn't turn around. "We're playing with fire."

"I want to touch you," she said in a voice so quiet, he half expected to have imagined it. He heard her hop off the bed, walk straight toward him and stop close to his back. "Will you sit on the bed?"

Refuse her. Send her away.

He intended to do just that.

But when she laid her hand on his arm, the words wouldn't come. "You know this is stupid?"

"Infinitely so."

At least they both shared that sentiment.

She ducked into the bathroom for the bottle of aloe vera still on the ground. Stepping back into his bedroom, she motioned to the bed. When he sat on the edge, she perched next to him, so light that the mattress didn't even shift under her weight.

His fingers twitched to pull her astride his lap, rip off her underwear, and sink into her. Instead, he sat stock-still and waited for what she'd do next.

"Turn your back to me," she directed.

As he did, he heard her squeeze out the gel and warm it between her palms.

"I don't want it to be too cold for you," she explained, her hands settling on his shoulders.

He had never experienced a sharper pleasure than her gentle touch as she smoothed the slick substance from his shoulders to his biceps.

When she pulled away to squeeze out more ointment, he almost demanded she continue her ministrations.

After what felt like an eternity, her hands settled on him once again and he groaned with delight.

She worked the cooling goop into his smarting burns, her fingers exploring the dips and valleys of his back. She traced his spine, swept to his shoulders.

"Turn around," she demanded in a husky voice.

He didn't think he could move without coming right there.

Struggling to shift, he now faced her. Her lips looked bruised and swollen. Marked by him, he realized with a thrum of possessiveness.

Her ragged breathing, the flush of red on her skin echoed the violent need that pounded through him.

Leaning closer, she mapped out his sun-reddened chest, the lavender soap scent of her intensifying. What would she do if he grasped her hand, dragged it across his stomach, and pumped into her tight fist? Or pushed her head down and waited for her to take him in her mouth?

He knew she could feel his heart beat wildly under her palms, could see his straining erection. Her hands lingered on his chest, traced across its span long after she had worked the gel into his skin.

Desire and curiosity played across her features. When her eyes lifted to his, he pounced, pressing her deep into the mattress as he captured her mouth.

Her fingers tangled in his hair as she kissed him

back. Cupping her breast that fit so perfectly in his palm, he traced along the hard tip of her nipple, but it wasn't enough. Desperate to feel her bare skin against his, he tore at her dress, ready to shred it to pieces.

"Zipper," she gasped, sitting up.

Finding the fastening, he slid it all the way down and pulled the dress and bra off her shoulders and arms to her waist—

He jerked back. "Holy fuck, what happened to you?"

Her entire torso—her belly, her ribs… Jesus, her *breasts*—was a patchwork of scars… tiny, close together slivers of long-ago wounds that marked every inch of the skin he'd exposed like silver needles.

Francesca wrenched the layers back up to her chest, but it was too late. He'd seen the agony that had been inflicted on her.

Rage blurred his vision. "Who did this? Who hurt you?"

The horror on her face undid him. He reached for her, needing to hold her—just hold her, while anguish and disbelief raged through him—but she leaped off the bed and ran into his bathroom. The door shut behind her.

***

In the framed bathroom mirror, Francesca stared at the disfigured skin Nate had revealed. The heat of the moment, the dizzying pleasure of his touch, had made her forget her scars.

Splashing cold tap water over her face helped cool her heated skin, but it took several rounds before the tremors left her fingers.

Still feeling unsteady, she readjusted her bra, rezipped her dress, and prayed that Nate had returned downstairs to give her space to recover. At least he hadn't recoiled in disgust. It had been shock—and all that pity— that froze him.

Opening the door, she found him waiting for her. He'd dressed in sweatpants and sat on his bed, but stood as she entered.

"Tell me what happened."

She really, really didn't want to, but she owed him an explanation. As she contemplated how to start, he spoke first.

"I know about the Righteous Hearth."

Blood thickened to clay in her veins. He *couldn't* know about the Righteous Hearth.

"What?" she croaked out, amazed she'd managed even the one word.

Reaching her, he took her hand. Although she tried to jerk away, he held on. "Sit. Please."

Cymbals crashed in her ears; her knees were about to buckle. Maybe sitting wasn't such a bad idea. She let him tug her to the bed. When she sat, he joined her, but kept a good foot of space between them.

"Jackson ran a background check. Don't worry, confidentially."

Her brain struggled to comprehend the implications. *Nate knew.* He knew the truth about her and the Righteous Hearth. He knew her past—had let her work at Zohra knowing that a cult was looking for her.

"I should have told you," she admitted. "Before you hired me."

He was shaking his head before she finished speaking. "No, it was none of my business."

But it *was* his business. He'd been upfront about needing to return home, but he'd never leave his club to a fugitive. "I don't think they know I'm in Italy. But if they do, I can quit. Accepting the job without telling you the whole truth was reckless. I don't want to drag you into my mess."

His resolute gaze met hers. "You're not."

She ignored his response. He didn't—couldn't yet—understand the slithery danger of the Righteous Hearth. "How much do you know?"

"You and Isa escaped from a religious sect in Nevada."

Pain gored her as she nodded. Did he know about Sofia? If he hadn't learned that from the background check, should she tell him?

He moved slowly, carefully, giving her every opportunity to turn away, to refuse. She couldn't if her life depended on it. His heat and scent surrounded her as he brought his face closer and brushed his lips over hers. "Tell me what they did to you."

Trust didn't come easily to Francesca; the last time she'd trusted someone, she nearly died. But Nate deserved to know who he'd hired to run his club.

"The Righteous Hearth believes that God passes on his wishes through the Spiritual Leader. Girls don't go to school because their job is to birth healthy sons. The boys are also discouraged from studying. Because labor is a way to please God, we raise and sell cattle and poultry. Some crops too."

He laid his hand on hers. "You've spent most of your life there."

In the spinning room, the weight of his hand was her only constant. Because she knew better than to rely on anyone but herself, she pulled her hand away. "My parents joined when I was five. The Spiritual Leader was always strict, but he's become paranoid. He's building a new compound, deep in the Nevada desert. The compound where we lived was pretty remote, but at least it wasn't guarded by barbed wire and armed men. Isa and I knew we had to leave before everyone moved to the new compound—we had no choice. *I* had no choice. The Spiritual Leader had seen a vision, a vision that I was to marry his closest advisor. My ex."

"The guy you said won't take no for an answer?"

She coughed to clear the tears because she refused to cry. "Yes. When I was nineteen, he swept me off my feet. He was a little older, and charming, and… I fell in love with him. We dated for a year, but we dated in secret. Dating and any sort of intimate relations are strictly forbidden before marriage, and the Spiritual Leader has to approve the match first—only then does he give you permission to court. But he only approves the matches he himself arranges."

"How convenient."

She ignored his dry retort. "He didn't approve our match, but we were in love—or so I thought." Taking a deep, pained breath, she let the words fall. "And then he did something… reprehensible, and I ended it. He wasn't happy. He told the Spiritual Leader that I seduced him, made him sin, that I was lustful and impure and I had soiled him with my immorality. My parents were horrified—the community shunned me. I had to repent—do penance for my sins."

His hand at his side flexed. "What kind of penance?"

"A common practice—one of the common practices in the Righteous Hearth—is to wear a cilice until the Spiritual Leader deems you atoned. I wore it for months."

He shot up from the bed. "Holy shit. A hair shirt?"

She nodded. "They make them out of goat hair because it's coarse and uncomfortable, and cuts the skin in a million little scratches. The Righteous Hearth sews spikes into the shirt too. Sort of like thumbtacks, only the pins are shorter. They hurt *a lot* and the pain gets worse the longer you wear it. Awful, sheer agony. After a while, the wounds got infected—the Spiritual Leader wouldn't let me see the doctor. My fever was so bad, I couldn't stand. Finally, my parents did something. They stood up to the Spiritual Leader and took me to the hospital—they saved my life. No one defies him. I am still so grateful. I'd be dead if it wasn't for them. The antibiotics helped and, when I was released, the Spiritual Leader came to our house—announced me repented." Her palm flew to her rib cage. "All these years later… these scars are just there. I've accepted them. I forget about them—I hadn't even thought when we—"

"Let me see them."

The rough request had her shaking her head. "No. One look was enough."

He sat back on the bed next to her. "I need to see them, Francesca."

The edge of desperation in his voice undid her. If he wanted to indulge his morbid curiosity and gawk at her disfigured body, she'd let him. Drawing down the zipper, she pulled at the sleeves until the dress collected around her waist and her scars were revealed to him.

She couldn't gauge his reaction; his lowered lashes made it impossible to even guess at his thoughts.

"May I?" He lifted his hand.

Later, she'd wonder why she'd given him clearance to touch her. But in that moment, abraded raw by the memories, she gave in to her need for just a little human contact. Agreeing with a jerky nod, she forced herself to sit still.

With a gentle finger, he traced across the old scars on her ribs and belly—the ones that years had smoothed but never healed.

He thought her ugly, marred, tarnished.

What am I doing?

Suddenly, the need to escape his gaze, evade his touch, made her tremble. The room seemed too cold, the pad of his finger too rough, his attention too stifling.

When she lurched away, his eyes lifted to hers. The rage in his face, when she'd expected revulsion, stunned her. So she made herself stay, even as her body shook with the effort.

"Can I hold you?"

She wanted to be held so badly, but accepting was impossible. Once, she'd trusted and relied on Miles, and it had made her weak. Remaining strong for Isa—for Sofia—was imperative. Letting herself be comforted would lead to dependence, and she couldn't allow it. He'd be leaving on Sunday—and she'd remain here, alone, working hard to save up, to study, to build a life she and her sisters deserved.

"No."

Nate didn't contest her refusal. Instead, his hand drifted to her arm—to the fresh markings there. His eyes met hers, seeking permission. That, she couldn't refuse him. When she offered the smallest of nods, he brought her arm to his mouth, brushed a soft kiss along one welt. Careful as though afraid to hurt her, he kissed across each raw slice.

"These are new."

She nodded as memories churned. "After the Spiritual Leader told me that I'm meant to marry my ex, I refused. He tried to get me to agree in several sessions with him… and left these."

"He tortured you." The clipped words bounced off his lips like hailstones.

Unable to sit half naked with her arm in his grip any longer, she pulled away. Dragging up her dress, she rezipped it, stood. "He'd make me come to his office, sit at the desk with my arms out across the table. He'd talk at me, and as I continued to refuse the match, he'd flog me. Session after session."

The rage in his gaze kept her from telling him the rest—her time in the Sinners Shed.

"Don't leave." Nate rose too. "If you can't tell me more just yet, that's okay. Just… don't go. Not like this."

"I don't want to talk about it anymore."

"Okay. We won't talk about it."

The question that had lassoed her lungs fought its way through her. "Are you going to fire me?"

His head jerked back in surprise. "Of course not."

The anxiety left her, and it robbed her of her ability to stand. She sank back to the edge of the bed. "*Thank you.* I need this job."

"And I need to leave on Sunday."

Resolution and reluctance warred in his features.

She sought to soothe the reluctance. "I know."

"I can't stay." He paced now, striding from corner to corner like a just-caged wild animal.

Did he want reassurance? "I'll take good care of Zohra while you're away."

He stopped then, faced her. "I'm needed in Manhattan."

"You've said."

"You'll be by yourself to deal with the Righteous Hearth and the Morettis. I'll ask Jackson—better yet, Hayes to fly out. Hayes has a web of government connections—"

She stood, interrupting him. "No need to send a babysitter. I can handle Giorgio Moretti, and the Righteous Hearth doesn't know I'm here. I'll be fine, Nate. I'm used to handling things on my own."

Before he could argue, she hurried to the door, facing him one last time. "I need to call the locksmith. Moretti can't have access to this building again. And you and I should keep some distance—what happened today, and yesterday, can't repeat."

Chapter 13

The rest of the week zoomed by in a whirlwind of activity, and without a single Moretti sighting.

Nate had left it to Hayes to dig up what he could on the Morettis. His brother produced a long history of the crime family, which was founded after a blood-filled fallout with Frascati in the '90s. Because the Morettis operated so deep underground, Hayes couldn't generate a verified list of their illicit businesses or of Giorgio's brother's whereabouts, but he promised to keep looking.

In the meantime, Nate had a club to officially launch this week. He'd put months of work into Zohra and he wouldn't settle for a culmination that was anything short of spectacular.

Margaux Martin, Zohra's go-to event planner, flew in from the States to prep for the official opening. Jackson tended to go all-out for Zohra launch parties and big events, bringing in aerialists, singers, burlesque performers, all spotlit perfectly by elite production companies, but Nate kept Zohra Rome's opening night more low-key.

He opted to recreate Italian Renaissance paintings using detailed sets and live models: *Venus of Urbino*, with Venus reclining on a red couch; *Sleeping Venus,* with her on white satin; *The Birth of Venus,* with her on a scallop shell; and *Apollo with His Lyre*. The Roman goddess of sex and Roman god of music and dance seemed fitting to showcase. The local production company had been working on the sets, lighting, and props all week, and Nate had to admit they looked pretty damn good.

Although he and Francesca agreed to keep far away from each other, his reckless pull toward her deepened as the week progressed. Despite studying for her GED, she worked long hours and made insightful suggestions that Margaux and the production team readily implemented. Her typing abilities improved drastically. She had shared that she spent evenings practicing her typing, and she must have practiced a lot, because by the end of the week she could out-type him.

She was smart, resourceful, bubbly, easy to like. She became good friends with the temporary chef he had flown in from Zohra Paris, who kept feeding her. Nate didn't appreciate the Frenchman's hovering over Francesca, but she didn't seem to mind, so he let it slide, though he scrutinized them with feelings bordering on resentment.

He found himself seeking her out for silly little questions, bringing her a cup of coffee from the kitchen or a cream-filled maritozzo from a local bakery. She reacted to each item with such pure joy, it left him swaying. The Righteous Hearth had hurt her, tortured her, kept her away from technology and schooling, tried to confine her. But they hadn't managed to destroy her.

Thinking of the cult pierced him with a fresh fit of fury. They'd hurt her badly—mentally, physically, emotionally. He'd never been bloodthirsty, but the scars crisscrossing her body made him want to track down every single member and make them pay. She hadn't shared more since Tuesday, and he hadn't pushed. Pressing her for details would hurt her, and that was the last thing he wanted to do.

But he intended to find out everything he could about the Righteous Hearth and destroy it—he had resources at his disposal and legal connections in Nevada. There would be nothing left when he was done with them.

As he watched Francesca laugh with the mixologist and the kitchen crew, sampling some sort of pink bubbly drink that Giacomo had prepared for everyone, a pang of reckless longing stabbed through him. Her inviting enthusiasm drew people into her sphere, like a sun others sought to orbit. He wanted to be a part of that orbit, even if he knew better.

He approached the group sampling fizzing drinks, intent on joining them, but everyone quieted as though he were a tropical lightning storm interrupting pool time.

Francesca set her glass down immediately. "Am I late?"

Batting away his frustration at everyone's reactions, he shook his head. "We still have a few minutes. What are you having?"

"Giacomo created a new drink. It's ginger ale, pomegranate juice…"

She went on to recite the ingredients, but his brain turned off listening to the list. Instead, his eyes focused on the tinge of pink staining her lower lip, a trace of the drink she had sampled, and he fought the urge to lean down and taste it from her lips. She wore a white T-shirt dress today, which covered her chest and arms, but left a scandalously lot of leg bare, golden skin he longed to explore.

Giacomo slid a pink drink his way too. "Try it."

Nate tore his gaze away from Francesca and reached for the glass, surprised that his hand remained steady. The bubbly concoction was too sweet for his taste, but he offered the right compliments before setting it back down and heading for his office. Francesca promptly followed.

"I don't pay you to drink on the job," he said when she closed the door behind her.

Her eyes rounded. Color fled her cheeks. "I'm sorry. They insisted. It's our new signature drink, and I wanted to try it in case the guests asked about it. There's no alcohol in it, of course. Giacomo made the ginger ale in-house. It won't happen again."

"Stop being so *nice* to everyone here."

Two parallel lines cratered between her eyes. "What do you mean?"

"You're the club manager. *Manage.* Don't *befriend* everyone."

"But…" She paused, looking genuinely confused. "I like everyone. They're all so nice. We spend so much time with them, why… why would I be mean to them?"

"Why are they all hovering around you like you're their mama duck?"

"They're not! We were just sampling the new drink."

He knew he was being irrational, but now that he had her alone in the privacy of their office, he couldn't restrain himself. "Yeah, and yesterday when the chef gave you those fried artichokes to try? What's your excuse then?"

"He needed someone to tell him if it's seasoned enough."

"He's a Michelin-star chef. He *knows* when it's seasoned enough."

Her brows knitted together. "You don't want me to speak to my coworkers?"

"I want you to do your job," he spat out.

Her voice took on a razor's edge. "What part of my job am I not doing?"

Good, let her be angry. She was too pleasant lately. Too accommodating.

Frustrated, he grasped for anything. "Do you have the guest list for Saturday?"

"Yes. I've memorized all the attendees, and their likes and dislikes, and allergies, and... sexual preferences, so I know which room to recommend to them when they arrive. I'm good at my job, Nate. I value it. I don't know anyone in Rome, and, besides Isa, I have no friends here, and I like having colleagues I can chat with. It makes me feel less lonely here. And I don't understand your problem."

He leaped across the small office before he could stop himself, his fingers closing around her upper arms. Her eyes widened as he bent his head. This close, the trace of the drink looked especially pink on her lower lip, almost matching the blush that suffused her face, intensifying the aqua of her eyes.

Her erratic breathing lifted her breasts against his chest, and a perverse part of him pulled her in closer until he felt the sharp points of her nipples through his shirt, then closer still. Her gaze bonded to his lips, as if expecting him to kiss her, anticipating it. Instead, he released her. She stumbled back a step.

"Noémie will be joining the Zoom soon," he muttered in a thick voice. "We should hop on too."

"All right," she said, but didn't move away. "Are you okay?"

He exhaled a humorless laugh. "No. All I want is to take you against this wall."

Her gaze widened. She turned her head to look at said wall. Her teeth nibbled her lip as she twisted back to face him. She didn't look that outraged. She opened her mouth to say something, closed it.

Not trusting himself to pursue the conversation further, he strode toward the desk. "We should join the Zoom."

***

Holy moly, what just happened?

One instant, she was trying a drink with her new friends. The next, Nate's strong arms were holding her close and his mouth was lowering to hers and… and he said he wanted to take her. Despite her better judgment, she'd found the words electrifying.

After launching the video call, Nate pulled over a chair for her to join him at the laptop so they could video chat with Noémie Fournier. Francesca had never met Noémie, but Nate had mentioned how much he respected her work.

A beautiful woman in maybe her late thirties popped up on screen, wearing a red lipstick that suited her flawless complexion. Her eyes lit up instantly. "Nathaniel!" —she pronounced it Na-ta-niél—"How are you? Find any horse heads in your bed yet?"

He chuckled. "I would have appreciated a warning."

Noémie shrugged. "I'm like Cassandra. No one ever listens to me. Hi, you must be Francesca."

"What horse heads?" Francesca asked.

"A silly *Godfather* reference," Noémie responded with a smile.

Whose godfather?

Before Francesca could ask a follow-up, Noémie moved on. "Ignore me. Are you two excited for opening night?"

"I'm a little nervous," admitted Francesca.

"That is absolutely normal. Do not worry. As long as the clients are happy, and safe, you have done your job."

"Do you have any tips for me?" Francesca asked.

Noémie didn't even have to think. "I greet the guests and then I stay far out of everyone's way. They're not there to speak with me—they're there to have fun. Keep the food flowing, the nonalcoholic cocktails pumping, and the rooms well-stocked, and they'll be happy clams. And be discreet. The members value their privacy."

"Of course," Francesca assured her.

"Address them by their first names. No Signore this or Signora that. You want to establish yourself as their equal. You're young, so that'll be more difficult with some guests, but don't be diffident. You're their peer. Speak to them as such. Otherwise, they'll treat you like a servant or won't take you seriously."

"That's helpful, thank you." Francesca jotted down Noémie's advice in her notebook.

"Nate will give you my number. Text or call me any time, and I will walk you through any emergency. Trust me, I've seen it all."

"Bye, Noémie," Nate said.

Surprised by the abrupt way he'd ended the call, Francesca didn't even have time to add her goodbye before he slammed the laptop shut.

"What—" she began, but his strong hands closed on either side of her waist, and he hauled her into his lap, slanting his mouth over hers in a bruising kiss. A kiss that tasted of anguish.

As his hands roamed freely over her body, her dress rode high up her thighs, exposing the full expanse of her legs. His rough palms cupped her butt through her underwear, explored heated skin. The layers of sensation sent moisture flooding, and she undulated against him in an attempt to alleviate the building pressure.

He released her just as abruptly, transferring her back to her own chair as though she weighed nothing.

Francesca struggled to find her breath, but every inhale seemed to be scented with him, making her want to crawl back into his lap.

His roughened voice cut through the silence. "I hate that I want you."

Ouch. Before she could gather herself to respond, he left her.

The door creaked as he shut it behind him.

***

The hurt his words had brought to her eyes sliced through him with each cowardly step away from the club.

He was losing his mind. Steven and his clients needed him back next week, and instead of preparing, he was salivating after Francesca. *Why the fuck did I kiss her?* They'd had a deal.

He was done with playing club owner. He wanted his life back.

Before he'd run to Rome, he'd been a rainmaker at his corporate law firm. Clients flocked to him; senior partners promoted him. Nate liked the parties, the clothes, the respect. Padma loved the lifestyle his job afforded them. Until she didn't.

What relationship could he possibly have with

Francesca, when he was in New York and juggling a full caseload? Absolutely none.

The more time he spent around her, the more of his thoughts she consumed, and he couldn't afford the diversion. His mentor had saved twenty-five lives in his classroom that day, and now lived with the bullet fragments. Nate's every waking moment would be spent on their lawsuit against Clary Guns. He couldn't allow Francesca to splinter his attention.

Why was staying away from her such a fucking challenge?

He checked the time on his watch. Enough roaming the streets; he had to get back in time to drive her home.

Returning to the club, he found the ballroom empty of staff. The office, too. Unease kicked in. *Did Francesca leave to walk home alone?* He'd driven her ever since the goat memo, and the idea of her out there by herself bothered him.

Not finding her in the kitchen either, he checked the courtyard. *Fuck. She did leave.*

Pulling out his phone, he intended to call her, but soft footsteps on the main stairs returned him to the ballroom.

Francesca.

Elation at seeing her surged through him, followed by unease. He shouldn't *want* to see her.

She took the rest of the stairs down and faced him, eyes snapping. "What you said—"

Knowing he'd hurt her, raring to apologize, he interrupted. "I'm sorry, I didn't mean it the way it sounded. I can't think straight around you, and I can't seem to stay away."

Her lips sloped down at the corners. "It wasn't very nice."

"No," he agreed, stabbing his fingers through his hair. "It wasn't."

The anger and hurt were still there in her eyes, and now sorrow too. He'd wounded her with his words.

He needed her to understand why he'd lashed out. "I want you, Francesca. Bad. But I can't allow myself to want you. I go back to the States on Sunday. Steven needs me back in Manhattan. He is the reason I made something of myself, and I'm scared that I'll let him down because I can't get you out of my head."

He battled the need to touch her, and lost. Threading his fingers through hers, he brought her hand to his lips.

"I admire what you're doing for him, Nate."

No one fully grasped the extent of what Steven meant to him. Maybe if he explained, Francesca would understand why his mentor had to take priority over all else.

"I don't know where I'd be without him. He's the reason I became a lawyer."

Realizing he still held her hand, he forced himself to release his fingers one by one. He waited for her to move away, but she didn't budge.

Slanting her head, she smiled that joyful Francesca smile. "Did his class inspire you?"

Unable to look at her, he stalked to the bar, poured himself a whiskey. "*Steven* inspired me. My parents didn't have much confidence in me growing up. Jackson lived with his dad, so I grew up with Hayes and Oliver. Oliver was the baby, and Hayes excelled at everything. I was the disappointing one."

She inched closer, but didn't join him behind the bar. "No, don't say that."

"They had cause to think that. I partied my way

through the first two years of high school, but eventually I wised up. Got a job, started volunteering, took AP classes. I got into a couple of colleges, and even one Ivy League. I was so proud of myself. My parents, in times of frustration, told me I'd amount to nothing, but they were wrong. Or so I thought. I accepted the offer from the Ivy. And then I learned I didn't get in on merit. My father had made a seven-figure donation to that school—and they found a way to offer me admission."

Her swallow was audible. "I didn't know such a thing was possible."

He laughed, even though he found no humor in the truth. "Very much so. I was ashamed. My dad had paid millions of dollars to get me admitted. I worked hard, but he still hadn't believed that I could get in on my own merit."

Swirling the amber liquid in the crystal glass, he slung back his drink. It had happened so long ago, but the memory still drew nausea and embarrassment deep from within him.

"I declined the acceptance. Couldn't go to the school my father bribed to take me. Even if it was his alma mater. What if he bribed the other schools too? I needed to make it on my own. So I went to a community college—transferred to a university from there."

Her eyes, full of compassion and understanding, held his. Finally stepping behind the bar, she took his hand between hers, held tight. "And you went to law school. Your parents must be proud of that."

"They were proud to have something to brag to their friends about. The only reason I even applied to law school was because of Professor Douglass. Steven saw something in me, and I set out to prove him right."

"And now he needs you."

"Even after I quit my job, almost crashed my life, he still wanted me to represent him. My old firm hired me back, accepted my terms that I take Steven's case pro bono. My job starts officially in three weeks, but I promised to be back earlier—start wooing my old clients back to the firm on Monday. I already have dinners lined up. It's the least I can do after the firm overlooked my… sabbatical. That's why I can't allow myself to get distracted by you."

Her lashes pressed together as she squeezed her eyes shut. When she opened them, tears gathered at the corners.

Shit. He'd hurt her again.

"Francesca—"

"No." She put up her hand. "No, wait, you have to understand. It's not what you think. *I can't get distracted by you either.*" Her voice broke, and she sniffed back gathering tears. "When Isa and I left the Righteous Hearth… we left our baby sister, Sofia, there. She's ten. We couldn't take her with us because she's underage and it would have been kidnapping." Her eyelashes fluttered as she blinked to clear the tears. "I left her, but I will get her back. This job means everything to me. The money will give me the opportunity to take her away from there."

Fuck. Her heartbreak panged through him. "Maybe I can help—"

"No. I won't be indebted to you. Favors come with stipulations. I have to do this on my own. I only told you so you'd know that I understand. Neither one of us can afford to get distracted."

Chapter 14

Saturday came sooner than Francesca anticipated. Tonight's opening would launch Zohra Rome officially, and she'd be a manager of a fully operational sex club. She never in her wildest imagination would have considered this possible. Growing up the way she had, a sex club wasn't even something she'd heard of until Isa had showed her that article.

As if understanding that Francesca couldn't handle any more upheavals, Isa had quieted down and occupied her time at home over the last week, studying on her phone. She had found a study buddy through some sort of online language program and was learning Italian.

Whatever kept her out of trouble.

Because the party wouldn't begin until ten that evening and would go all night, Nate had told her that he'd pick her up at five, which provided her with an extended opportunity to study.

Putting away her study materials just as the clock struck four, she began to get ready. After showering, she loitered in front of the armoire in a towel, trying to decide which of her dresses would work best for the evening.

Her grandmother knocked on her door. "May I come in?"

Francesca waved her grandmother into the room. "Of course."

Nonna carried a garment bag with her. "I got you a little present."

Reluctant to see her grandmother spend money on her, Francesca faltered. "You didn't have to do that."

"I could not resist. You don't have to wear it tonight if you don't want to, but I saw it and had to buy it for you."

Her grandmother laid the garment bag on the bed. Francesca, not used to receiving gifts and unsure what to expect, slid the zipper down. She stared at the one-shouldered gold gown. "This is gorgeous, Nonna."

"Try it on," her grandmother encouraged.

Cautiously, scared to accidentally damage it, Francesca pulled the dress off its hanger. "This must have cost a fortune. We can't afford this kind of expense."

Nonna waved off her concern. "It was on sale."

"You're sure?"

Her grandmother smiled. "Yes."

Francesca touched the shimmering fabric. "It's beautiful. Thank you for this."

"I wanted to get you something to celebrate tonight. I'm proud of you, Francesca. You fight for what you want, and I admire that in you."

Shedding her towel, Francesca undid the zipper and wiggled into the body-hugging dress, the fabric cool and silky against her skin. Although the skirt fell to her feet, a daring slit exposed most of her thigh.

"Do you want me to sew up the cut?" asked Nonna. "Is it too much?"

The old Francesca would have insisted, but as she spun in front of the narrow mirror, all she could think of was Nate's reaction to her in this dress. "No. I love it, Nonna." She held out her arms. "Are these too noticeable?"

"In the dim lighting of the party, no one will see."

Glancing down at her healing marks, Francesca prayed Nonna was right. She couldn't bear to see disgust in the club patrons' faces. They'd remind her too much of the disdain she'd faced when the community condemned her as a whore.

"Cessie! Nate's here!" yelled Isa from the vicinity of the front door.

Stupefied, Francesca frowned at her grandmother. "Why's he here so early and why'd he come up? He always waits downstairs."

"Looks like I can finally meet him," said her grandmother.

"Cessie… did you hear me?" Isa popped her head in. "Whoa! You look hot. Where'd the dress come from?"

"Gift from me," said Nonna.

Isa's eyes rounded in excitement. "Cessie, may I *please* put some makeup on you, *please, please?* I've been watching tons of YouTube makeup tutorials and practicing and Nonna took me to buy some earlier this week, and I think it would look amazing on you."

"I don't know…"

"It's a party." Nonna headed for the door. "Go crazy, put on some makeup. I'll go see if Nate would like a coffee."

***

Isa had left Nate to wait by the front door, where Francesca's grandmother found him. The older woman's lemon-yellow dress elucidated where Francesca had been borrowing her fruit candy-colored clothes.

"Come in, please." She waved him into the apartment. "I'm Graziella Rizzi. You must be Nate. Francesca will be out in a minute. I'll make you a coffee."

Nate couldn't explain what had spurred him to come up to Francesca's apartment, but he stepped farther inside.

"Sit, sit. It'll be another minute or two," her grandmother insisted, pointing to the small table against the kitchen wall. A faded linoleum tablecloth hung over its sides.

Setting the moka pot on the stove, she crossed the small space to place a chipped sugar bowl in front of him. "I wanted to meet the person who hired Francesca, especially after all the trouble Isa caused you."

"Francesca said you haven't seen each other in a while?" he asked, curious about her grandmother and their relationship.

"Too long. I'm glad the girls are with me now."

The moka pot began to gurgle, filling the small kitchen with the aroma of fresh stovetop espresso. Graziella placed a cup of steaming coffee in front of him and another cup across the table.

"Thank you." He stirred a spoon of sugar into his coffee.

She slid into the chair opposite him. "It's the least I can do after all you've done for Francesca. When do you go to New York?"

"Tomorrow afternoon. There's one issue I had hoped to deal with before I left, but I didn't get to it."

Graziella took a sip of the black liquid. "The Morettis?"

Ah. Francesca had told her grandmother. "We've upped club security, but Giorgio might still sniff around."

"If he does, he'll be castrated."

He'd lifted his cup, but Graziella's statement halted it halfway to his mouth. "That—"

"Ta-da! Here she is!" Isa pranced into the kitchen.

"Will you stop that?" grumbled Francesca behind her.

Nate's heart began to thump as Francesca entered the small space, tucking a bobby pin into her loose curls.

The gold dress clung to her figure as if painted on. As she walked, her long, tanned legs played peekaboo through the thigh-high cut in the fabric, revealing more of her than he'd seen since Tuesday.

His fingers loosened as he remembered the feel of her under his hands. The cup of coffee clattered to the table, hot liquid spilling out across the linoleum tablecloth.

Graziella stood. "I'll get a rag."

He barely heard her as he dragged his gaze to Francesca's face. Her darkened lashes emphasized the blue of her eyes. Her lips were slicked with gloss. He wanted to wipe off the sheen with his thumb and taste her.

Graziella dabbed at the mess on the table.

Realizing what he'd done, he reached for the rag. "Allow me. I'm sorry. I don't know how I did that."

Graziella's lips curved as she released her hold on the soaked cloth. "I do."

After he and Graziella finished cleaning the table, he turned to Francesca, cleared his throat. "We should go."

He hadn't realized he was still holding the rag until her grandmother took it from him and tossed it into the sink.

"When will you be back, Francesca?" asked Graziella.

"Party ends in the morning."

"I'll drive her back here myself," added Nate.

Graziella looked between her two granddaughters. "Dante and I leave tomorrow morning. I won't see you until next week. You are positive that you two will be all right here? Maybe I should cancel."

"We'll be just fine," singsonged Isa, handing Francesca her leather bag.

"You two go and have fun. You deserve a break after everything you've done for us," Francesca assured her.

Graziella hesitated. "You are sure?"

Francesca walked over to give her grandmother a tight hug. "Positive, Nonna. You and Dante have a great time." She turned to her sister. "Isa, I'll see you tomorrow."

Nate followed Francesca out the door, his eyes glued to the sway of her hips in the skintight dress.

"Where's your grandmother going?" he asked as they took the stairs to the lobby.

"Her boyfriend, Dante, is taking her to Positano for their anniversary. Their flight leaves pretty early tomorrow, so it'll just be Isa and me for the rest of the week."

"God help you."

She laughed, glancing up at him. Her eyebrows had changed, he noticed. They'd been trimmed back and now arched higher. Oddly, he missed the curlicues at the wings. "Isa hasn't been so bad. She's been learning how to do makeup." She motioned at her face. "This is all her doing. And she's met someone online who's helping her learn Italian."

He paused. "Who'd she meet online? That isn't safe."

Francesca shrugged. "Someone in a languages study group. I'm sure it's harmless. He doesn't even live in Rome."

***

As he drove them to Zohra, Francesca ran through the guest list, but he couldn't focus. Hands fisted on the steering wheel, he kept his gaze on the road, tried but failed to ignore the scent of her. *Did she always have to smell like lavender soap?* It made him think of taking a slippery, soapy bubble bath with her.

Don't look at her. One glance and he'd be slanting across the console, tugging down her dress, and sucking her nipple deep into his mouth.

He took his first full breath once he'd parked and leaped out of the Fiat. The warm evening air didn't erase the need churning through him. He avoided touching her as they entered Zohra and found the club deep in preparation. Florists arranged flowers in massive ceramic vases and models practiced their poses across the opulent sets. Francesca peeled off to greet Margaux and the security team. He hated the lascivious way the guards watched her approach.

Instead of going upstairs to change as he had planned, he strode forward, reaching her just as the new members of the security staff completed introductions. She glanced up at him as he joined her. This close, he could see the shimmer dusting her lids, her cheeks, her cupid's bow. As he slid his hand around her waist, her eyes widened.

Mine.

The unexpected thought made him drop his hand from her waist.

He had no business laying claim to her. He was leaving for New York tomorrow.

Giving him an odd look from beneath her thick lashes, Francesca took a deliberate step away from him.

If Margaux noticed the tension, she ignored it. "We'll do check-in here, and we'll have extra masquerade masks available for anyone who forgot theirs. Nate, I heard the lockers for the cell phones had issues last Saturday during preview night. Has that been fixed?"

"Yep. They should work fine now."

"Should isn't will," said Margaux. "Francesca, come with me. We'll test them. Nate, you join too."

He watched Francesca's ass all the way to the lockers.

***

With less than a half hour to go until the party officially kicked off, Francesca looked around the ballroom in disbelief. The flowers, the staging, the decorations were immaculate, and she had a hand in every aspect of this. She'd only been on the job a week, and already she had organized a launch party. If she could do this with the little work experience she had, anything was possible.

Hang in there, Sofia. Cessie will get you soon.

The security guards were in place, as were the models, the mixologist, the servers, the check-in crew. They had upped security in case Giorgio chose tonight to return, and the giants lined the perimeter of the club, attempting to look discreet. Margaux had gone off to have a word with one of the production crew members, but Francesca hadn't seen Nate since he'd joined them at the lockers. The burn of his hand on her waist had imprinted itself into her memory, as did the loss of his touch when he had drawn away.

She strolled to the check-in desk and pulled a feather half-mask off the table. Anonymity was key at Zohra. She tied the elaborate concoction around her head. There. Now she would be anonymous too. Although the mask left the lower half of her face exposed, emerald-tinted feathers jutted from the black satin in an opulent display across her brow and black crystal beads dangled across her cheekbones, doing an efficient job to distract from her features.

Hearing the familiar footfall, she turned toward the stairs. Nate, dressed in a dark emerald-green suit, a minimalistic mask dangling from his fingers, took the rest of the steps down until he faced her across the ballroom.

The blood rushing to her ears muted the ding of the jostling staff around her. Her heart beat painfully against her chest as she fought for control of her breathing. Nate beelined straight for her, erasing the distance with quick strides.

He stopped when he was close enough for her to smell his citrus cologne.

"You ready?"

Unable to restrain herself, she took a step closer until they were bare inches apart. "I am. Are you?"

"All packed."

He'd leave tomorrow; she already knew that. Having prepared for his departure with the fortitude of a soldier about to embark on a solo mission, she felt equipped to run Zohra without him. Yet imagining being here alone, without his easy presence, expanded the hollow ache inside her. Despite knowing better, she'd come to *like* him. Being around him made her happy—a feeling she'd learned to cherish after living for years in misery.

"I'm leaving my car here," he told her, "for when I visit. I want you to use it. Find an instructor who speaks English and take some driving classes. It's an important skill to have."

"I can't accept—"

Before she could voice her full protest, he interrupted. "It's not a handout. I want to keep the Fiat here, and someone needs to drive it or the battery will die."

She had always yearned to drive—knowing how in case of emergencies was indispensable. And she'd have to drive her siblings around when she and Isa returned to the States and had Sofia living with them. So she forced herself to agree. "Thank you."

"What're you up to tomorrow?" he asked, as though his leaving wasn't changing the very fiber of her days in Rome.

Thankfully, needing something to focus on besides Nate's departure had inspired her to make plans. "I'm taking the train to Florence."

"Florence? Why?"

"You know that we only have the Parisian chef here for another week. Zohra Rome deserves an Italian equivalent. I found a chef in Florence who I think would be great here. I want to offer her a job."

Something like pride flashed in his eyes, but she didn't dwell on it, in case she'd imagined it.

A smile tugged up the corners of his mouth. "Think she'll accept?"

"I don't know, but I hope I can convince her. The

club will be closed Sunday anyway, so it's a good time for me to go."

"I'm leaving Zohra in good hands."

Pleased, she grinned.

His gaze dropped to her mouth.

Oh no. Do not *kiss me. Saying goodbye tomorrow will be hard enough as is.*

She had to escape. Desperately, she looked at the closed door. "I should go."

He studied her mask with a frown. "Turn around. I'll fix your mask ribbons."

Her hand flew to the ribbons. "Oh no, did I tie them wrong?"

"Just a little crooked." When she presented him with her back, his deft fingers untied and retied the bow. "Not too tight?"

She released her hold on her mask, testing it as she faced him again. "No, feels fine, thank you."

He put on his own mask. Unlike her borrowed feather extravagance, his simply covered his eyes in black silk.

"Where do I get a simple one like yours?"

"I'm meant to be recognized. I don't want people seeing your face."

Panic singed her at the implication. "You think someone from the Righteous Hearth could be here?"

"I am not taking any chances with you."

Before she could respond, his lips caught hers. A split second of a kiss, yet when he lifted his head, she struggled to calm her wild lungs.

Staying away from him became just that much more imperative.

Good thing he was leaving tomorrow.

"The clients will be arriving soon. I should go." She stumbled over the words, but she got them out. Maybe he called her name as she fled; she wasn't sure. The sound of the blood whooshing through her ears drowned out everything else.

As the evening progressed, Francesca tried to focus on the decorations, the check-in table, the guests, the passed appetizers, the color of the darn walls—on anything but Nate—but her body had become hyperaware of his whereabouts at all times. Even without looking for him, she knew exactly where he was in the room, whether he was greeting guests at the door, helping Giacomo pour drinks, laughing with newcomers. Francesca didn't wish to follow his every move, but she couldn't help herself.

Effortlessly, he greeted guests, welcomed local politicians and celebrities, and met the Zohra members in town from the States for summer vacation. The way the women stared after him, she bet they came today just to ogle their host.

Her eyes drifted to him as he spoke to two beautiful women clad in scandalously sheer lingerie, standing by the naked redhead who posed as Venus on the half shell. As if sensing her attention, he turned his head and met her gaze, sending a bolt of awareness to throttle her breath. Whirling away, she hurried to their office, fighting the overwhelming need that seared her veins.

She entered the office and shut the door against his approaching footsteps. She hated that she knew the exact tempo of his walk. His strides slowed as he neared the office door. A pause strained before he knocked.

"Francesca?" His tone remained low, but she heard it even over the thump of the music in the ballroom beyond him.

No use pretending she wasn't inside. "It's unlocked."

He took off his mask as he entered, shutting the door behind him. "I shouldn't have done that earlier. We'd agreed."

The stupid feathers in her mask made it hard to see him. She reached up to tug the bows free. They knotted instead. She pulled wildly at them, but it only made the tangles worse.

"Need help?"

Her shoulders drooped. "Yes."

"Turn around." When she did, he undid the knots one by one until she felt the mask loosen. As the last ribbon released, she let the mask fall into her hands.

"I wanted you to do that earlier," she admitted with a dejected sigh. "I like it when you kiss me. I tried to fight it, but I want you. Since you're leaving tomorrow…"

What if she set aside all her burdens for just one night? That night would be worth it. Then, when the dust settled and Nate was back in New York, she could look back on the one thing she had gifted herself—a brief, torrid one night with him to wipe out the pain and shame her relationship with Miles Decker had brought her.

It took every ounce of her strength to meet his gaze.

She drew in a deep breath, whizzed it out to keep her voice steady. "What if we give in for just one night?"

His brow knitted together. "Francesca—"

She covered his lips with her hand to stop the flow of words. "Nate, my life is going to get very complicated really, really soon. I want to have one fun night, to be young and careless for just a little bit."

The dubious expression never fled his features. "How do I know you won't regret it?"

"That's not for you to worry about."

"Nate, you in there?" Margaux's irritated voice reached them, along with her knock. "The damn lockers aren't working again."

He spat out a curse. "We'll continue this later."

Francesca followed him to the lockers, hastily refastening her mask.

Chapter 15

When the guests' clothes started to come off, Francesca removed herself from the party. Not that she minded the nudity. Growing up where shame reigned above all and nakedness was a sin, it was oddly freeing to see consensual adults being so free with one another without fear of being smote. Or sewn into a hair shirt.

These people paid a lot of money for a night of pleasure, and they were intent on getting their tickets' worth, and that was A-okay by her. But she was no longer needed in the ballroom, Nate was deep in conversation with one of the bouncers, and her limited free time necessitated she make the most of her minutes.

She stepped into the office, pulled off her mask, opened her laptop, and launched the mathematical reasoning portion of a GED practice test while the music beyond her walls turned dark and sexy.

She didn't hear Nate open the door until his voice cut through her concentration.

"We have a problem." He strode inside.

"What is it?"

His lips tugged upward at the corners. "The Mildners are upstairs, and they lost the key to the cuffs they're using."

She stood, sure she'd misheard. "How?"

"Frankly, I'm too nervous to ask."

"Won't a key from a different set work?"

"That's the thing… they brought their own cuffs. They said ours were too frou-frou."

It took her a moment to process his words. "Mrs. Mildner is cuffed upstairs and there's no key to uncuff her?"

Nate shook his head. "No. Mr. Mildner is. Problem is, the locksmiths are all closed already."

Exhaling, she glanced down at her test. She'd have to resume it later.

She closed the laptop. "I can help."

"How?" He raised a brow. "You got a spare key to their carbon steel cuffs?"

"Better." As she hurried past him, his fingers wrapped around her hand, stalling her. "What?" She fought the sizzle of need.

He pulled the mask off his head and arranged it across her face, slipping the band over her hair. "There."

"Oh." She had forgotten about the mask policy. "Thanks."

Her fingers traced the silk that now lay against her cheeks as she followed him upstairs along the back stairway.

He stopped when they reached the Mildners' room. "They're in here."

Ever the gentleman, he held the door open so she could slip into the lushly appointed private suite. Sure enough, Mr. Mildner lay cuffed to the bed, fully naked. Something like… cooled wax tangled in his matted chest hair. Mrs. Mildner sat on the bed next to him. She had wrapped herself in one of the Zohra-branded robes.

"I don't know where the key could have gone," she

said. "I can go back to our hotel and look, but I'm almost certain I brought it."

Francesca, politely avoiding looking at Mr. Mildner, skirted the bed to peer at the lock. Yep. Standard issue, and they hadn't engaged the double lock. This would be easy.

She reached into her hair for a bobby pin, one of several she had secured like a safety blanket into her otherwise loose hair. Pulling it out, she tugged the two sides apart until the bobby pin flattened. Leaning over Mr. Mildner, she popped off the plastic tip and, just as she'd done dozens of times before, inserted the pin halfway into the lock. When the tip bent to the right angle, she repeated the process. Satisfied with the S-shape, she guided the bobby pin deeper, turned it to release the locking mechanism, and the cuffs slid open.

"Wow! How did you do that?" exclaimed Mrs. Mildner as Francesca stepped away from the bed.

"I can feel my hands again," sighed Mr. Mildner, sitting up to rub at his wrists.

"How *did* you do that?" Nate watched her as though she were an illusionist.

She shrugged, her lips twitching at their shocked expressions. "Releasing accidentally restrained guests is in my job description."

"That was impressive," said Nate as they left Mr. and Mrs. Mildner to resume their activities.

She kept her voice light as she responded. "It's a skill that's come in handy once or twice before."

"In Nevada?" he nudged.

Because she didn't want to think about it, she offered a shallow nod. He seemed to understand, waving her to precede him down the staircase.

Gathering all her courage, she stopped and faced him. "I meant what I said earlier, Nate. Just one time, I want to have fun. Think about it."

Before he could answer, she tugged up the long skirt of her dress and raced down the stairs.

Even though several more incidents required her attention, the night mostly went off without any major hitch. The festivities ended as the sun began to rise, though a few guests had fallen asleep upstairs, overstaying the club's close.

Nate brought in several bottles of chilled champagne for the staff to celebrate the conclusion of opening night. Zohra Rome had officially launched.

After the toast, the staff set down their champagne flutes and streamed out of Zohra, heading home to catch up on lost sleep. Tomorrow, production would return to tear down the sets, stage, and lighting, and the cleaning crew would put the place back to rights. For now, they left all as was, and Francesca, who'd barely slept the last couple of days, finally hit a wall. She had been so anxious that the evening go well, her body felt like it had been through a marathon and needed to recuperate. Muscles tense and achy, she sank into a nearby couch, leaned her head against the velvet back, and closed her eyes.

Nate's voice came from somewhere just above her. "Go upstairs and take a nap. Some of the rooms weren't used, but sleep in mine. Sheets are clean."

She kept her eyes closed. "I should go home, sleep in my own bed." She hoped Isa was still snoozing. They shared a room, and she didn't want her sister's exuberant questions to delay her from a very long, very deep slumber.

"If that's what you wish, come on. I'll drive you."

She squinted open one eye. "No, you're exhausted too. Go upstairs and sleep. I'll figure out how to call a cab."

He placed his hands on the sofa back and leaned over her. "It would be much easier if you just get a few hours of shut-eye here."

It was a tempting offer. Francesca glanced beyond him to the ceiling, as though she could see through the stonework to which rooms were clean and unoccupied.

"Sleep in my bed," he encouraged again. "I can guarantee no one was in there."

She sighed, exhaustion making her movements lazy. "Oh, all right. I'm so tired, I don't think I can make it back to Nonna's even if you drive me."

He bent lower, pressing a brief kiss to her forehead. The gentle gesture shouldn't have sent her heart skittering.

She stood on wobbly legs.

"I better show you which room is mine."

She remembered very well which room was his, but Nate's familiar hand grasped hers and she yearned to hold on to the thrill of his touch a bit longer. She clung to him like an anchor, a buoy amid the battering waves of apprehension that clamored through her. The Spiritual Leader had always dictated what she should think and feel and do, but she was finally free to experience life on her own terms. Free to make her own decisions, and she wanted this. She wanted him. Just as he wanted her.

He tugged her along behind him as they ascended the steps until they stopped in front of his room. Reaching for the key in his pocket, he unlocked the door and walked inside with her, her hand still clutched in his.

"I'll sleep in one of the other rooms." But Nate didn't leave. His thumb traced over each knuckle; when she inhaled at the drugging touch, his head dropped forward, as though in agony. "I should go while I still can."

Her eyes strayed to his packed duffel bag and laptop case all ready and set in the corner. He'd be gone in just a few hours.

Until then, she wanted him. Just like the world she had stepped into, he was different and terrifying and scintillating all at once, and she longed to learn him.

Every single one of her pulse points beat a disjointed staccato as she stepped into him. "Stay with me before you leave for the airport."

Cupping her face with his large hand, he brought his eyes level with hers. "You know that this can't go anywhere."

She relaxed into his touch. "I don't want it to. I'm not asking for more than just this once."

"God, I've been waiting for this." His lips were a breath away from hers, but he didn't kiss her. "From the first moment I saw you, all stormy and irritated, all I wanted to do was taste you."

"I was very irritated that day."

"You had every right to be." He trailed the pad of his finger along her collarbone. "I can't believe you're here."

Guilt for this moment she was taking for herself prickled her, but Nate's hot hands skated along her skin, chasing away her reservations. Just one morning with him, and then she'd resume her life and he'd return to New York.

But when he found the pull of her zipper, the memory of his earlier reaction to her disfigurement clawed to the surface. She couldn't endure if he focused on her scars as he did the last time. Laying her hands on his, she stopped him.

"Could you... ignore the remnants of what happened to me? I can't bear if you only see them when I'm with you."

Nate produced a sound somewhere between a growl and a wheeze. "Trust me, I'm much more interested in other parts of your body right now."

The comment loosened the tension squeezing her insides, and she released her hold on his hands.

Sliding down the zipper, he tugged the one beaded strap off her shoulder, and the shimmering fabric pooled around her feet.

Standing in front of him in her sensible underwear, she wished she'd worn fancy lingerie to entice him, but his gaze turned black as he swallowed, and color rose on his cheekbones—he didn't seem to mind.

He tugged her underwear down her legs, the air-conditioned air swirling around her flaming skin as she stepped out of them.

Although he had stripped her of every layer, he faced her fully clothed and looked intent on remaining so. When she reached for his suit jacket, he grasped her hands, lifting them to press a kiss to the inside of each wrist. His eyes burned into hers.

"If you touch me," he explained in a voice so gravelly, she barely heard him, "I'll come all over your stomach. I've been semi-hard all night just thinking about getting you alone in a room. I want to make this last."

"I've wanted to get you alone in a room all night too."

He nipped her jaw. "You don't know how much I want you. I smell lavender anywhere and I need you. Do you know how wild you drive me? Every time I watch your lips move, I want to feel them close over my cock."

Before she could process his dark confessions, he scooped her up, laid her across his expansive bed. Shrugging out of his suit jacket, he kneeled next to her and bracketed her with his arms. She lifted her face to him, felt his pleased groan vibrate through her as he took her mouth. But when she settled her hands on him, he captured her wrists and anchored them to the bed above her with one hand.

"Sometimes I hate how much I want you," he said. "You're all I think about when I shouldn't be thinking about you at all."

His hot palm hovered over her breast, and she gasped in a lungful of air, anticipating sweet pressure, but it never came. Instead, he traced barely there circles against her aching nipples, weaving featherlike figure eights from one breast to the other, but not settling the weight of his hand on her.

She arched into his touch, needing more pressure, but he moved his hand away, only returning to graze her when she settled.

"Do you have any idea what it's like to want someone so much?" he asked.

Sweat sheened her skin as she struggled feebly against the manacle of his hand holding her wrists immobile, desperate to touch him, to sink her fingers into his midnight hair and make him press his mouth to her breasts.

"Nate," she groaned in frustration.

He pulled back to watch his palm play with her nipples. "You're so fucking hot when you beg me," he said. "Do you want your pretty nipples in my mouth?"

"Yes," she gritted out, trying to bow into his hand, but he eluded her again.

"I want to show you how desperate I am for you every fucking day." Lowering his mouth, he exhaled a teasing gust of warm, moist air over her throbbing flesh. "I need you to be as desperate for me too."

"I am. Please."

When he dipped his head further, and the slick heat of his tongue traced her areola, she sobbed with relief. He blew across the wet trail… and then the hot pull of his mouth surrounded her swollen nipple. With singular focus, he licked, tugged, bit the tender surface before switching his attention to her other breast.

Moisture slicked her thighs as her hips rose restlessly into the air, seeking him, finding nothing but cool air.

This time, when she tugged to free her hands, he released them, his mouth descending on hers. He scored her lip with sharp teeth, tickled the tender bow with his tongue. Desperate to touch him, she curved her fingers into the strong muscles of his neck, traced the curvature of his shoulders.

He trailed a teasing finger lightly down to her belly. Demanding he stroke her aching center, coil the raw pleasure higher until she found that elusive, unfathomable relief, she flattened her feet to the bed and pushed her pelvis toward him.

"Are you ready for me?" He set his palm flat on her stomach.

The heavy weight of his hand made her feel every single one of her fluttering internal muscles.

"Hurry up." Patience gone, she grasped his wrist and dragged his hand between her legs, clasping it with her thighs, a silent warning that he better keep it there. A satisfied growl vibrated against her as his fingers slipped through her arousal.

"Have you ever…" he began in a velvety voice. When she stopped breathing, he took her sudden tension for confession. "You have. My naughty girl."

She gasped as he stroked.

"One day, I'll make you show me how you touch yourself."

Did he not remember that they only had today? "No. I can't."

Returning his mouth to her breast, he murmured against her skin, "We'll negotiate. If you agree to it now, I'll let you come."

She shook her head.

"Ah… I guess a more serious negotiation has to take place."

Finally, she panted out what he'd forgotten. "We only have today, Nate. There's no other day."

He stilled, as though that particular fact really had slipped his mind. Incrementally, his body relaxed, and he released her nipple. "Then we better make the most of it."

Standing from the bed, he pulled her closer to the edge in one quick swoop. As he dropped to his knees in front of her, he used his hands to spread her wider.

When she felt his breath against her moist curls, she gasped. "Wait—"

He looked up. "Want me to stop?"

Her head rolled back. "No, continue, *please*."

She balled his sheets in her hands as he dipped lower and licked her. No one had ever done that before.

Arching off the mattress, she balanced on her forearms to watch him. His hot gaze bored into hers as he tasted her again. It seemed so naughty and hot and surreal and real all at the same time.

He lashed her with wet heat until her arms gave out and she plopped back on the bed. When he darted his tongue inside, the jolt of pure sensation lifted her hips into his mouth, seeking more. Pleas clamored inside her head, but she didn't realize she moaned them aloud until they echoed against the walls of his room.

Spurred by her throaty cries, he teased her with insistent flicks. She begged, panting, beaded with sweat, her head thrashing on the bed in desperation.

Slowly, he worked one thick finger into her, his mouth still on her.

"Yes… just like that… yes…" he murmured against her.

Her body shuddered as pleasure tightened and swirled, inner muscles fluttering. She searched out his hand on her stomach, loved how his fingers sought hers, intertwined, held. Bowing off the mattress, she gripped his hand with the power of her release, his name tumbling from her lips before she could stop herself.

Taking a playful nip of her inner thigh, he stood and flashed her a pleased grin. Although she didn't have the energy to tell him to strip, he moved to do so unbidden, pulling off his tie, reaching for the top button of his shirt.

As he undid each button, he watched her as though he were half-afraid she would disappear in a poof of glimmering smoke. She loved his hot eyes that seemed to memorize every inch of her. Once naked, he joined her on the bed and her entire body tightened with anticipation.

Trailing wet, stirring kisses up her neck, he stopped when his mouth hovered inches from hers. "You're so hot when you come. I love the sounds you make when you're close. I want to feel you drench my cock."

She tasted herself on his tongue as he kissed her. "Hurry then."

A whoosh of air teased her cheek as he chuckled. "So impatient."

Fisting her hands in his hair, she made him meet her eyes. "Why are you so slow?"

His face was serious when he responded. "From the moment I saw you, I wanted you, but you were so untouchable."

"I wanted you too," she confessed, gasping as he slid his heavy length against her through the flooding slickness. Each deliberate stroke pierced her with pleasure. "I couldn't sleep the first night I met you."

"What were you picturing?" His seductive voice curled around her as he continued the inexorable glide across her sensitized flesh.

"Kissing you."

"I jacked off to thoughts of you, picturing you like this, naked, with me."

Her thoughts began to slur as she focused on the sensation of him moving against her. "Nate…"

"You want more?" he asked. "You want to feel me fill you?"

She raised her hips in response, gasping as the head of him lined up to her entrance.

He shifted away with a groan. "Protection."

Returning, he settled between her legs; his mouth branded hers as he guided himself into her.

"You're so tight," he growled. "So hot. Yes, more… take more."

He slid in to the hilt, brushing a gentle kiss against her cheekbone, her cheek, her lower lip.

"God," he inhaled.

His expression turned feral as he withdrew, only to return impossibly deeper, sending sparks of white-hot pleasure to burst through her. She lost herself to the power of him, to the words he slurred in her ear, to the claim he laid with each stroke. When she clamped around him, he didn't let her settle, stretching out the dazzling spasms racking her body, pumping into her with increasing wildness until he too exploded, burying his face in the curve of her shoulder.

"Holy shit," he mumbled, withdrawing from her. He left her briefly before returning, pulling her to his chest with trembling hands.

She wrapped her arm around him and settled her ear against his thumping heart.

"I never—" he began, but stopped. "That was—" As their breaths began to steady, he traced circles against her sweat-sheened back. "Watching you come on my cock was the hottest thing I've ever seen."

"I don't want to leave your arms." The realization of what she'd just said made her start. Not as much as it freaked out Nate. His body tensed under her as he processed the comment. "Because you're so warm, and the room is so chilly," she hastened to add.

It rankled that he relaxed at the hurried explanation. Undoubtedly, Nate remembered their one-time-only agreement and feared she'd get attached to him. He didn't have to worry. Falling in love with Nate was not part of her plan. She didn't have room for him in her future.

As she drifted off to sleep, she thought of his packed duffel bag in the corner with a squeeze of gratitude. Being around him longer would make it that much more difficult to say goodbye. How fortunate that he was leaving in a few hours.

Chapter 16

"Francesca!"

At first, Francesca thought she'd imagined her sister's voice calling for her from somewhere in the club. Isa couldn't be here.

"Francesca, *where are you*?"

Fully awake now, she sat up, surprised to find Nate asleep next to her. What time was it? He had a flight to catch.

"Cessie!"

Definitely Isa.

Her cries had woken Nate too. He blinked at her. "Was that…?"

Naked, she rolled off the bed, attempted to pinpoint the exact location of her dress as she called out to her sister. "Isa, I'll be right there!"

Spotting the pile of gold, she yanked it on with trembling hands. The zipper caught on the fabric on her first attempt to zip up, but closed on the second try.

Nate had pulled his clothes on too—the ones he could find, she guessed, because he ended up in his pants and shirt. He reached the door first, waited for her to dress. Once she was fully clothed, he opened it.

Her sister was halfway up the stairs and looked frantic—red, sweaty, like she ran the whole way from Nonna's.

Panic unlike she'd ever known slammed into Francesca. She ran to her sister. "Isa. What's wrong?"

Isa fell into her arms, holding tight as she hiccupped mid-sob. "The Righteous Hearth. They've found us."

"Explain." Nate's voice sounded harsh in the ensuing silence.

Isa stared at him but remained mute.

"It's okay," Francesca encouraged her. "He knows everything."

Isa focused on her sister. "After Nonna and Dante left, I wanted to go for a run. I went later than I'd intended, and it was so hot by then, I didn't make it far. When I jogged back, I saw him near our building. Miles. He was trying to get inside. I backtracked before he saw me, turned the corner, and *ran*."

"Who the fuck is Miles?" demanded Nate.

Isa craned her neck to look at him. "He's Cessie's fiancé."

Chapter 17

"He's not my fiancé," Francesca hurried to clarify. "That's the ex I told you about. He's why Isa and I left."

Footsteps at the top of the stairs hindered her explanation. A couple who'd fallen asleep in one of the rooms, now fully dressed but sleep-rumpled, appeared at the top of the landing. They slipped past them on their way out of the club. She'd forgotten about the straggling guests.

Nate pointed down the steps. "We should take this to the office."

Isa looked at Francesca. "I want water. I'm thirsty."

"Come on." Francesca kept her arm around her sister. "We'll get you water on the way."

They stopped by the kitchen to get Isa a cold glass of water en route to Nate and Francesca's office.

Once inside the small space, Isa hopped on the desk and took a long swig, but Francesca hovered at the edge of the room, too nervous to sit.

Nate closed the door behind them and faced her. "Tell me everything. From the beginning."

The directive set Francesca's teeth on edge. "This is for me and Isa to figure out."

"Stop. Tell me, and we can go from there."

Isa drained the rest of the water and slammed the glass down on the desk. "Just *tell him*, Cessie."

Surprised by her sister's outburst, Francesca plopped into the chair in the corner. Nate remained standing, arms folded across his chest, and kept his focus squarely on her.

She filled in the blanks. "Our parents dedicated their lives to the Righteous Hearth, but they have never been part of the advisory echelon. When the Spiritual Leader declared that he had a vision of me marrying Miles Decker, my parents rejoiced."

"They want him for a son-in-law because it would move them higher up the ranks in the church. So they approved the match without asking her," Isa supplied.

"The wedding was supposed to happen once I agreed, since I have to agree. But I wouldn't agree. I couldn't after what he'd done to Isa when we'd dated…" She didn't know how to continue.

"He came on to me," Isa explained. "Cessie and our parents were out when he stopped by the house. I let him in because he said he wanted to hang out. But then he said some gross stuff, and he tried to touch me."

"I had just turned twenty—Isa was thirteen then. Of course I broke it off immediately with Miles."

"Did you tell your parents?"

"I told them everything once I learned he was my intended. They said I was lying."

"They didn't believe me either," Isa added. "One fight got particularly bad. So they locked Francesca and me in the Sinners Shed."

Nate spun between them. "What the fuck is that?"

Francesca didn't want to think about it, so Isa explained.

"It's where the Righteous Hearth locks those who disobey. It was so hot outside that day, but inside felt even hotter. We had no water, nothing to cool us down, and the shed continued to heat. What they didn't know is that Cessie is real good at picking locks. She has been ever since Mom and Dad would lock me in my room when I'd misbehave as a kid and she'd always undo my cuffs when they weren't home, but then would have to put them back on when they returned."

Nate looked horrified. "They'd cuff you guys?"

Francesca waved off his question, refusing to think of their parents' preferred punishment. The Sinners Shed had been so much worse. The bobby pins in her hair had heated in the shack. Ridiculously, she felt their burn against her scalp even now.

"The Sinners Shed was the final straw, and we were prepared," she said. "Prior to that, my friend Haley, who's married and lives outside the compound, helped me open a bank account and get passports for Isa and me."

"We waited for nightfall and ran. Haley took us to the airport."

Restless, Francesca stood, facing Nate across the emerald rug. "We had nowhere to go, but Isa and I had been saving all our money that we earned helping Mr. Orson take care of his farm animals, and we came to Nonna. We hadn't spoken to her in years because Mom and Dad wouldn't let us, but I had her number."

"Cessie called her when we landed—someone at Airport Information let us use their phone—and she answered and came straightaway to the airport. How did Miles know we'd come to Rome?"

Francesca considered her sister's question. "Maybe the Righteous Hearth figured we'd have nowhere else to go but to our grandmother's? We never thought they'd suspect we'd have passports, but we were wrong."

"Was he able to get into the building?" Nate asked Isa.

Isa shrugged. "I don't know. I didn't stick around to see." She turned to Francesca. "Should we call Nonna?"

Francesca couldn't let their grandmother get entangled in their mess. "Not yet. She and Dante are celebrating their anniversary. She can't do much to help, and I don't want to get her mixed up in this."

Isa's eyes filled with sadness. "We need to find another place to live."

"Stay here." Nate appeared as surprised by his words as Francesca, but he seemed to commit. "I mean it. No one will guess this is where you'd be. The nights will get rowdy, but you can block off the top floor. No one will disturb Isa there."

Touched by the offer, Francesca wished to accept, but she couldn't. "That's too generous. We can't get Zohra involved. The Righteous Hearth is dangerous. They hold a lot of power. They control a huge chunk of Nevada. The police, the prosecutors… they're all on their payroll. They're probably worse than the Morettis."

"And Sofia is stuck there," said Isa.

"I'll help you get your sister back."

Francesca's feathers ruffled. "We don't need your help."

"I know you don't need my help. You're to a fault independent and self-sufficient, but I want to help. I have family in Nevada. I know attorneys there."

Francesca kept the bitterness out of her tone. "We can't afford the good ones."

"I can."

"No." She lifted her chin. "Isa and I don't want to owe you. The price is too high."

He looked like he wanted to shake her. "I'm not bartering with you, dammit. There is no price."

"There's always a price."

A muscle began to tic in his jaw. "Tell me your plan then."

"It's an uphill battle. On paper, my parents are exemplary. Pillars of the community. My father owns a chain of gas stations across Nevada, which the Righteous Hearth made happen, so they can provide for her. What can Isa and I offer? We aren't Sofia's parents, and we have no money."

"The way you and Isa reacted that one time I gestured too sharply? They hit you."

"Not often, and only when we were younger. The Righteous Hearth demands obedience in children, encourages discipline. Besides, all that is hard to prove. And they're more lenient with Sofia," Francesca explained.

"I don't want to be in Rome anymore, Cessie," said Isa. "But I won't go back to Rose Falls, and I won't let you marry some pervert just so Mom and Dad can lord it over their friends."

Francesca crossed to her sister, taking her face between her hands before engulfing her in a hug. "I won't ever let you go back, Isa."

"You sure we shouldn't tell Nonna?" Isa asked against her shoulder.

"Not until she's back." But she knew how they could escape—just for a little while. "You're coming to Florence with me today."

Confusion marred Isa's features. "Why would we go to Florence?"

"To see a chef. I was going to do a day trip, but we can stay the night."

"Shit," Nate cursed, his eyes flying to the clock ticking against the wall.

Francesca looked too. Almost eleven.

His flight.

***

"I have to go."

His flight was leaving in less than three hours, and he would be on it.

After Padma left and he lost Sammy, he blew up his life like an asshole. Now he had his job at Rhyme, Ryan, & Shuster back. Even knowing that he'd quit law, Steven trusted him to represent him. He wouldn't fuck it all up again now.

When he turned for the door, he didn't look at Francesca because he couldn't. He wasn't so sure he could walk away if he did.

His leaden legs took him up to his room, but as he stared at his duffel and computer bags, he couldn't bring himself to pick them up. Irritated, he stalked to the bathroom to get his toiletries, tossing them into the small case he'd left there last night.

He was leaving Francesca at the mercy of a cult that had tortured her. On top of that, he'd dumped a club on her that was under tangible threat from the Morettis, and possibly from Frascati too. Yes, she claimed to be okay with it. But he'd stupidly become protective of her, and abandoning her to known and unknown elements was a physical ache he couldn't shake.

Could he live with himself if something happened to

Francesca? When she'd tried to disobey the cult before, they'd mutilated her. What would they do if they found her now?

Returning to the duffel, he unzipped it with an angry jerk and stuffed the toiletries case inside. Then shut it closed again and hoisted it to his shoulder.

Francesca would be fine. It's not like the Righteous Hearth knew she worked at Zohra, and the Morettis would probably lay off once he was back in New York.

Francesca Brook is not my responsibility. She is capable of taking care of herself.

"Fuck." He dropped the duffel bag to the ground.

His new position at the law firm wouldn't start for another two weeks. There was time—plenty of it—to wine and dine his clients back to the firm. The thought of postponing dinner with his mentor churned his stomach, but Steven would understand. In fact, he'd insist on it. Leaving Francesca to deal with the Morettis and the Righteous Hearth in a strange country alone went against everything Steven stood for.

No, it wasn't work or Steven rushing him back to Manhattan today.

The hurry came from him.

The longer he stayed here, the more time he spent with Francesca, the more he felt toward her. And he refused to feel anything toward her—toward anyone. Padma had taught him that lesson. Trust—love—brought nothing but devastation. He had to get out while he still could.

Steven's case, shutting down Clary Guns, would require his full attention...

But not tomorrow. He still had two weeks.

Running away now would leave Francesca to deal

with the Righteous Hearth and the Morettis alone, and he'd never be able to look at himself in the mirror if he deserted her like that.

He studied his calendar on his smartphone. He'd stay two more weeks—less, if possible—to handle the Morettis and figure out how to deal with the Righteous Hearth.

And he'd purge Francesca from his system.

A few more bouts of wild monkey sex with her should do it. Then he'd return to Manhattan, having put his obsession with her to rest.

Ignoring the odd skip of his heart now that he was staying with Francesca just a little longer, he checked the time in Manhattan. Too early to call his clients, but Steven would be up. He called his mentor first, then sent off the necessary emails to his clients and law firm.

After he changed his flight, he returned downstairs.

Play it casual. Don't let her read into this.

If Francesca suspected he'd stayed to safeguard her, she'd revolt.

Following Isa's voice, he found them in the kitchen. While Francesca held the fridge door open and looked over the leftovers the chef had organized there last night, Isa volleyed questions at her about the Zohra party.

Isa saw him first, and didn't seem thrilled about it. "You're still here."

The comment made Francesca turn. Her gaze scanned around him, indubitably searching for his luggage. Finding none, she gave him a wary look. "Did you miss the flight? Are you taking a later one?"

"I moved it to two weeks from now."

She closed the refrigerator door, looking as happy about him staying as Isa. "Why?"

Well, didn't that just make one feel welcome. Feigning indifference, he lifted a shoulder. "Haven't tied up the loose ends yet."

When her eyes flashed, he put up his hands. "I know you've got it all under control. But for my own peace of mind, I'd rather not rush off while Moretti is hanging around."

"So you're staying because of Giorgio, and not the Righteous Hearth?" she clarified. "Because they're my problem, not yours."

"You handle them. I'll handle the Morettis." That division of labor seemed to pacify her. Or maybe she didn't want to fight in front of Isa. He pushed it a hair further. "And I'm going to Florence with you today."

He could practically see her shields go up. "Why would you do that?"

In response, he opted for an easy smile. "Zohra is closed tonight. What else am I going to do?"

She didn't buy it for a second. Her eyelashes swept over her eyes, but not before he caught a flare of alarm there.

Before Francesca could contend further, Isa spoke up. "Don't you have a hobby? Florence is a girls' trip."

He arched a brow at the teen.

With an annoyed roll of her eyes, Isa sighed. "Fine. Are we at least going to drive? If we do, can I drive? Maybe on a remote street?"

Nate inwardly cringed at the thought of the teen behind the wheel of his car. "We're taking the train. It'll be easier."

Francesca made a frustrated sound. "Okay, you can tag along. But we have to go back to Nonna's to get a few things first. I can't travel in a ballgown."

Nate raked his gaze over the aforementioned gown, the one he'd stripped off her just hours earlier. When Francesca's face flushed, he made himself look away.

"Give me the key and a list," he told her. "I'll grab them for you. Isa, you know how to use an espresso machine?"

"Nope."

"Well, this is your day to learn."

After Isa and Francesca wrote out a list of items they'd need from their apartment, Isa circled the espresso maker with the determination of a matador. Leaving her to figure it out, he folded the list and tucked it into his pocket.

Giving Isa a careful look, Francesca waved him toward the ballroom. "I'll walk you out."

She didn't speak until they reached the side exit. "There's one last thing I need from there. Isa wouldn't want you to know about it, but I need you to bring it."

"What is it?"

"Under my bed, there's a folder. Could you grab it for me? But don't look inside."

***

Less than a half hour later, Nate packed up the items that Isa and Francesca had wanted. Walking through their grandmother's apartment, seeing the two narrow beds in the tiny room Isa and Francesca shared, the small dresser and armoire that stood almost empty because they had so few things, had ratcheted his admiration for the two women. They had escaped to another country with almost nothing, and now were saving up to rescue their sister.

Kneeling next to Francesca's bed, he pulled out the folder she'd tucked deep beneath. Keeping his word, he didn't open the file, just added it to the two half-empty totes he'd packed with their few things.

Returning to Zohra, Nate set the bags at the bar and found Isa and Francesca in the kitchen. Francesca looked up from the greens she was chopping. Three dishes loaded with last night's leftovers lined the counter next to her. To his deep satisfaction, Francesca's eyes heated as they focused on him. He moved before he thought better of it, walking around the counter to stand next to her.

Isa was at the espresso maker, expertly managing its many handles and knobs.

"Any sign of Miles?" asked Francesca.

"No, I didn't see anyone."

"The idea of him knowing where Nonna lives… it makes me sick." She dropped the knife to the cutting board before facing him. "How do they always do this?"

"Do what?"

"Somehow, they *always* have a way of bringing people back. Last year, the Righteous Hearth found Louise and her son when they'd run—somehow coerced them to return, locked them in the awful Sinners Shed, kept them there… The heat, the lack of food and water, almost killed her little boy."

Fuck. There were more people like Francesca and Isa who'd sought to escape. "Are they still there?"

Francesca nodded. "After the shed, Louise lost the will to fight. Now, she sings the church's praises, acts as an exemplary member—but, Nate, I saw that bleak, hopeless look deep in her eyes where she couldn't hide it. She abhors being there, but she knows she can never leave. If she does, they'll find her again—and the punishment will be even worse."

"How are your parents a part of that?"

Her shoulders lifted in a semblance of a shrug. "They trust that God speaks through the Spiritual Leader… and, they've been there so long now, that community is their family. Their finances are tied to the Righteous Hearth. They don't see a way out."

"They don't want a way out." Isa slid a white porcelain cup, steaming with a decent-looking espresso, to him. "Here, this one is for you."

Reluctantly leaving Francesca's side, Nate went to the fridge to grab milk for his coffee.

"Cessie, coffee?"

Francesca didn't answer her sister. Concerned, Nate twisted his head to see why. Concern morphed into satisfaction. Her gaze was glued square to his ass. *Good.* He was proud of his butt.

"Cessie?" Isa asked again, her tone now sharper.

Francesca tore her eyes away from him and resumed her chopping. "Oh, yes please. Thanks."

"You know we weren't allowed to have any caffeine by the Righteous Hearth?" Isa said to Nate. "No stimulants of any kind, including coffee and tea, though I'm pretty sure Mom and Dad had a stash of teabags under the sink."

Francesca's lips twitched. "They did. They hid them behind the dish soap."

"What other rules did your parents break?"

"A few to protect us as kids," said Francesca. "They weren't as strict as the Spiritual Leader deemed parents should be. When I got sick, they defied him and took me to the hospital. They prioritized Isa's and my needs."

"Until Miles Decker came calling." A thick thread of resentment tightened Isa's tone.

"That's only because, if I married him, it would guarantee them higher standing in the community."

"So they sold you for clout," said Nate.

Her hand squeezed the knife handle. "They didn't sell me. No money was exchanged."

"But they refused to take her no for an answer," clarified Isa.

Francesca portioned her makeshift salad among the three plates of leftovers. "It's odd… they were good parents in so many ways and awful in so many others. The deeper they got in the church, the more under the Spiritual Leader's influence they fell… the worse it got. But when we were kids, before they got too ingrained, they were pretty wonderful."

Nate touched her shoulder. "You miss them."

"I do. I'm so angry at them, but I miss them. It's hard to explain."

"I'm just angry at them," said Isa.

"That's because you were too little to remember our road trips and game nights and camping weekends before the church banned all that."

Isa clanked Francesca's coffee in front of her. "Hurry up and eat. I want to see Florence."

Chapter 18

After a hurried lunch, Nate reserved them a hotel in Florence despite her insistence she do that herself. Nate refused to listen, which peeved, but because it really was only one night, she'd let it slide.

Having changed into the navy dress Nate had brought her from Nonna's, she came downstairs to meet him by the main door. His eyes raked over her on her descent, lingering on her legs. She savored the thrilling bite of pleasure at his perusal, even if she knew not to get used to the feelings he continued to draw from her.

Making love with him had been freeing. She'd broken away from the Spiritual Leader's mandates, the Righteous Hearth's decrees. She'd wanted to have wild sex with a man she found attractive, and did.

If he'd just gotten on that plane, she'd be celebrating their time together. But he'd stayed. Worse, when she'd heard he was staying, she'd been *elated.* She'd recognized the feeling with dawning alarm—the man she'd come to like had chosen to stay with her longer. It was horrifying.

Isa joined them after changing too, and Nate called them a cab for the Roma Termini train station. Although Francesca had read that Roma Termini was one of Europe's largest, she didn't find it as overwhelming as the airport.

The station brimmed with people—tourists rolling large suitcases, well-dressed men and women carrying newspapers under one arm, laughing teens jostling one another. Some travelers lined up in cafes, waiting to order coffee or snacks; others browsed the shops; yet even others waited by the platforms for their trains.

Francesca appreciated the chaos of the crowds around them, as it gave her a sense of anonymity, a way to remain hidden even while they were out in the open.

Once they bought their tickets from the ticket machine, Isa turned to her. "Can I go check out the shops?"

"Don't stray far," Francesca warned. "Our train arrives soon."

"Would you like to explore too?" asked Nate. "We have a few minutes."

Isa's eyes lit up at his suggestion, and she grabbed Francesca's hand. "Ooh yes, let's go, Cessie."

"I guess it wouldn't hurt to look around."

When they entered the first shop and Isa skipped ahead to explore, Nate stepped closer to Francesca and intertwined his fingers with hers. Not used to PDA, she found holding his hand thrillingly indecent, but she wouldn't have let go if the entire population of the train station suddenly stopped and looked at them.

If only he'd just gotten on that plane.

Isa glanced up from perusing the items. Her gaze zeroed in on their clasped hands. She skirted the display and caught up to them, face stormy. "Let's go to the platform. Or we'll miss the train."

Isa threaded her arm through Francesca's free one, pulling her forward and away from Nate.

As the train, painted a shiny red with gold letters across its side, approached, Isa craned her neck to look at Nate. "How long will it take?"

"About an hour and a half."

"You said our tickets come with snacks. What kind of snacks will they have?"

"You'll have to wait and find out."

They boarded and found their spacious, leather-bound seats. Isa grasped Francesca's hand. "Sit with me."

Francesca threw Nate a rueful smile and sat down next to her sister, while he claimed a seat behind them.

A prickle of awareness made Francesca turn toward the people lining the platform next to their train.

Her gaze settled on the familiar swirl of blond hair, the long neck, the sharp slope of the shoulders…

It couldn't be.

The man's head turned, as though he felt the weight of her stare.

Their eyes collided.

Miles.

Recognition and surprise launched his eyebrows high. His mouth released as if to call out her name. He leaped toward them, but it was too late. The train pulled away with a jolt.

Francesca squeezed Isa's hand.

"Ow. What?"

The response dried up in her throat. She had to force herself to say his name. "Miles. He just saw me."

"*Where?*"

Isa's sharp question had Nate leaning forward. "You okay?"

Francesca swallowed against the enveloping panic. "I just saw Miles on the platform. He saw me too. How did he know we were here?"

Nate's gaze shot to the window. "Which one is he?"

"You can't see him anymore. But he knows where our train is going. He'll know where to find us."

Chapter 19

As the train picked up speed, Nate abandoned his seat to kneel next to Isa and Francesca's row. Isa, sitting rigid-straight, face ghostly pale, stared blindly into space, as if her thoughts were worlds away.

"Isa? You okay?" he asked, concerned for the usually outspoken teen.

Francesca wrapped her arms around her sister and pulled her close.

Isa collapsed against her shoulder, clearly fighting tears. "He can't find us. I will never go back. Ever, ever."

"I'll never allow that to happen," promised Francesca. "I just need to think." Her gaze met Nate's. "How would he know to look at the train station?"

Nate had a niggling suspicion he didn't voice. "Either way, Florence isn't this train's only stop—if Miles was at the station by coincidence and saw you, he still doesn't know where we are heading. And even if he ends up in Florence, looking for you will be like trying to find a needle in a haystack. Impossible. If he does find you, he'll have to go through me."

"This isn't your battle to fight, Nate," Francesca said. "If Miles is here… he must have a way of getting us to cooperate. I don't know what it is, but he wouldn't fly to Italy without a plan. The Righteous Hearth has endless means at their disposal. It frightens me to think what they intend to hold over our heads. As far as the church is concerned, I'm already his."

The comment irked. "You're not his."

"You don't know what it's like to be raised in a place like the Righteous Hearth. You're not your own person. We are there to follow the Spiritual Leader and do God's bidding to save the world."

"Do you still believe that? That Righteous Hearth will save the world?"

"No, but it's… it's hard to shake. Sometimes I feel guilty for running away, for not heeding the Spiritual Leader's guidance… but mostly, I'm just sad I left Sofia there."

Nate laid his hand on Francesca's knee, squeezed before Isa could swat him away. "We'll get her out."

No matter how much Francesca fought his offer to help, he couldn't look the other way while a helpless child waited to be rescued.

Isa lifted her head off Francesca's shoulder. "If they found us here, that means they know everything—what if they go after Nonna?"

"Nonna is far away," Francesca assured her, "and Dante is with her. She'll be okay."

As the conductor made her way down the aisle, Nate returned to his seat, pulling out his phone to review the timetable for trains leaving Roma Termini in their direction. If Decker managed to get his ticket in time, he would catch the train departing only ten minutes after theirs. A sorry head start.

Someone had tipped off Decker to Francesca's

whereabouts. Nate had a feeling that someone was Giorgio Moretti.

***

When they reached Florence and the train pulled into the Santa Maria Novella station, Nate hurried them onto the platform.

"If Decker moves fast and attempts to look for you here, he'll be on the train that arrives in ten minutes."

They navigated the crowded train station to the exit and bypassed the cab line, their strides brisk. Weaving around throngs of slow-moving sightseers, Francesca could see his earlier point. Miles was determined, driven by the wishes of the Spiritual Leader, but even he wouldn't be able to find them in this swarm.

She checked the time on her phone. Just past three. "Our appointment is in twenty minutes."

The restaurant was a fifteen-minute walk or a twenty-minute cab ride with the traffic. They settled on walking. As they moved in the direction of the restaurant, she avoided getting too close to Nate. It would be too easy to grow attached to him if she wasn't careful.

They bypassed the Basilica di Santa Maria Novella, a beautiful fifteenth century church that Francesca had read about on their flight to Italy, walking until they reached the Cathedral of Santa Maria di Fiore. She and Isa stopped, staring up at its red-tiled dome. The span of its façade was inlaid with white, red, and green marble in intricate geometric shapes.

The tightly pressed crowds slowed their progress around the cathedral, but eventually they turned onto the street that took them to the two-Michelin-starred restaurant. Because the restaurant wouldn't open until later, she knocked on the glass front door to let Chef Camilla Morino know they'd arrived. Chef Morino approached from somewhere inside the restaurant and unlocked the door.

"You certainly caught me off guard with your offer," she said with a laugh, letting them inside. "And you brought a whole team. Come in, I made plenty of food."

Francesca instantly liked the older woman, with her kind eyes and ready smile. She'd accessorized her otherwise casual outfit with heavy gold earrings and a substantial gold necklace, looking elegant and expensive. Zohra would have to pay her a lot to get her to move to Rome and work at the club, Francesca surmised.

"It's kind of you to think so highly of me," Chef Morino continued. "As I told you on the phone, I'm happy here, but I'm curious on why you want me."

She gestured to one of the white tablecloth-covered tables across the pristine space. The table brimmed with a selection of antipasti laid out on simple dishes.

Francesca had half expected Isa to leap toward the table and dig in, but her sister, comprehending the seriousness of the meeting, stayed to the back and waited for her cue.

The appetizers were delicious, as was the coffee that she'd served afterward. As they ate, Francesca laid out the hiring package she'd prepared last week in efficient points, then painted a picture of what she saw for Zohra Rome and the partnership the two would have.

"To be honest, I planned on refusing you today," said Camilla. "But you've intrigued me. I'll think about your offer and will let you know next week."

Meeting adjourned, they thanked Camilla and stepped out on the hot, summer streets of Florence.

Nate's teeth sparkled as he grinned at her. "You are remarkable. One day, you'll be running a Fortune 500 company."

The suggestion was ludicrous, but it held its appeal. Anything really was possible once she got her degree. She'd ensure her sisters got their education too—as soon as she had them both with her. Pleased by the compliment and relieved that the meeting was over, she allowed herself to grin back.

Nate took her hand. "Let me show you Florence."

Although the lead in her gut screamed at her to go to the hotel and hide, she didn't wish to deprive Isa of a brief break. And Nate seemed to have a lot of energy to burn.

After she yielded, he secured tickets to the Galleria dell'Accademia to visit Michelangelo's *David*. Francesca had only read about the sculpture, and seeing it in person brought out goose bumps across her skin. The Righteous Hearth had kept its members scared of the world outside its teachings, yet that world was beautiful, and historic, and magnificent, and Francesca thirsted to experience all of it.

Afterward, they traversed Ponte Vecchio, a medieval stone bridge over the Arno River, pausing at the elaborate window displays of the jewelry shops that lined the bridge. Isa asked Francesca to take a photo of her in front of the Arno. When Francesca snapped it using Isa's phone, Isa snatched back her cell phone and promptly texted the photo to her Italian language study buddy.

While Isa skipped ahead, taking photos and texting, Nate took advantage of their private moment. Pulling Francesca to a stop, he tilted up her face with a gentle finger and kissed her right there in the middle of the crowded bridge. The brief kiss was hot enough to burn her, and she wanted it to go on forever— *Uh oh.* There was no forever for her and Nate.

Someone behind them whistled, but Francesca was already stepping away.

After the bridge, they walked to the Piazza della Signoria, studying the sculptures on display in the Loggia dei Lanzi.

"Oliver is obsessed with sculptures. He got his PhD in ancient Greek statuary." Even as Nate rolled his eyes, he took a photo of the displayed statues and texted it to his brother.

It warmed Francesca to know how close Nate was with his siblings, even as guilt stabbed through her. Here she was, free and happy in Florence, while little Sofia was trapped in Nevada.

Soon, Sofia. She vowed to show her baby sister the world the Spiritual Leader was intent on keeping from his followers.

For dinner, Nate chose a Tuscan restaurant nearby. Isa, who'd been bubbly throughout the day, began to wane as their meals arrived. She picked at her food without much interest.

"I want to go to the hotel," she said.

Nate directed his response to Francesca. "I think tonight calls for an early bedtime."

The lick of flames in his eyes contradicted his careful tone.

Francesca swallowed, understanding his intent. They'd only agreed on one night—well, technically *morning*—together, since Nate was supposed to be well on his way to New York by now. Did they dare continue their brief affair? The tingling excitement that bubbled through her screamed *yes* even as logic argued otherwise.

After dinner, they walked to the boutique hotel, which took up two buildings—once a medieval church and a Byzantine tower.

"Whoa." Isa practically danced into the lobby comprised of exposed stone walls, carved-wood ceilings, and neutral furniture arranged around a fireplace. It smelled tantalizingly of lilies of the valley and something crisp and fresh, enveloping them in a white floral fragrance.

Taking advantage of Isa's preoccupation with the surroundings, Nate took Francesca's hand and leaned close. "Stay with me tonight."

The anticipation in his gaze mirrored the eagerness detonating through her. *Yes, yes. One morning with him wasn't enough.* But that morning had scraped at her defenses, exposed a softness for him she shouldn't feel. It would be dumb to agree to more sex with him—she liked him too much as it was.

But it's not like he was staying forever. He'd be gone soon enough; she just had to steel her heart until then. Decision made, she nodded.

The concierge, an older gentleman in a pristine suit, waved them over to the check-in desk with a hospitable smile.

Nate reached for his passport and extended it to the concierge. "We have two rooms reserved. Make sure they're next to each other."

Francesca leaned against him. He understood she'd want Isa's room near theirs on the off chance that Miles came snooping around.

"Dibs on rooming with Cessie."

Crap. She should have seen that coming.

Francesca opened her mouth to set Isa straight, then closed it. Leaving her sister alone in a strange city felt wrong. Isa was scared, and Francesca couldn't force her to sleep in a hotel room by herself. It was the first time either one of them had stayed in a hotel in adulthood, though Francesca could still remember the occasional stays from their family vacations before the church banned outings.

Resigned, Francesca gave Nate an apologetic look. His lips curved up in reluctant acknowledgment.

The concierge checked them in and gave them a thorough rundown of the hotel and its amenities, including the breakfast that would be served early the next morning.

Isa swirled toward Francesca. "I want to see our room, Cessie."

Nate waved them toward the elevator.

They reached Isa and Francesca's room first. Before Francesca could unlock the door, Nate stepped forward and brushed his lips across hers. The kiss was brief, but it spoke of promises.

"Gross. Get a room," groaned Isa.

"I did," Nate pointed out. "But you called dibs on Francesca."

Isa's eyes flashed. "She's my sister. I'm tired. Cessie, can you let me into our room?"

Francesca ran her hand across Nate's arm in a regretful gesture and went to unlock the hotel room for Isa.

Their room had a startlingly beautiful view of the Duomo of Santa Maria del Fiore. The air conditioner blew cool air with a low hum, a welcome respite from the hot evening that swirled outside the windows. The streets below teemed with life even in the fallen evening, with tourists and vendors and locals, and Francesca was glad they stayed in Florence, even if Miles was out there roaming the city.

She refused to be bound by fear. She had spent the last few months of her life terrified that her and Isa's plans would be found out, that she'd be forced to marry Miles, that she and Isa would be caught before they reached Italy. Fear no longer ruled her life. Screw Miles. Screw the Righteous Hearth. And screw the Morettis, to boot.

She and Isa had escaped. They were free. Soon, they'd rescue Sofia too.

They took turns showering. Once dressed in their usual sleep getups that Nate had procured for them from Nonna's, they climbed into their respective beds and turned on the TV.

"Isa," Francesca said. "Can we talk about Nate and me?"

"No. Not right now. I'm sleepy. I don't want to talk."

Francesca wanted to explain that Isa had nothing to be concerned about, but she knew her sister. Isa would talk when she was ready. "Then tomorrow maybe?"

"Maybe." Isa plugged in her phone to charge and set it on the nightstand. She turned her back to Francesca and burrowed deeper into her pillow. "Night."

Francesca waited for Isa's breathing to become steady and even.

"Isa?" she whispered, just to triple check.

Her sister was fast asleep.

Careful not to wake her, Francesca climbed off the bed, tugging down the hem of her sleepshirt. Lifting the spare room key from the table, she tiptoed to the door, which seemed so much farther away now that she attempted a temporary getaway.

Five more steps…

Four…

Three…

Stopping, she peeked at Isa, still sound asleep. *Now or never.* She crossed the rest of the distance, turned the handle, and peeked into the hallway. Finding no roaming guests, she closed the door behind her, making sure it didn't make a loud click.

In the hallway, anxiety at leaving her sister skyrocketed. She reached for the keycard again. But before she could bring it to the sensor and unlock the door, she hesitated. Nate's room was only a few feet away—within shouting distance. She'd only be away a half hour—Isa would be safe in that time, and Francesca would return promptly.

She turned toward Nate's door.

I'm a terrible, terrible sister. She's scared and alone in a new place. I can't leave her.

She turned back to Isa.

But I'll be gone a half hour—twenty minutes tops. She's fast asleep, and I'll be back before she knows it.

She padded to Nate's door.

But what if Miles finds her in that time?

She tiptoed back to Isa's.

I'll be able to hear footsteps in the hall. And I'll be gone fifteen minutes—ten, tops.

Decision made, she crossed to Nate's room, raised her hand to knock—

The door swung open before her knuckles made contact. She faced Nate, dressed in nothing but a pair of sweatpants.

His eyes creased in satisfaction. "I was coming to find you for a made-up work emergency."

Nate was on her the moment she stepped inside and

the door locked behind them: his mouth on hers, his hands roaming brazenly, curving into her back, fisting her shirt, sliding over her butt.

He explored the shell of her ear. "I've been thinking about getting you alone all day."

"Me too," she admitted, tilting her head to give him better access. "Every time you'd inadvertently touch me, I'd forget to breathe."

"That wasn't inadvertent," Nate said against her neck. "I exhausted all ideas of how to get my hands on you without Isa scratching my eyes out."

"She's being protective." She traced the breadth of his shoulders. "We can't take long tonight. I waited for Isa to fall asleep to sneak out, but I have to go back. I can't leave her alone—not when Miles is lurking somewhere nearby."

"Give me two hours." He slid his hands under her T-shirt, traced her ribs.

"Ten minutes. Tops."

"Thirty slow ones."

She squashed down the guilt. "Fine. But if we hear anyone roaming the hall, I'm returning to Isa."

"Deal."

The ground dropped out from under her as he lifted her against his hard chest. When he set her on the bed and pulled her shirt off, his eyes met hers in the soft glow cast by the bedside lamp. They were dark with hunger, with need, but there was something else there—something tender and sweet, and she couldn't trust it.

She'd believed Miles once; she knew better now. The only real thing between her and Nate was sex—nothing more.

Chapter 20

A sharp rap jolted Francesca awake.

No, no, no.

What time is it? How did I fall asleep?

She had been so intent on returning to Isa's room within a half hour *at the most.*

Nate slept soundly next to her, his arm snug around her waist. They had left the bedside lamp on, and its low gleam bathed the otherwise dark room. It had to still be night—*right*?

"Cessie? You in there?" Her sister's voice sounded loud and insistent through the door. And infinitely annoyed.

She cleared her throat, hoping her voice sounded even. "Yes! I'll return to our room in a minute."

Struggling out of Nate's tight hold, she leaped from the bed, searched for her shirt.

"Don't bother," Isa snapped. "I'm tired and going back to bed."

Francesca didn't wish to upset her sister. "Isa—"

Her sister cut her off. "Stay with Nate, I don't care. Good night."

The conversation had woken Nate. Taking in the scene, he cursed. "We fell asleep."

"I need to go," she told him, already halfway to the door.

He lifted his watch from the bedside table. "It's past midnight. Wait until tomorrow. Let her cool off."

She twisted to face him. "I can't. I left her alone and frightened—she must have been so scared when she woke up and I wasn't there. I'll… I'll see you tomorrow."

Moving from the bed, he dragged on his sweatpants. "Stop bending to her every whim."

Guilt made her turn on him. "*Whim*? I wouldn't have had the guts to leave the Righteous Hearth without her. And I left her tonight *alone*. Nate, I owe Isa my life."

He walked past her. Cold, distant. Frustrating. "I'll walk you to your room."

"Isa won't want to see you." And she needed some time alone, to work through the guilt that swirled like a sandstorm inside her.

"I don't plan on seeing her. I'll leave as soon as you unlock your door."

He looked like he wanted to do anything but accompany her, so she gave him an out.

"My room is all of six steps away."

He didn't take it. "Then it won't take long. Let's go."

***

Returning to his room after taking Francesca to hers, Nate stalked to the window and threw it open. The cool night air did little to help his mood. What the fuck was he doing in Florence? He wasn't Francesca's boyfriend, or her bodyguard. The urge to protect her had seized him in a death grip, and he fought to loosen it, to *breathe*.

He should be in New York right now. Instead, he

was running around after Francesca like a besotted puppy. He came with her to Florence, for Christ's sake.

If he wasn't careful, he'd get lost in her… Get too involved in her problems with Isa, with her other sister…

Her pull on him would eventually demand too much of him.

More than he could give.

Chapter 21

In the morning, Isa was gone.

Waking early, intent on having the conversation Isa had rejected last night, Francesca rolled to face her sister's bed.

She'd expected to see Isa sprawled across it, but in the shadows, the bed looked empty. *Must be a trick of the light.*

Francesca blinked—hard. *Nope, still empty.* Sitting up, she flipped on the bedside lamp.

Isa did not miraculously reappear.

Where would she go this early?

Springing out of bed, she hurried to the windows and pulled apart the curtains. The morning sunlight did not make her sister materialize from some shadowed corner. Just to make sure, she checked the bathroom and found it empty too.

Confused, exasperated, panicked, she looked for her sister's belongings.

Crap. Isa had taken her small bundle with her.

Where would she go?

Francesca surveyed the room again for good measure. That's when she saw it—a folded piece of paper smack in the middle of the table, with her name written across it in Isa's messy hand.

She read the hastily written missive.

Off to see Teddy. See you back in Rome.

The urge to go to Nate was strong, but she fought against it. Instead, she dialed Isa. The call went straight to voicemail. Although she suspected Isa had turned off her location, she checked anyway.

Only then did she seek out Nate. He opened the door, looking awake and very irritated. The sun hadn't risen that long ago, but he was already dressed.

The annoyance on his face flipped to concern. "What happened?"

She extended the note to him. "Isa left."

"Left to go where?" Nate pulled the note from her fingers, scanned the brief message. "What the hell? Who's Teddy?"

Her racing heart made her dizzy. "Her Italian study buddy."

"The random dude from the internet?"

Panic licked at her. "Yes."

"Last name?"

She couldn't breathe. When she stalked back to her room, he followed. "I don't know. She's always just called him Teddy. I didn't think to ask for his last name."

"You got his number? Email?"

Tears burned her eyes. "Nothing."

"Where does he live?"

That, she knew. "Venice. He's studying at the university there. I tried calling her, but she isn't answering."

"Want me to try?"

"She'll ignore you too." Her fingers flew across the screen as she sent a string of messages to her sister. She didn't expect a response, and she didn't get one.

Nate paced the room, ratcheting up Francesca's nerves.

"You follow her location. Can you see where she is?"

She shook her head. "She turned it off. She doesn't want to be found."

"Fuck. Where do we even look?"

Francesca was absolutely certain when she responded. "Venice." Gripped with anger at her sister's foolishness, she dropped onto the edge of the bed. "I can't believe she'd be stupid enough to leave. What if Miles finds her?"

Nate's reticence made her even more nervous.

"Did she take her things?" he asked.

"Yes. And her phone charger." Suspicion flashed. *What else did she take?*

She ran to the room safe, where she and Isa had tucked away their precious documents—their scorched earth chance to get Sofia back. The safe was unlocked. The file was gone.

"Crap, crap, crap." She ran her fingers up and down the felt that lined the safe, as though the papers may still be there, just invisible.

Nate reached her at the safe, understood immediately. "What was in that file?"

Unwilling to share that part of their escape with him, she shook her head.

Irritation flared in his tired eyes, but he didn't press her. "She could be anywhere in Italy."

"Teddy is in Venice, so that's where she'll be. You don't have to come. Someone has to be at Zohra tonight, and I have to bring her back. If you need to fire me and hire another manager, I understand. Zohra comes first."

He spun her around to face him, just as he did the

first time they met. "You come first. I'm not letting you traipse all over the country looking for your idiot sister."

"She's not an idiot. She doesn't know how to handle… us."

"So she ran away like a child?"

"She is a child. We grew up so sheltered, Nate. She doesn't have the ability to handle this like a normal eighteen-year-old would. She and I've always had only each other—we were always together, and now… now she sees me with you, and she doesn't know how to process it."

"So she ran away in a strange country while a nutjob is looking for you both?"

"I'm going to get her back."

"I'll go with you."

The reluctant agreement was worded so low, Francesca barely heard him.

"Isa isn't your responsibility."

"I know that, but I'm not sending you on a wild-goose chase across Italy. We don't know Teddy. Is he a teenage boy or an old perv using some teenage boy's photos?"

Francesca gasped. *"People do that?"*

"Of course they do that. All the time."

It would be too much to ask him to accompany her. "I'll be careful. You should get back to Zohra."

"With luck, we'll grab her today and be back in Rome tonight." His brow furrowed as he studied his phone. "The first train to Venice left a half hour ago. We're not too far behind."

"You think she took the train?"

"I doubt he'd have driven through the night to get her by car, and she doesn't drive."

Francesca considered the argument. "Good point."

She swapped her sleepshirt for her gray linen dress, collected her scant belongings, and checked Isa's whereabouts on her phone again—Isa's location remained off. Frustration with her sister deepening, she followed Nate to his room so he could grab his things before heading to the lobby, where the concierge called them a cab.

While they waited for their driver to arrive, Nate dashed into the breakfast room, snagged a couple of pastries for the ride to the train station, and presented one to her in a crisp white napkin.

Starving, Francesca bit into the flakey croissant, grateful for the quick breakfast.

The cab driver dropped them off at the train station brimming with people.

Weaving between the crowds, his hand around hers, Nate checked the timetable. "Train leaves in fifteen minutes."

"I can't believe Isa would do something like this," she said, overwhelmed. "What if she isn't in Venice? I don't even know where Teddy lives. Maybe this was a stupid idea, but I can't go back to Rome and wait for her to show up. She's never traveled across a foreign country before. Heck, she's never even traveled across the United States before. She must be so angry with me to run off like this."

"It's not your job to adjust your life to keep Isa comfortable."

Frustrated by his inability to understand, Francesca struggled to explain. "She's my little sister. I'm all she's got. Maybe she's mad because she had a crush on you? And I stole you away."

"You didn't steal me. I'm not interested in your baby sister. I'm interested in you. Have been from the moment I saw you."

She pretended to be studying the people around them. "I wish she and I had talked last night. It's not like her to madly dash out and meet a stranger."

Nate raised a brow. "Really? From my experience with her, it sounds exactly like something she would do."

"She's going through a hard time."

"So are you. And she's making it even harder for you."

He kept her hand in his as they hurried to their platform. Francesca, who'd never had anyone to rely on besides herself and Isa, didn't know how to process his presence. Couldn't allow herself to get used to it.

It took every last bit of her willpower, but she forced herself to move away from him, to walk by herself as they made their way to their train. Switching her purse to her other shoulder between them, she preceded him up the train step into the railcar and slid into the window seat.

"I don't know how I'm going to sit still for over two hours," she told him. "I'm so mad at her. Didn't she think we'd follow her?"

"She expected it."

Distracted by the sheer presence of him next to her, Francesca almost overlooked her phone buzz. She looked at the screen. "It's my grandmother. She'll worry if I don't answer." Exhaling, Francesca attempted to sound jovial. "Hi, Nonna."

"How are you girls doing?" As her grandmother spoke, Francesca could hear waves crashing in the background.

"We are good…" She contemplated whether or not

to reveal their location, decided to not hide it from Nonna. "We are in Florence."

A pause. "Oh?"

"I had a business meeting. Isa went with me. Nate's here too."

"A neighbor said a strange man has been asking about you two earlier this week. You think that it's someone from your parents' cult?"

Francesca fought a groan. "Yes. It's Miles. Isa saw him Sunday morning. That's why she and I came to Florence."

"I don't want you two staying in the apartment alone now that Miles knows where we live. Dante and I can return today, if you need me."

"No. Don't be silly. You and Dante enjoy your trip. I've got it all under control."

A wistful note weaved into her grandmother's voice as she responded. "You always do."

Fighting a storm of melancholy, she ended the call and sank deeper into her seat. The train took off with a subtle lurch, picking up speed as it left the train station.

She studied the passing scenery outside her window. Although her mother was born in Italy, she hadn't spent much time there as a kid. Nonna and her mother had several fallings-out during her mother's teenage years, so things had already been fraught by the time Francesca was born, and then her mother and father joined the Righteous Hearth and cut off ties when Nonna protested.

Francesca, obsessively now, checked Isa's location. The location appeared. Fearful that she was imagining it, she spun to Nate. "She turned her location back on."

Nate took the phone from her, studied the screen before returning it. "Venice."

"She wants us to find her."

"She's testing you, to see if you'll follow her."

Francesca knew he was right, and it made her even more aggravated with her sister. Isa would have a lot of explaining to do when they caught up to her. Change was hard on them both, but Isa had inadvertently jeopardized her job and, by extension, their ability to get to their sister.

What if the Italian study buddy was Giorgio Moretti? Or someone from the Righteous Hearth trying to lure Isa away?

She was going to be sick. Nauseated, she rested her head on Nate's shoulder, allowing herself to seek comfort from him. Just for a moment.

He shifted as though to wrap his arm around her, and she waited for the solid feel of him to surround her, make her feel safe, but it never came. Instead, he jerked his arm back down to his side and kept it there.

Telling herself she was a big girl, she didn't need him to comfort her, she lifted her head from his shoulder and resettled herself in her seat.

When the train came to a stop at Venice's Santa Lucia train station, she jumped up. Lifting her phone, she confirmed Isa's location. "She's currently at St. Mark's Square."

Nate walked ahead of her as they exited the train, navigated through the crowds, and stepped into Venice. Francesca, who'd spent most of her life in Nevada, had never imagined she'd have the chance to see Venice, and the first glimpse of it made her breath catch.

A vast canal stretched out before them. Gondolas, water taxis, and what she assumed were the vaporetti she'd read about zipped along the water. The sun-speckled buildings lining the canal appeared to float.

Even in the late morning, humid heat hung over the city, mixing with the cloying odor of sweating tourists.

As throngs of visitors jostled around them, Francesca plastered herself to Nate. "It's… crowded."

He swept her in front of him, his broad back a shield against the enclosing mobs. "Guess Venice is the place to be today." He sounded like he'd rather be anywhere else.

Francesca took comfort in knowing that Isa was so near. As she tried to locate her on her phone, the location pin disappeared.

"Crap."

Nate understood immediately. "She turned off her location. Can she track you too?"

"Of course."

"She knows you're here and doesn't want to go home yet."

Her annoyance with Isa grew. She had to return to Rome by the time Zohra reopened tonight, and Isa was wasting precious time.

Her shoulders drooped as she comprehended the unfeasibility of their task. "We'll never find her in these crowds."

"Turn off your location."

Confused by his terse command, she frowned. "I don't…"

He glared at her, that muscle in his jaw jumping. Nate's patience with Isa had run out. "I have no time for cat-and-mouse games. If you keep your location on, she'll know when you're close and turn her location off every time."

"She's just upset. We weren't raised in a place that allowed us to discuss our feelings and emotions. She doesn't have the tools to process that she's upset."

But Francesca turned off her location regardless. Desperate times called for desperate measures, and she had to find her sister before Miles found them… or before whoever this Teddy was did anything bad to her.

The tension did not flee Nate's features. "I need coffee and food. A pastry from two hours ago isn't going to cut it."

Nate was indisputably hangry. The heat of the day and the crush of the tourists weren't helping either one of their moods.

"Can we try to find her first? Then eat?"

She felt his resignation as he sighed. "Keep an eye out for her location popping on. We'll go to St. Mark's Square. Want to go by water or foot?"

"By foot will give us a better chance of finding her," she said. But after studying the slow-moving tourists, she wasn't so certain that was true.

They made their way along the bridges and across canals until they reached St. Mark's Square.

Nate stopped in the middle of the piazza. "Anything?"

She glanced down at her phone. "Location is still off."

"You know what Teddy looks like?"

Francesca shook her head.

"Which university is he attending?"

"If she told me, I don't remember. I'm a terrible sister. I never even thought to check who she's been spending all her time with online."

"You didn't know."

She should have known, though. She had failed Sofia by leaving her behind, and now she was failing Isa. Guilt and despair spun inside her. "She's a kid and she's lost in the middle of a strange place."

Nate didn't seem to share her soft spot for Isa. "She left on purpose to make you prove she comes first."

***

Nate was hungry, and hot, and irritated. He'd postponed seeing his mentor to deal with Moretti and the cult, not to chase a spoiled brat across Italy. Remembering how his heart had bounded when he'd decided to prolong his time with Francesca shoved him into a darker mood.

He didn't have room for Francesca and all her problems in his life. Refused to make room. His job and, soon, the trial would inhale his time. His focus needed to stay on his mentor. On making Clary Guns pay. Prioritizing Francesca would chip away at the life he'd just rebuilt for himself.

They crisscrossed the square twice and stalked its surrounding arcade, peeking into shops and cafes, a futile attempt to find a needle in a very packed haystack. When he saw Francesca eyeing a nearby gelato shop with wistful craving and heard her stomach gurgle, he pulled her to a stop.

"Lunch time," he said. "I'm done running around Venice on an empty stomach."

He had expected her to argue, but she surprised him by agreeing. It spoke to how hungry she must be.

"It'll be good to eat. Should we pick one of these places?" She pointed to the restaurants that lined the piazza, each one distinguishable by the colors of their chairs.

Nate eyed the tourist-heavy restaurants. Although he was starved, he wanted good food, and none of the options in front of them sounded appealing.

"No, but I know just the spot."

Steeling his muscles to not reach for her hand, he directed them through a pattern of walkways and bridges—some empty of all people, others packed with tourists. Finding the quiet street he knew well, he stopped in front of a small restaurant tucked into a row of houses.

"This is my favorite local spot."

"How'd you know to find it so quickly?" she asked as he swung open the door.

"My family visited Venice a lot when I was a kid. It almost became a backyard for my brothers and me."

He already knew that inside would look much bigger than the narrow door implied. Tables were packed with gondoliers in their striped outfits and jovial locals digging into hearty dishes. Italian conversations flowed like the wine.

Francesca's attention fixed on the giant with shiny, pink cheeks who hurried toward them.

"Nataniele! It's been too long. And you brought a girlfriend."

Nate shook Gigi's hand. "We're in town for a bit. Gigi, this is Francesca. Francesca, meet Gigi. He owns this place."

"It's been in my family for three generations," Gigi told her proudly. "Come in, come in. Got a table in the back for you, Nataniele. What's the latest?"

Nate pulled out Francesca's chair, but remained standing as he caught up with his friend. The restaurant, with its dark-wood paneling and tables wrapped in cheerful tablecloths, smelled of home cooking and sent his stomach growling.

"Sit, sit." Gigi motioned to Nate. "I'll bring you wine."

He knew Francesca would enjoy the house wine, an ice-cold Lambrusco. Not wasting time, he rattled off a list of dishes, asked for them to be brought out as soon as possible.

Once Gigi danced away, Francesca took a sip of the wine. "Sweet and fizzy. I like." A cloud chased away her smile. "I can't believe Isa."

He wanted the smile back. "We'll find her."

"How? This is insanity. It's like looking for a lost earring in an alfalfa field."

He would never tire of her farming references. "Isa wants to be found. She'll turn on her location soon enough."

"What if this Teddy guy is a pervert of some sort? Or what if it's Giorgio? Or someone from the Righteous Hearth?"

"We'll cross that bridge if we come to it."

Reaching across the compact table, he finally gave in to the craving, closed his hand over hers. He hadn't expected for her to relax under his touch. When she did, he relished it. Although he knew he should let go, his fingers wouldn't release, so he settled in and let the pleasure of holding her hand sway through him.

Her fingers sought his, played, even as sadness threaded her voice. "I can't keep putting myself first, Nate. I have to find Isa."

The idea that she thought herself selfish bothered him. "For as long as I've known you, you've never put yourself first."

"You've known me barely a week. I could have married Miles, and not subjected Isa and me to this wild run across the globe. I thought I was doing what was best for Isa, too, but she's been acting out ever since we left the Righteous Hearth, and I don't know what to do. Now she's out with a stranger. She could get hurt because I thought it was a good idea to run away."

He didn't know why he continued to hold her hand, stroke across her skin, only that he couldn't make himself let go. "Don't ever regret leaving that place."

"It's hard not to when I've managed to lose Isa."

Gigi returned, setting out dishes piled high with fried and grilled seafood, succulent pasta, thick slabs of lasagna, and homemade tiramisu. They ate their way through the food-laden table in silence, scarfing down the savory and slowing down for the dessert.

Nate had expected to feel glue-trapped in Venice, Isa's disappearance another grating obstacle to his return to the life he missed. And he did at first, hungry and caffeine-deprived and annoyed. But now, the feeling fled. He was sharing a great meal and good wine with a beautiful, captivating woman he would soon tumble naked into bed. Things could be a lot worse.

Francesca didn't appear to share his sudden appreciation for the moment. Tension creased the space between her brows, made her cheeks hollow, drained her of her usual vitality. He missed the animated, effervescent Francesca he'd come to know.

As he watched the frown mar her perfect features, he knew he'd do anything to wipe away the fretful look. She didn't have enough days where she looked completely at ease. The woman was self-reliant to a fault. Frustratingly so. She had had to be, in order to leave the only world she'd ever known, move halfway across the world with no money and no safety net, and make a life for herself and her sister. If she'd only let him share her burdens—

Nate sat back in his chair, the move so abrupt he almost tumbled backward.

He didn't want her burdens, wouldn't repeat his patterns. All he wanted was to fuck her until he'd had his fill.

The change in his mood didn't escape Francesca. "You okay?"

No, he wasn't okay.

He shouldn't be here.

Downing the last of the wine, he couldn't meet her eyes. "We should go."

She didn't ask where. She knew as well as he that looking for Isa in the crowded city would be pointless, but they couldn't stay at Gigi's forever.

Because he couldn't help himself, he came around the table and tilted up her chin, waited until she raised her eyes to his. Her gaze softened as he leaned in and brushed a kiss across her lips. He'd remember this when he returned to New York—he'd remember her for the rest of his days.

Losing himself in the sensation of her, he deepened the kiss until she pulled away with an embarrassed headshake.

"Not here. It's crowded."

He'd almost forgotten where they were. "Let's go loop around. Maybe your fool of a sister will turn her location back on."

"She's not a fool. She's just… acting out."

His teeth ground together. "She's doing so in a foolish way."

Francesca sighed. "Very foolish. But she's not a fool."

No, she knew exactly which buttons to press to stress out her sister.

Francesca reached for her purse. Nate snagged the check, handing it off to Gigi with several folded bills. "Keep the change. I'll see you on my next visit, Gigi."

Nate led Francesca out of the restaurant and onto a small, sun-drenched bridge.

"Next time you try to pay when I take you on a date," he said in a low voice against her ear, "I'm going to wait until we're alone and find a way to teach you a lesson."

"This wasn't a date," she pointed out with an impish crinkle of her nose.

"We had wine. We had conversation."

"We argued about my sister. That wasn't a conversation."

"I kissed you."

"You kiss me all the time," she said, eyes dancing.

Warmth flooded his chest. He had a better time arguing with Francesca than he'd had making love to other women. Pulling her against him, he proved her point, kissing her on the bridge that traversed a small canal, loving the feel of her against him, the way her fingers curved into his shoulders to steady herself, the restless way she pressed herself to him as she kissed him back.

The stifling heat and the mosquito-buzz of tourists vanished. He could stand here forever, being baked by the sun, kissing her, and he'd be the happiest he'd been in his life. This felt right. This was home.

Don't be an idiot.

This wasn't real.

She'd walk away.

Just as he had to.

A low but insistent vibration against his side didn't register until Francesca pulled away.

"It's my phone," she explained, withdrawing it from her pocket. "It's Isa." She answered it hastily. "Where are you? What in the world are you thinking?"

He leaned in close to catch Isa's petulant voice. "I'm not coming back."

"You are most definitely coming back. Tell me where you are. I'll come get you."

"I'm with Teddy. I'm fine."

"You wanted me to chase you to Venice. Do you have any idea how irresponsible that is? What about Miles? What about my job? Nate's club?"

"That's not my problem."

"You're upset about Nate and me. Tell us where you are, and we'll talk about it."

The line went dead. Isa had hung up.

Nate wanted more than anything to tell Francesca *I told you so,* to point out how little regard her sister had for Francesca's needs, but he held his tongue. Francesca and Isa had always been a team, and Francesca wouldn't tolerate any disdainful comments. She was already grappling with guilt over Sofia. She'd never willingly disparage Isa, maybe the only person in the world who knew what she was going through now that they'd escaped the Righteous Hearth.

Francesca needed her sister as much as her sister needed her. Isa irritated him most of the time, but he'd never let anyone come between him and any of his three brothers, and he admired that Francesca felt similarly. Family meant a lot to them both.

She looked at him with broken eyes. "I can't go back to Rome without her, Nate. But you should. One of us has to be at Zohra tonight."

She was right.

He shouldn't be here. But something inside him wouldn't give, wouldn't move.

"Giacomo can manage the club tonight."

She cocked her head. "Why would you want to hang around Venice and try to find Isa? You don't even like her."

"I'm not doing this for her. I'm doing this for *you*."

Shit. Comprehending what he'd just said—realizing he'd meant the words—he released her, stumbled back. As if the few feet of distance between them would help him.

Laying his hands on the bridge's iron railing, he stared at the murky canal below them. The light pressure of her hand on his arm made him jerk.

Her voice was as soft as the breeze around them. "I'm not used to anyone helping me. I don't want to owe you."

Angling his head, he met her gaze. In it, he saw the same fear that swirled through him. Neither one could trust the other. They both had been through too much to let someone else in. But he couldn't leave her to deal with Isa alone.

"If Isa were my sister, would you run off to Rome?"

Her response was instant. "Of course not."

"Then why won't you accept the same from me?"

Her lashes lowered. When they lifted, her eyes radiated distress.

He couldn't believe he was talking her into letting him help when he should be distancing himself from her problems. "Will it help to know I'm in it for selfish reasons?"

The corners of her mouth turned up. "I have a feeling I know what those might be."

"Too bad. I was looking forward to spelling them out for you," he drew her into his arms, "in very thorough detail."

As she leaned against him, his heart nearly leaped out of his chest, reaching for her.

He ran a soothing palm down her back. "Give Isa some time to process. She'll reach out to you when she's ready."

"I can't just sit and wait for her to want to speak to me."

"Short of knocking on every door in this city, you don't really have a choice. Give her a few hours."

She raised her head. "Would that be enough time for you to spell out your selfish reasons?"

Her smile made his heart trip. Leaning toward her, he pressed a soft kiss to her lips. "It's a start."

Chapter 22

Nate reserved a hotel on his phone with a few efficient clicks.

Don't get used to this. Don't get used to him.

No, she could only depend on herself and on Isa.

She'd allow herself just a little bit more time with him, but that was it. Soon, she'd have to end this. It would be for the best; she couldn't grow to rely on him.

They meandered along bridges clogged with tourists until they reached the hotel displaying "Danieli" in simple gold script against a pink façade. White pointed arches framed the rows of windows and matched the main entrance.

Francesca stepped inside the grand lobby lined with marble columns and tall arches, and froze, mesmerized by the carved ceilings and skylight, the open staircase, and the flowers that filled the space.

"This is much too fancy," she whispered. "You and I don't even have real luggage. You bring real luggage to a hotel like this."

Nate chuckled next to her. "I'm sure they won't bat an eye."

They walked toward the circular reception desk made

of wood so polished it gleamed, where the concierge checked them in, unfazed by their lack of suitcases. He motioned for a bellhop to lead them to their room. The bellhop didn't question the lack of luggage either.

As they crossed the corridor, Francesca studied the historic building and the beautiful Italian architecture. What a far cry this was from her childhood in Rose Falls. It was hard not to feel as though her parents had robbed her of her Italian heritage by cutting off ties with Nonna and secluding themselves in their small religious community. Francesca's grandfather had died before she was born, yet the longer she stayed in Italy, the more she mourned not having the opportunity to know him.

The bellhop showed them into the room and discreetly slipped out once Nate handed over a few euros.

Francesca's gaze ran over the elegant space, with its rich fabrics, opulent wallpaper, and antique furniture. The Venetian Lagoon teased them through the wood-framed windows.

"This is so beautiful."

Although she felt Nate's presence at her side, he did not respond. Confused at this sudden silence, she glanced up at his tense face, at his eyes which turned black. The intensity scared her. "Nate—"

He didn't let her finish, taking her mouth with a desperation that left her reeling. She rose on her toes to kiss him back, interlacing her hands behind his neck, marveling at the tense muscles.

She pushed him to the bed, fell on top of him. When he rolled her under, she let him. When he plundered her mouth, she welcomed it. They tore at each other's clothes until bare skin pressed against bare skin. His mouth skimmed over her breasts.

His voice was as thick as scorched caramel. "I need to be inside you."

"Good." She lifted into him. "I want that too."

***

He groaned his approval as he cupped the triangle between her thighs. *Mine.*

Parting her swollen folds, he dipped, circled, plunged into her soaked channel. When he flicked her nipple with his tongue, muscles deep within her tremored around his fingers. He needed to feel her around his cock.

"You are always so hot for me," he murmured. "So perfect."

"Now, Nate… now."

It didn't take him long to grab protection. Frenzied to possess her, he interlaced their fingers and drove himself home. She arched under him, using her legs to pull him in even deeper.

In the maelstrom, his gaze locked on hers, saw the raw craving that consumed him mirrored there. Stunned, he realized she was as defenseless against it as he was.

As if unwilling to let him look deeper, she squeezed her lids together, shut him out.

But it was too late. He wouldn't allow retreat.

"Open your eyes," he demanded. "Look at me."

When she did, he lost all control, giving in to the boundless hunger that consumed them both, until she gave in to it too, screaming her release. He was sure his own shout could be heard to the outer reaches of Venice.

Nate hauled Francesca to his chest, his heart pounding against his rib cage. *Fuck.* He still wanted her.

He'd intended to drive away the desire she stirred in

him, dispel the longing, take her until they'd both had their fill, but it wasn't enough. Would it ever be enough? Somehow, someway, he'd have to make sure it would be. Losing Padma—and, God, *Sammy*—had almost destroyed him. Letting Francesca in only to lose her would annihilate him.

Snarled by his miserable thoughts, he hadn't noticed that Francesca had fallen fast asleep until he glanced at her next to him. She'd had little sleep last night and a mad dash across Italy that morning. She needed rest. He should slip out of bed, have a drink down in the lobby or a nearby bar. Staying in the peaceful web that they'd weaved around themselves would lead nowhere good.

He trailed a finger along her downy cheek.

Leaving the serene confines of their bed to sit in a crowded bar when she was soft and warm next to him held no appeal. He stroked over her with languor, memorizing the softness of her skin, the gentle rise and fall of her chest. Tracing along one cool nipple, he marveled as it heated and pebbled at his touch.

Gliding his hand lower, he parted her curls, stroked.

Her body responded to him as always. Liquid honey flowed, and she moved restlessly against him.

"You awake?" he murmured against her ear, closing his teeth over her sensitive earlobe.

Her arms wound around him. "Oh yes."

He needed more, needed all of her, so he could unshackle himself of his fixation with her.

"Sweetheart, I need to feel you again." He reached for the protection he'd left on the nightstand, eased her to her stomach, sank inside.

She engulfed him, drenched him, opened to him and let him take. His vision blurred as he plundered, scored her neck, soothed. She whimpered for more below him, and he gave, pleasuring her as much as he pleasured himself with her.

She clamped like a tight fist around him and still he moved, taking her with him, letting her feel the full force of her power over him. She cried out when she came again, and still he moved, powerless to his craving for her. It was never enough. He tunneled into her, trying to work this hunger out of his system, this need, plundering until she sobbed, clenched on him again. Only then did he give in, exploding deep inside her.

And still the craving remained.

Chapter 23

Nightfall descended over Venice by the time Francesca stirred. Nate's arm, heavy and protective, curled around her. He'd wrung every bone out of her body. Even now, hours later, she wasn't sure she could move. Gathering the last of her strength, she twisted toward him, not surprised to find him sound asleep.

How could a man be this beautiful? Unable to resist, she trailed a finger along his forehead, down his nose, over his full lips to his bristly chin. Like an addict, she pressed close, drank in his familiar scent, let it center her.

Glancing past him to the darkness outside, her heart plummeted. Isa was still out there with some stranger, and Francesca didn't know how to find her. Extricating herself from Nate's hold, she climbed off the bed and padded to the purse she had tossed to the floor in her haste earlier that evening. Reaching into the bag, she pulled out her phone.

No text messages, no calls.

Isa had never been this troublesome before. The escape from Righteous Hearth had been harder on her than Francesca had realized. On a last hope, she tapped on Isa's location.

It populated.

Francesca's hand trembled as she stared.

Her little sister was currently on the Rialto Bridge.

Crossing to the bed, Francesca shook Nate awake. "Isa is on Ponte di Rialto. We need to go."

Nate groaned but moved off the bed quickly, dressing as he blinked sleep from his eyes. "She text you?"

"No. She turned on her location again."

"Don't turn yours back on until we reach her."

"I won't. Not going to let her slip away now."

He snagged her linen dress off the ground, extended it to her, but held firm until she, confused, met his gaze. An emotion she couldn't name haunted his eyes.

"What?" she asked.

He released the garment, but his gaze remained unsettled.

Suddenly feeling very naked, she pulled on the dress. "I'm dragging her back to Rome tonight. I don't care how. She's been acting out for a silly reason."

Still he watched her with that troubled expression. "Because she thinks I'm coming between you two."

"Yes, and we both know that's ridiculous. She has nothing to worry about. But…" *Now or never.* She ripped off the Band-Aid while she still could. "I think… I think we should probably stop… what we've been doing."

He stilled completely.

"It's just that you're leaving soon, and I have to focus on Isa and on getting Sofia away, and I don't want things to get too… messy."

A tempest thundered in his eyes. "Messy?"

"Yes. If we don't stop now, it'll… it'll be harder to stop later. At least for me."

Anxious, miserable, she waited for a response, but received none.

Instead, a veneer descended over his features, hiding his emotions as effectively as one of the elaborate Zohra masquerade masks. He cleared his throat. "We need to go."

His brusque indifference almost undid her. Only when he reached for the doorhandle did she see that his hand trembled.

***

As they walked out of the hotel and into the warm evening, Francesca barely acknowledged their surroundings, striding along with one eye on Isa's location.

As self-sufficient as always.

He should be relieved. She didn't want him in her life, and he had no space for her either. Steven's case would take over his every waking moment. He'd be working 24/7, and in Manhattan, while she'd be here, in Italy, and eventually in Nevada to get Sofia. They had no future. Even if they wanted to make it work, it would be impossible.

Yet her resolution to end things irked. He wasn't done with her yet.

Ponte di Rialto was just over a ten-minute walk from their hotel, a relatively straight shot. As they hurried past the Palazzo Ducale, with its illuminated open-air arcades, toward the Piazza San Marco, he tugged her to a stop. Live orchestra music from the piazza drifted across the warm evening breeze, swaying around them. Her brows drew together. Tilting up her chin before she could glue her gaze back to her phone and Isa's location, he stole a kiss.

If she'd stiffened, he'd have let her go immediately. Instead, she opened to him so sweetly, relaxing against him. When he drew back, tracing her flushed cheek, she leaned into his touch. He couldn't stop himself from pocketing another kiss before they resumed their quick pace to the Ponte di Rialto.

Gondolas and vaporetti navigated under the softly lit bridge. Although most of the day tourists had already left, the bridge was far from abandoned. People scaled its stone steps, photographed the canal at night, and chatted jovially in all kinds of languages.

As they reached the base, Francesca studied her phone. "She's still here and her location is still on."

Nate settled his hand low on her back. "I'm sure she'll be easy to spot."

They climbed the steps, scanning for Isa along their way, as water lapped gently around the bridge.

"I see her. There, on the right."

Nate followed her gaze. Sure enough, there she was, a few feet from a family of tourists. She stood together with some skinny kid Nate assumed was Teddy.

Isa's head swiveled as she scanned the crowds. It was clear that she expected Francesca to track her down as soon as she made her location available again, and she was waiting. Once she saw them, her shoulders melted and her face lit up.

"Cessie!" she screeched and beelined for them.

Francesca raced to meet Isa halfway, stumbled back with the force of her sister's hug.

The loss of her warmth stung like icicles. He stopped within a few feet of them.

"I was so worried!" Francesca exclaimed. "What were you thinking? I'm so sorry, we should have talked…"

"I'm sorry, Cessie. I shouldn't have done that. I was mad and I wanted to hurt you and…"

The two spoke over each other, but they seemed to understand the jumbled apologies. They hugged each other tightly once more.

"Are you here alone?" asked Francesca.

"No, I'm with Teddy. Come meet him." As she took Francesca's hand, her eyes encompassed Nate. "You too, I guess."

He'd take the lukewarm invitation.

Isa led Francesca to the teen. Lanky, with nondescript brown hair, he looked no older than Isa.

"Nate Icefall." He extended his hand in greeting.

He had a solid grip for a kid. "Theodore Rutherford. It's nice to meet you, sir."

Francesca extended her hand next, introducing herself to the guy her sister had chased all the way to Venice.

Nate studied the teens. "Where the hell have you two been all day?"

"Sightseeing, sir. Isa had never seen Venice, and I was showing her around." Teddy's nervous gaze darted between him and Francesca, and his Adam's apple bobbed.

Well, he didn't seem like a pervert.

"It's been really strange, though," said Isa. "I thought I was being paranoid, but I felt like we were being followed. I don't know if Miles is here… or maybe the Righteous Hearth sent someone else, but I had to warn you."

Had to warn her? A phone or a text would have been a nice warning. Making Francesca check Isa's location all day until Isa finally deemed it time to make herself known was not a warning. But he bit his tongue. Isa was a flight risk. He couldn't chance her taking off again.

He scanned the sightseers around them. "I'll get you two rooms at our hotel. You can tell us everything there."

"There's nothing much to tell," Teddy piped up. "We couldn't find anyone Isa recognized, but it has been unsettling. I felt it too."

"Teddy is very intuitive," Isa explained, lifting her bag higher on her shoulder.

Nate had a choice response to the comment, but he clenched his jaw to keep it inside.

Thankfully, Francesca changed the subject in time. "You two hungry? Did you eat?"

"We ate," said Isa. "Teddy took me to a fancy restaurant for dinner."

Where did the kid get money for fancy restaurants? Who were his parents?

Francesca stepped into Nate's side. "Then let's go. I'll feel better once we are away from the crowds."

When she weaved her fingers through his, triumph surged through Nate. She wasn't done with him yet either. Lifting her hand to his lips, he pressed a kiss to her knuckles. He didn't have to see the blush that pinkened her skin—he felt the heat of it.

Isa rolled her eyes. "Can you two wait until you get back to your room? Come on, Teddy and I are tired, and I don't want to bring whoever is tracking me and Cessie to his apartment."

"You got an apartment here?" Nate asked Teddy.

The kid hesitated. "Yeah. My dad thought I'd be more comfortable in my own space."

"Who's your dad?"

"Does it matter?" Isa's annoyed voice cut in before

Teddy could answer. "Stop interrogating him. Teddy has done nothing but be my friend."

Kid looked decent enough. He'd run a background check on him later to make sure.

Motioning for the teens to follow them as they left Ponte Rialto, Nate set the direction for Danieli. Now that the day tourists had dispersed, a hush lay over nighttime Venice. As they weaved their way through narrow alleyways and footbridges, their steps echoed in the fallen silence.

He didn't see anyone out of the ordinary as they approached the hotel, walking along the gently lapping water of the Venetian Lagoon. Yet the feeling at the base of his skull indicated something was wrong seconds before Francesca's hand in his tightened and she froze.

A blond man strode toward them from the direction of Danieli.

Isa gasped behind them.

"Run!" she yelped and took off, setting Teddy to take off behind her.

"Isa, *stop*," Francesca called, taking off after her sister and Teddy.

Are you fucking kidding me?

On a groan, Nate followed them. The last thing he needed was for Francesca to get hurt chasing the two idiots, but hauling her back without them would be useless. She'd never stop until Isa and Teddy were safe.

The teens ran fast, sprinting along the Riva degli Schiavoni waterfront before taking a sharp left and darting into a narrow alley, darkness closing in around them.

They weaved in and out of Venice blindly, running like their life depended on never stopping.

"Isa, slow down! Wait!" Francesca kept gasping out, but her sister and Teddy were too fast. Just like Nate, she too had to concentrate on breathing.

The pace felt grueling to him, even as a runner.

Fear kept Isa going, Teddy at her heels. Nate and Francesca had to speed up just to keep them in sight. They crossed an empty footbridge, traversed another narrow alley, found another bridge.

"Francesca." Nate reached her side when the alley widened enough to allow it. "Let her go."

The response wasn't surprising. "Never. She's scared. She can disappear again."

Abruptly, Isa ran out of steam. Stopping, she slid down the wall of the nearest building. Teddy fell to his haunches beside her, taking her in his arms.

"I won't go back, I won't!" she cried against his shoulder.

Reaching her in a few steps, Francesca sat down on the ground next to her on her other side. Isa collapsed into her arms, sobbing.

Doubled over to catch his breath, Nate let the sisters have their moment, Teddy a silent presence next to them.

"Shhh, it's okay," soothed Francesca. "I won't let him take you anywhere."

"What if we can't stop him?" Isa hiccupped.

"He'll have to go through my dead body," Nate promised.

Teddy wiped the dripping sweat from his forehead. "Yeah. Mine too."

"We're not alone anymore, Isa," Francesca crooned. "We have people with us now. We don't have to do this alone."

Isa's voice registered skepticism. "What are they

going to do? You know how powerful the Righteous Hearth is."

Teddy puffed out his skinny chest. "I'm not scared of them."

Isa narrowed her eyes at him. "You should be."

"I won't let them take you anywhere," Nate said. "They can bully two young women, but they have no idea who they're dealing with now that I'm involved."

Isa rolled her eyes. "All you got is bravado."

"I've got more than that." Nate directed his question to Francesca. "You trust me?"

She paused before answering. "I do."

The hesitation sliced him.

"Don't be stupid. We can't trust anyone," said Isa.

"We can trust Nate," Francesca replied, her voice certain now.

The simple comment unraveled the barbed coil inside him. Francesca didn't trust many people; he knew that. Yet despite all she'd endured, and the walls she'd built around herself, she chose to trust him. He would make sure she never regretted her decision.

"And me," Teddy added.

Isa wiped at her tears. "We should tell Nonna."

"No. She and Dante are far away. I don't need them to get tangled up in our mess. I think we should confront Miles."

Isa looked horrified. "Are you insane?"

"No, I'm not. I'm tired of running. It's time I stand up to him. I don't wish to marry him, and I won't."

"I'm scared," Isa confessed in a small voice.

Francesca tightened her hold on her sister. "Me too. But it's for the best. We can't keep living in fear, scared of every stranger walking by Nonna's building."

"How'd he know we were here?" asked Isa.

"How did he know you were in Italy at all?" asked Teddy.

"It's the Righteous Hearth. They know everything," Isa explained.

"I doubt that," said Nate. "A small sect from a tiny part of Nevada? Someone had to tip them off."

Francesca froze as she thought through the possibilities. "I can't imagine who that would be. We were so careful."

"What about Haley?" asked Isa.

Francesca was already shaking her head. "Haley would never."

But Isa insisted. "Maybe she told her husband?"

"She didn't," said Francesca. "And even if she did, it doesn't explain how Miles knew to go to the train station at the exact time we'd be there."

Nate still suspected Moretti. But how would Giorgio know Miles Decker?

"Let's go back to our hotel," Nate suggested. "I want a word with Decker."

Francesca tensed. "No. I don't need you to speak to him, Nate. It's something that I must do myself. I have to stand up to him or he'll never leave me alone."

A muscle in his jaw beat in tune with the fury that seized him. *She expected him to let her speak to her stalker alone?* "You're not to meet, see, or speak to him unless I'm with you." As she opened her mouth to argue, he continued. "You want to face him alone?"

She didn't respond for a tense minute, during which he wound up for an argument. But the response that followed her long sigh disarmed him. "No. I don't. All right. You may join me. Let's go and confront my obnoxious betrothed."

The statement bothered Nate. "You are not his betrothed."

"It was a joke." A bite of annoyance colored her explanation.

"It wasn't funny," he told her, fighting the irritation that surged at the thought of her being engaged to another man.

"Definitely not funny," Isa chimed in, agreeing with him for once.

He extended his hand to Francesca. She took it readily, letting him help her up. If only she always accepted his assistance with this little argument.

Chapter 24

The sweat that had risen across her skin from the mad chase across Venice began to cool and evaporate from her frame as they made their way to Danieli, leaving Francesca exhausted and anxious. She never wanted to see Miles again, didn't want to hear what he had to say, but she couldn't keep running from him and the Righteous Hearth.

She was ready to begin her life. Cutting it off with the Righteous Hearth once and for all was step one.

Placing her free hand over where hers and Nate's joined, she glanced behind her. Isa trudged alongside Teddy, looking like she was walking across the Bridge of Sighs.

As they reached the warm glow of Danieli, Francesca expected to see Miles in the exact spot they'd left him, but he was no longer there. Had he run after them? If so, where along the route had they lost him? Was he still out there searching for them or would he double back to the hotel?

Her questions were answered when they entered the opulent lobby. Miles sat in one of the armchairs, waiting for them.

He rose in recognition. As he crossed to them, Nate

placed himself between her and her wayward ex-boyfriend.

Miles stopped a few feet away, eyes burning with unconcealed satisfaction. "I've found you."

"You've wasted your time," said Nate. "Francesca is mine."

She stepped around him. "I belong to myself, thank you very much. But you have wasted your time, Miles. Isa and I aren't going anywhere with you."

Miles's eyes flashed. "You don't have a choice. God wants us to be together."

"God doesn't want us to be anything."

"You're wrong. The Spiritual Leader saw it in one of his dreams. I've come after you to prove my commitment to you. You and I are meant to be together for all eternity. I felt it from the moment I laid eyes on you years ago. The Spiritual Leader confirmed it. Come home."

"You tried to touch my underage sister. I'm not going back, and neither is Isa. We are done with the Righteous Hearth. We are done with it all."

"What happened… then… it was a misunderstanding. You know your sister. She's—"

"Don't make me hate you more than I already do, Miles. Don't make up lies when we both know the truth."

He changed tactics. "I'll be a good husband. I was lost, Francesca, lost for so long. But the Spiritual Leader showed me the way. I'll be head pastor once we are wed. We'll have real roles in our community, true responsibility to lead the others."

"I'm in no position to lead anyone. And neither are you. Miles, you said I *seduced* you when we both know that's not true. I almost died because of you."

All pretense at civility and passion fled his eyes,

leaving them flat and cold. "I have no time for trivial arguments. I've come to collect you. We will be on our way."

Francesca, suddenly seeing the ridiculousness of the situation, couldn't contain her laughter. "Collect me? I will never marry you. Miles, this ends here."

He gave her a superior look. "Sometimes we have to do things we don't want. The Spiritual Leader understands things you and I cannot even begin to comprehend. We mustn't question. You and I are simple creatures. The Spiritual Leader has a gift. He sees all."

"He's just a man. An insane man."

"How can you say that?" Miles's face swelled to a bright red. "He's our guide."

"Isa and I are done."

He took a sudden step toward her. "You're not done. I am building a home for us on our new land. A place to raise our family. You haven't even seen the new grounds."

Every pump of blood in her body screamed for her to back away from this unpredictable man, but she stood her ground. "I have seen it. It's a prison."

"It's to keep out the sins of the world."

This close, each word layered sticky moisture across her skin.

"It's to keep us in." She itched to run to the nearest bathroom and wash away the coat of spit his enunciation had left on her face, but she forced herself to stay. "I won't do it. I won't go. Nothing you say will convince me otherwise, so you're wasting your time."

"The Spiritual Leader is being kind to you because of how much he respects your father. Refuse me, and he'll send more men after you. The next ones won't be so nice."

Nate took a step forward.

She squeezed his arm, indicating that she had this. "Send every single member of the Righteous Hearth here. Without my consent, they can't do anything."

He snorted disdain. "How do you know so little about our ways, Francesca?"

Done with the conversation, Francesca jerked her head toward the exit. "You need to go. Tell your leader that he can try, but Isa and I are out."

Miles's perfectly formed lips pursed. "What about your parents? You'd cut off all ties with them?"

The thought crushed her. Despite everything, she missed her mother and father every day. But she couldn't show weakness. Miles was a predator. He'd go for the jugular. She kept her voice even. "They made their choice when they let Isa and me be locked in the Sinners Shed because I refused to marry you."

Still Miles pressed on. "What about Sofia? Will you let her live her entire life without you? Without Isa?"

She laughed then, the sound knocking Miles back a step. "If you think I'll let you guys have Sofia, you're crazy. Sofia is mine. She comes with us."

"Sofia isn't yours. She is a member of the Righteous Hearth." A greasy sheen of glee filled his face. "And what about your newest sibling?"

The question paralyzed her. Maybe she'd misheard. "What newest sibling?"

Miles's face twisted. "Oh, don't tell me that you don't know. Your mother is pregnant. She's having another baby. Would you let that child grow up without you as well?"

Dizziness swirled through Francesca as the lobby emptied of oxygen. "Mother isn't pregnant."

Miles *tsked*. "She is. You'll have a new baby brother or baby sister soon. Isn't that exciting? Would you really turn away from your entire family? We want you with us, Francesca. We want Isabella too. We love you. You belong to the Righteous Hearth. Come back with me. Come start our lives together."

His features, ones she'd at one point loved but had since come to hate, blurred.

Her mother was having another baby.

She may have another one after that.

No matter how far she and Isa ran, no matter how hard they'd fight for custody, their parents would bear more and more children, and her siblings would be left in a cult.

She wouldn't let that happen.

Francesca lifted her chin. "Goodbye, Miles. I hope to never see you again."

"You're making a mistake."

Nate stepped in front of her. "No, you are. Come near Francesca again, even as much as whisper her name in your sleep, and it'll be the last thing you do." The phrase, delivered in such a soft, casual tone, chilled her, even as Nate continued. "You or anyone else from your douchebag cult even think about Francesca or Isa, I'll annihilate every single one of you until not even a footprint remains in that prison you call your land."

"You'll be sorry you said that." Miles flattened his lips.

"You got two seconds before I prove my point."

Miles backed up a hasty step and slipped past them and out of the hotel.

He'd regroup and try again, Francesca was certain, but at least for now he retreated.

"You okay?" Nate turned to her but didn't touch her.

Francesca was grateful for his restraint. Her entire world was disintegrating around her, and she didn't know whether she'd lash out on instinct if he tried to confine her in any way.

"Not really," she said through a painfully tight throat. "Our mother is having another child? No matter what Isa and I do to get Sofia out of there, there will always be another baby left behind."

Isa stopped at Francesca's side. "We can't let our siblings be raised in that mess, Cessie. It's bad enough we had to leave Sofia for a bit. But you know the Righteous Hearth is getting worse. When Mom and Dad move to the new compound, we'll never get to Sofia. Or the new baby."

Her sister was right. They had to act now. "I have to go back."

"Like hell," Nate spat out.

"No, Cessie, no, you don't. That's not what I meant," Isa said at the same time.

She wished they could understand. "Maybe if I reason with Mom and Dad, they'll give Sofia to me. Maybe… maybe they'll consider giving me the new baby too."

"Does that sound like something they'd do?" Nate asked in a tone she knew he was struggling to modulate.

Tears burned her eyes. "Maybe before… yeah. Lately, as Dad has become more involved, they've both changed, have become more devout… it'll be harder now. But not as hard as when they move. They'll be behind barbed wire, with no access to even a landline phone. They'll be shut off."

"You're not going back." Nate finally reached for

her, his hands locking around her shoulders to emphasize the edict.

Francesca didn't take kindly to edicts. She shook off his hold. "I have to. This might be our only window of opportunity."

Nate folded his arms in front of him, not attempting to touch her again. "What are you proposing to do? Grab Sofia and run?"

Isa's face paled. "What if they lock you in the Sinners Shed again?"

"I'm great with a lockpick."

"They may have new locks now. Don't do this. I can't lose you." Her sister's eyes brimmed with tears, splintering Francesca.

She pulled her into a hug. "You won't lose me. I just have to talk to Mom and Dad is all. Just talk. Maybe we can work it out."

Isa clung tighter. "I'm going with you then."

Dread crystallized in her blood. "Absolutely not. If something goes wrong… at least I'll know you're free."

Her sister straightened away from her. "What will Nonna say?"

The question sliced through Francesca. She had just rediscovered her grandmother. How would she explain the need to return to Nevada, however brief? How would she convince Nonna to not accompany her? She'd probably make Dante tag along too.

"She'll understand that there's no other way."

A muscle pulsed in Nate's jaw at her response; he looked primed for a fight. Tensing to counter-parry, she waited for his next argument, but he surprised her. "Let's get your sister and Teddy rooms for the night. We can all discuss this in the morning."

"One room," said Isa. "I'm staying with Teddy."

Nate looked at Francesca. "Your call."

She shrugged. "They're both of age. But I'm paying."

He flashed her a dark glance. "We've talked about this."

"Nate—"

He leaned close. "One word of protest, and I'm taking you to our room and explaining how things work around here."

Hot need stabbed through her at his low tone, yet she refused to back down. "How many times do we have to have this argument?"

"You want to learn that lesson right here?"

Francesca thought it wise to refrain from further quarreling. Nate seemed near to snapping, and she didn't know what would happen when he did. He stalked to the concierge, waving over Isa and Teddy.

Francesca refused to sit while she waited for Nate to secure a room for her sister and Teddy. The adrenaline rush of confronting Miles had faded, leaving her headachy and exhausted, but the armchairs in the lobby felt tainted.

Now that she'd made her decision to return to Nevada, she was certain it was the right one. Neither her mom nor dad would leave the Righteous Hearth, but maybe they'd be open to maintaining a relationship. For all their flaws, she still loved them, wanted them to be part of her and Isa's and Sofia's lives. Maybe they'd understand her and Isa's need to leave, would be open to letting them have Sofia… and the new baby…

Hopelessness closed over her like muck. They'd never let Francesca take her younger siblings… unless she used the financial documents to put them away.

She hadn't heard him return, but all of a sudden, Nate loomed over her. "All checked in— You okay? I know it's been a long day. Let's go to our room and unwind a bit."

"Sure." The word sounded more exhausted than she had intended.

"I got Teddy and Francesca a room a few doors away from ours. Figured you'd want her close."

Her cracking heart shattered. *Why did he have to be so thoughtful?* She gave him a wobbly nod, fighting the despair that invaded her veins.

"Come on. I'll draw you a bath and go wrangle us something for dinner."

She did want a bath. The thought of it had her moving, but when he reached for her hand, she jerked hers away. It would be hard enough to say goodbye. She couldn't get used to the comfort he continued to offer.

No, she had to prepare herself to be alone and self-reliant. Her time with Nate had come to an end.

Chapter 25

Francesca drew more and more into herself as they approached their hotel room. Once inside, he couldn't resist. Wrapping his fingers around her hand, he tugged her close.

She hesitated for the briefest of moments, as though unsure whether a kiss was prudent, before sealing her lips to his with a low whimper. When her tongue teased his, he groaned, walking backward with her in his arms until the back of his legs hit their bed.

He tumbled onto it, with her falling on top, her legs on either side of his hips as she kissed him. Greedy hands roved over his shoulders, his arms. Balancing on his thighs, she sat up with a deliberate wiggle along his aching dick.

A mischievous sparkle lit her eyes, but there was something else there, hiding in the shadows. *Despair.*

"Don't move." Slipping her hands under his shirt, she tugged it up until she exposed his stomach, explored the bunching muscles there, scored them lightly with her nails. "I love how beautiful you are."

He released a low chuckle. "The crunches are paying off."

Her gaze found his, and she shook her head, sending

her hair dancing. Her palm settled over his heart. "You're beautiful here."

How could he ever give her up? For what? The life in New York he'd longed to return to for so many months now seemed dreary without her.

Seized with want, frantic to feel her grip him, to make her forget her plans to leave him, he crushed his mouth to hers.

I love her.

The realization washed over him in a wave of clarity, the thought so sudden and sharp, it stopped him.

He pulled back.

Let her go.

She froze above him, concern widening her eyes. "What's the matter?"

What would she do if he said the words right now? He knew all too well that she'd run. Already dealing with too much, she'd see his declaration as nothing but another burden.

She wasn't ready for the words yet, and he wasn't ready to say them. He had too much to sort through first.

In response to her question, he tucked a stray curl behind her ear and kissed her again, infusing the contact with every emotion she could not yet accept.

He'd planned to make love to her slowly until she couldn't imagine a world without him, but a frenzy had taken over Francesca, and she ripped at the clothes between them until they were both naked in their bed. He pushed her into the mattress, his lips skimming along the curve of her stomach, but she wouldn't let him take the time to linger.

Rolling on the condom, he sank home. When he was fully seated, she wrapped her legs around him, and he lost the ability to think. He brought her to the brink again and again until she pleaded and begged and gasped. As independent as Francesca was outside of the bedroom, here she was his, and he needed her to accept it. To understand that they were forever intertwined, imprinted on each other's DNA, and no cult or decree or distance would tear them apart.

He took her with the power of the desperation coursing through him. Her body bowed under his as her orgasm burst through her, taking him with her. As he pulled her into her arms and felt the wild beating of her heart echo his own, he knew that he'd figure out a way to make it work. He had to; he wanted her forever, and he'd ensure she'd want him for just as long.

Feeling her shiver, he pulled the sheets around their cooling bodies.

Francesca shifted to look up at him with a teasing glimmer. "I believe I was promised a bath?"

Rocked by the force of the feelings her sparkling eyes drew from him, the answer caught in his throat. "You can have anything you wish."

Yet when he moved to leave the bed, her arm around him tightened.

"No, stay just a little while longer." She snuggled in.

He kissed the top of her head and held her close, certain beyond doubt that they could make this work. Somehow.

***

Warm lips found her cheek, her temple. "Wake up, sleepyhead." She opened her eyes to Nate's brilliant blue gaze. "Your bath awaits."

Anticipation curled through her. "I've wanted to get into that tub from the moment I saw it."

He extended his hand to her, looking very pleased with himself. "You shall have your wish, signorina."

Nate led her to the bathroom, where the bubble bath waited. Steam, redolent of midsummer flowers, rose from the frothy water. Nate's fingers tightened on her hand as he helped her step into the tub.

"Water too hot? Does it sting your arms?"

Soothing heat and fizzing bubbles lapped around her as she settled against the high back. "It's perfect. Join me?"

He looked like he wanted to refuse, but as his gaze roamed over her body, barely covered by the gleaming white suds, he lost the fight. The water level rose dangerously high as he settled himself behind her.

"This is perfect." Leaning her head against his shoulder, she sighed in pure bliss once, then again for good measure.

He pulled her tighter against his chest. "Yes."

Seeking a kiss, she turned her head. The frown etched into his beautiful face startled her. "Why so serious?"

He answered her question with one of his own. "When do you want to leave for Nevada?"

This time, distress instead of delight infused her sigh. She had hoped to put off that conversation just a few hours longer, but she had to face facts.

"I'll stay long enough to hire a new club manager. Don't worry. I'll handle my replacement. I won't mess up your club, and you can still go to New York."

"When do you want to go?"

"Soon. But how will Zohra operate without me if I can't find—"

"I'll ask Noémie to fly in for a bit."

Her muscles relaxed, and she let her head drop back on his shoulder. "Oh, that's a good idea. She can probably do this job with her eyes closed."

"I don't doubt that."

She played with the hair on his forearms, loving all the textures of him. "Thank you for everything you've done for Isa and me. We'll never forget it."

"I'm going to Nevada with you."

Confused, she swiveled her head to look at him. "What?"

"You're not confronting the Righteous Hearth by yourself. I'm coming with you."

Was she hallucinating? Needing space in the small vessel, she moved away from him, sliding to the other side of the tub. "You can't do that. You have… your job, your mentor's case. Nate, tonight is it for us."

"You are insane if you think I'd let you go into some barbed-wire compound alone."

"I'm not insane," she bit out. "And Mom and Dad haven't even moved to the new compound yet, I don't think. As I told Isa, I have to do this by myself. If this backfires—" She took a steadying breath. "I have a contingency plan."

"You can fight and argue all you want, but I'm not changing my mind on this."

"I don't need you to control my life. I know what I'm doing."

"I'm not trying to control you," he snapped out through the flower-scented steam rising between them. "When have I ever tried to control you?"

"I don't need to be bound to you. I don't want to owe you."

"You don't owe me. Sometimes, people want to help out without expecting anything in return."

"Well, that hasn't been my experience in life." The words spilled before she could catch them. "Don't you see? The reason my parents are in the Righteous Hearth to begin with is me. I'm the one who dragged them into it."

She had never shared that with anyone before.

"How?" he asked from across the tub.

Remorse and shame thudded with each heartbeat. Her parents would never be part of the Righteous Hearth if it hadn't been for her stupid mistake as a child. She was the one to blame for everything.

Maybe if she told him, he'd understand why she couldn't accept his help. Assistance always came with strings attached.

"When I was a kid," she began, unable to meet his gaze, "I broke my leg. We didn't have money, or insurance. Isa wasn't even born yet. Sometimes we attended Righteous Hearth on Sundays, but Mom and Dad weren't official church members. Dad went to the church to ask for help paying for my medical bills. The church agreed. They paid for everything, for my surgery and the cast, but no one offers help without expecting something in return. My parents have been bound to them since."

She chanced a glance at him then, preparing to see the disgust on his face now that he knew the role she had played in getting her family embedded in the Righteous Hearth. But there was no disgust.

"It's not your fault your parents are part of that cult. Whoever in Righteous Hearth demanded your parents join for offering to cover their kid's medical bills is majorly screwed up. They are the ones to blame, not you."

"If I hadn't jumped off that tree…"

"You were a child. Your parents were desperate to make you better. Someone took advantage of desperate people. That's who I blame. Not your parents, and certainly not you."

"We'll have to agree to disagree on that."

"Do you really think that I'm going with you to indebt you to me? Have I ever done anything to make you think that?"

She shook her head.

"Would it be so terrible to have me go with you?" Taking her hand, he pulled her across the tub, back into his arms. "Think about it… you can have your way with me any time you want…" His tongue trailed along the curve of her ear. "Anywhere you want…" His hand cupped her breast. "Any way you want."

He tugged on her nipple until it swelled and tightened, sending moisture to pool between her legs. With a pleased rumble, he traced his fingers across her stomach to the juncture of her thighs, slipped through her slickness.

Need made her dizzy. "You don't play fair."

"Never have," he murmured, drawing out the nectar, gliding it over her throbbing center. Gentle, unhurried. Intentional.

"What about Steven?"

"I see him in two weeks."

"I'll think about it…"

"I'm not asking for permission. You're not going to Nevada without me."

She gasped as he probed with a teasing finger. "I do what I please."

"Another finger joined the first. "Not when you put yourself in danger."

"You don't get to decide my life," she said. But it didn't come out as forcefully as she'd hoped. She grasped for the remnants of her self-control. "I don't like it when you dictate to me."

"And I don't like when you won't listen to reason. I'm not deciding your life for you. I'm simply coming with you so you don't have to go through this alone."

He knew how to tempt her, speaking to the deepest desire she'd always had—to have someone to depend on during the roughest of times. But she'd learned a long time ago that trusting someone came with painful consequences.

When he curved his fingers, she bowed into his touch, needing more. He really didn't play fair at all. She could barely think with those clever digits inside her, and he wanted an answer from her while deliberately scattering her thoughts.

She could play that game too.

Reaching behind her, she curved her hand around his hard shaft, reveled in the way his entire body stilled in anticipation.

"I want to take you in my mouth." The huskiness sounded foreign even to her own ears.

After a beat, he recovered. "Your answer first."

Not giving her time to respond, he resumed his ministrations, sending need to bead across her skin.

Answer to what…

Focus… Have to… focus…

"My answer… is no. You can't come with me."

His thumb circled her clit. Her hand on him tightened.

"Try again," he growled.

She wheezed in air to respond. "I go alone—*Nate, no fair.*"

His mouth descended on her neck, nipping gently, as his hands lifted, leaving her aching and needy.

"Say yes."

She let go of him, sliding her own hand between her legs.

He grasped her wrist, stilling her progress. "Francesca… just one word. Is it so hard?"

She breathed through the need, turning to fully face him in the tub. "Why would you even want to go? I know the sex is great, but why would you inconvenience yourself to go to a small little desert town?"

"For you, damn you," he spat out. "I want to be there for you. You're scared that I'll demand shit from you? That I'll control you? Don't you realize? *You* control *me.* You can ask anything you want of me, and I'll do it, damn it. I'll do it gladly. *For. You.*"

Confusion swirled like the cooling bathwater. "What are you saying?"

He opened his mouth to respond, but swiftly closed it. His throat worked as he swallowed. His shoulders sagged. "Nothing. I'm not saying anything. Water's getting cold. Let's get out."

Nate moved to stand, pulling her up with him, steadying her as she stepped out of the tub. Following her out, he padded to the towels and wrapped her in the warm cotton. "I know you want to go through this alone, but this isn't me making decisions about your life. This is me wanting to help, to share some of the burden."

She chewed her lip, craving to give in, to say yes, while alarm bells went off in her head. What if this was how her parents had felt when they'd accepted the supposed strings-free handout from the Righteous Hearth?

Her pulse beat a wild panic in her ears, but she chose to leap. "All right. You can come with me."

***

The softly spoken words sparkled through Nate like fireworks, when they should have sent him running for the hills. He just signed up to go with Francesca to Nevada and demand that her parents relinquish custody of her little sister. If her parents agreed, he'd have three Brook sisters under his protection. If they refused, Francesca would stay in Nevada until she got Sofia and, eventually, her new baby sibling out of the Righteous Hearth.

But he'd be in New York. A disaster if not handled well.

He waited for alarm bells to squawk, yet all he saw was Francesca dropping her towel.

"I meant what I said," she whispered against his mouth. "I want to taste you."

His body clamored to have her lips close around his cock, to push into her welcoming heat, to feel her tongue curl around him.

When she pressed her warm, naked body against his, his feet melded to the floor. Her hair fell over her face as she ducked her head, watching herself take him in her hand, stroke.

"God help me." He huffed out a laugh while he still had the brainpower to do so.

She glanced up at him with a vulnerability he hadn't seen in her before. Drawing a finger along her velvety cheek, he mapped the plump fullness of her lips. Leaning down, he tasted them, infused his kiss with all the emotions he couldn't communicate to her with words.

254

Still gripping his length, she lowered to her knees, and closed her kiss-swollen lips around him. Fighting the intoxicating pull to surge deeper, he kept his hands fisted at his sides, letting her set her own pace as she explored.

She used her mouth and her hands to learn him until he shook with need. It took the last of his control to pull her away.

Her eyes flew to his. "Did I do something wrong?"

"Everything you do is right," he promised, barely able to get the words out.

Lifting her, he walked them out of the bathroom and toppled them to their bed. He only left her long enough to grab protection. When he slipped inside, the emotions that suffused her features mirrored the ones that beat through him.

This was where he always wanted to be.

With her.

If anyone could figure out how to make it work, it was them.

Now he only had to convince Francesca.

Chapter 26

Even cocooned in the safety of Nate's arms, Francesca failed to bat away the reality that ate through her moment of respite like corrosive sludge.

Although she'd given in to Nate's demand to accompany her, she had to figure out how to keep him as far away from the Righteous Hearth as possible. They were a mean group to outsiders, and she'd die before she let any fallout so much as graze Nate.

"I can feel you thinking." Nate's fingers searched out hers, lacing.

"How open are you to negotiating?"

The languid path of his thumb across her skin didn't falter. "I think you know by now how to sway me."

"So if I had to go to the compound, but asked you not to go inside with me—"

His hand squeezed hers until the pressure edged on painful. He whipped over her, the full weight of his body pinning hers into the bed.

"Let me explain something to you," he breathed, even as his eyes stormed. "I won't let you traipse into a fucking cult alone. I *need* to go with you. If something happened to you, I couldn't bear it."

She tensed, expecting panic to manacle her, but none came… only a bright warmth that melted through her body.

Confused by her own reaction, Francesca laid a hand over his chiseled cheek, an attempt to calm his rapid breathing and the flush that climbed high on his cheekbones. "I don't want to go back alone. I'm glad that you're coming with me."

His body incrementally relaxed, and he turned his head to place a hot kiss into her palm. "Good. We're finally on the same page."

Inscrutable emotions burned in his eyes, but when he blinked, they were gone. He resettled himself next to her.

She draped herself over his chest, resting her chin on the back of her hand. "We need to find a safe place for Isa. I can't leave her with Nonna now that Miles knows where Nonna lives, and she can't stay at Zohra."

He traced tingly patterns along her back. "I know of a place. You haven't met Jackson yet, but his father owns a house on the French Riviera. I'm sure he'd let Isa stay there for a little while. It's safe as a fortress, and no one would think to look for her there."

"Think his dad would agree?"

"I can't imagine why not. I'll text him. If it's a go, we'll send her there the same day we leave for the States."

He stretched for the phone on his nightstand. His fingers flew as he typed and sent the text. As he read the almost instant response, his face lit up in a grin.

"Isa—and Teddy, if he wants—can stay with Valentin. They'll love his house. It's next to the beach and has a pool."

She sat up, considering. "I don't know how I feel about letting her stay with a stranger I don't know."

"Valentin is a good guy. You actually might know of him—he's the French actor, Valentin Auclair."

Francesca shook her head. "We weren't allowed to watch anything for so long, I don't know him."

"I'll video call him later so you can meet him. He's got a pregnant wife, who'll also be there… and they've got a whole army of staff. Isa will be in great hands. What? You look confused."

"Why would your brother's father want to help?"

"Because that's what families do."

The simple statement cut through Francesca. Her parents had wanted to help her—and her shattered bone—once too. Now, the Righteous Hearth had taken hold of them. "Not my family… at least, not anymore. Righteous Hearth discourages disobedience."

"For the record, I encourage it," he said in a voice that sent blood rushing to all her special parts. "Want me to show you how much?"

She did. She wanted him to make her forget that she'd be returning to Nevada, facing her parents and the heartbreak that would inevitably result when they'd turn down her request for Sofia.

"We should tell Isa and Teddy about the new plan first…"

He watched her lips move with darkened eyes. She suspected he no longer heard a thing she was saying.

"I should look at—"

He rolled over her, hard and insistent, his mouth cutting off her words.

She submerged her fingers into the silky strands of his hair, arched as he found a potent spot under her ear.

"I can't get enough of you," he whispered against her lips. "I always want more. You're all I think about."

He consumed every one of her waking thoughts too. It would hurt a lot when they said goodbye.

"Nate—"

"One more word and I'll find better things for your mouth to do." He took a greedy bite of her lip.

Her body reacted to the familiar scent of him, the protective feel of him around her. In the course of a very short time, she'd become addicted. Seeking to deepen the kiss, she lifted to him—

The insistent ring of Nate's phone snapped through the moment.

With a curse, he searched out the cell phone among the sheets, glanced at it with reluctance. "It's Giacomo."

She sat up. "You should take it."

When he did, Giacomo's voice projected on the speakerphone. "Hey. There's someone here asking about Francesca."

"Who?" Francesca demanded before Nate could.

"They said they're your parents."

Mom and Dad are in Italy?

Francesca grabbed the phone from Nate. "Are they there now?"

"They're waiting outside. I told them you're away tonight. Should I tell them to come back tomorrow?"

Francesca heard the tremor in her own voice. "Yes. Please tell them to come back tomorrow. I'll be back in the morning and will speak to them then."

Giacomo assured her he was on it, and the line disconnected.

Her parents... in Rome.

The very idea was so surreal, Francesca didn't know how to process it. She leaped off the bed, tried to pace away the stinging nervous energy. Realizing she was naked, she snagged a hotel robe, tied it around herself, and faced Nate.

"If Miles knows I'm in Venice, why would my parents think I'm in Rome? How would they know where I work?" She found her own phone. "I have to call Haley…"

Haley picked up on the first ring, and Francesca almost wept at the sound of her best friend's voice. She tamped down the tears. Now wasn't the time.

"Miles, Mom, and Dad are in Italy," she said by way of greeting.

Haley's detached tone had no inflection. "Hey, can you hang on a second? I'll call you right back."

The line went dead.

"What was that?" asked Nate.

"They have a landline. She's probably not alone."

The phone rang less than two minutes later. Francesca set it to speaker so Nate could hear too.

"Sorry I had to hang up. Greg forgot his lunch so I had to wait for him to leave. I wanted so bad to call you, but I was too nervous. I miss you so much."

"I miss you every day."

"Cessie, when I dropped you off at the airport, Lucilla and Jimmy saw my car there."

Francesca's eyes collided with Nate's as Haley continued.

"They told Greg. I denied it, but he figured out I'd dropped you and Isa off there. He told the Spiritual Leader, but I don't know how they realized you're in Italy. Francesca, I'm so sorry. I wanted to warn you, but I was too afraid to call in case Greg checked our call records."

Francesca's head pounded with concern for her friend. "Are you going to be okay? Did he take it out on you? Did they—"

"No, no, I'm fine. Greg was thrilled. He had something to share with the Spiritual Leader—he expects the news will promote him up the ranks for his loyalty. Miles left soon after that, but I didn't know where. And then your parents came to me. They wanted to know if you were in Rome. I told them nothing. I had no idea your parents went to Italy. I don't think anyone knows that here."

"So they aren't here with Miles…"

"I don't know. I don't think so."

"Do you know where Sofia is?"

"No, but I'll try to find out."

"Call me if you learn anything. Are you going to be okay?"

"Oh yes. Greg is scared of my father. He would never do anything to me. And you know the Spiritual Leader won't touch me."

"And what about your dad?"

"I'll be okay," Haley assured her. "But what are you going to do?"

"I don't know… I will figure it out. Let's speak again soon."

After Francesca hung up, Nate took the phone from her shaking fingers and tossed it to the bed.

"Who's her dad?" he asked.

"He's one of the Spiritual Leader's closest advisors and the Righteous Hearth's biggest donor."

"Should we call my brothers? Does Haley need a place to go? One of them can go get her."

There he went again, offering his family to help her as though it were the most natural thing in the world. The gratitude overwhelmed her. She squashed it down. She couldn't get used to this. She couldn't keep him.

"If she was concerned, she'd tell me. Her father's pockets are deep. He's single-handedly financing the new compound. No one will touch her." She worked her fingers into the tense muscle between her brows. "I never expected Mom and Dad to come here. I wonder where they left Sofia. We should tell Isa."

Once dressed, they strode along the empty hall until they stopped at Isa and Teddy's room. Sleep-rumpled and groggy, Teddy let them in.

Isa, sitting up in bed, took the news better than Francesca expected. She squared her shoulders, raised her chin. "Let's go back to Rome and see what they want."

"First thing tomorrow morning," promised Francesca. "On the first train out."

Isa crumpled the thick duvet under her fingers. "Where do you think Sofia is?"

"Haley is going to try to find out for us."

Isa's voice caught. "What if they already sent her to the new compound?"

Chapter 27

The train left the station just as the sun rose over Venice Tuesday morning. Tucked in next to Nate in her seat, unable to shed the feeling that she was being watched, Francesca twisted her neck to see whether Miles lingered like black mold.

Nate squeezed her thigh just below the hem of her white T-shirt dress. "You all right?"

With one last prolonged scan of the train car, she met Nate's concerned gaze. "Ironic, isn't it? We were ready to go to the States, but my parents came here."

"If they dare threaten you or Isa or Sofia—"

"They won't," she said with full conviction, though she couldn't be certain. She let her head rest on his shoulder. "You're a good guy, Nate."

When we're over, I'll miss you for the rest of my life.

They made it back to Zohra from the Roma Termini train station in record time. Entering through the side door, they found Giacomo enjoying a cup of coffee at the bar.

The nerves that spiraled through her made it impossible to start with pleasantries. "What did my parents say to you exactly? Have they been back?"

Giacomo rose. "All they said is that they were looking for you and Isabella and that they knew you worked here. They were so intense, it made me uncomfortable. They left after I told them you'd be back in the morning. I haven't seen them since."

"Were they alone? Did they have anyone with them?" asked Isa.

Francesca, realizing Giacomo had never met her sister or Teddy before, made quick introductions before Giacomo responded.

"No. It was just the two of them."

Nate studied the mixologist. "And no one has bothered you since we left?"

"No, but I saw a man in a bow tie near the club last night. He stayed until security attempted to speak to him. I don't know who that was."

Nate cursed. "He works for Frascati."

Giacomo blanched. "Frascati, as in… Wait. You know him?"

"He stopped by once before. The Morettis have been the aggressive ones, so I didn't give Frascati much thought."

"The Moretti family has had to be aggressive, playing second fiddle to Frascati for decades now. But Frascati are the ones you should be concerned about. They're ruthless."

Teddy's explanation froze everyone. They turned toward him.

Nate's gaze pinned him. "How do you know that, Teddy?"

He shrugged. "My father is finishing up a documentary on the Frascati-Moretti rivalry. I interned on it for a while."

"Teddy, who's your father?"

Teddy looked uncomfortable with Nate's question, but he answered. "My father is John Rutherford."

Nate's face lit with recognition. "Rutherford? I saw his documentary on the Ukrainian war."

"That one won an Emmy. Dad's third. He likes to collect them."

Isa took Teddy's hand. "What's an Emmy?"

"I'll tell you later." He grinned and squeezed her hand.

Isa's troubled eyes met Francesca's. "I think we should go to Nonna's. Maybe Mom and Dad are there."

"I doubt Mom still has the key to that apartment," Francesca said, "but we could try."

"Can we call Nonna now? Ask her to come back?"

"Not yet," Francesca told her sister. "I don't want to put her in any awkward situation with Mom and Dad." She wasn't certain Nonna would want to see them.

A frown creased Isa's forehead. "We've been keeping so much from her."

"She's on vacation. Let her enjoy it for a bit. Before reality intrudes."

Reality had already swamped Francesca. Maybe she could spare her grandmother.

"Should we go look for them? Mom and Dad don't have phones. We can't call them to learn where they are. Where might they go?" Isa wondered out loud.

"It's been a long morning," Nate said. "I'm starving. I'm not going to go chase your parents around Rome."

Francesca laid her hand on his arm. "What do you propose?"

"We eat. We wait for them to return. If they are eager enough to fly to Italy to speak to you, they'll be here sooner rather than later this morning."

They ate at Zohra, feasting on day-old tartlets Giacomo was able to scrounge from last night's surplus. Francesca liked the kid's resourcefulness. Maybe he could take over Zohra as manager when she left, if Noémie took him under her wing. After making them coffee, Giacomo left for his apartment, citing his need for sleep after a long night of Zohra revelry.

***

They barely finished breakfast when a rapping at the front door had Nate rising.

Isa leaped up so quickly, the last of her tartlet crumbled around her feet. "Is that Mom and Dad?"

"I'll go check," said Nate. When Francesca stood too, he fixed her with a warning glance. "You stay here."

She rolled her eyes. "Fine. Go. Before whoever it is leaves."

Nate recognized Francesca's parents instantly, even without meeting them before. They were both tanned, lean, and tall. Francesca had inherited her mother's dark hair and her dad's blue eyes. Even in the boiling late morning, they wore long sleeves, their wide linen pants skimming their ankles.

"We understand our daughter is here," said her father.

Instinct to protect Francesca urged him to send them away, yet he couldn't make the decision for her. "Wait here," he instructed, and closed the door.

"It's them," Francesca said as soon as he returned. She looked as eager as someone seeing the blood-dulled blades of a waiting guillotine. "I'll go talk to them."

"I'm coming too," Isa said.

Francesca cut in front of her sister. "No. You're not. You're staying out of sight. We don't know what they want."

"I won't sit here while you—"

"You will. Stay with Teddy."

Isa opened her mouth to protest, but Nate interrupted. "You really want to hear what they have to say?"

Isa thought about it, then shook her head. "Not really. Not right now."

"Let me see what they want first. If I think they've come to be more reasonable, you can speak to them too."

Teddy squared his shoulders. "You need me to come along as backup?"

Francesca smiled at the gallant gesture. "That's very kind of you to offer, but I think Isa needs you more right now."

Teddy wrapped his gangly arm around Isa and stood taller. "We'll be here."

Nate took Francesca's icy hand.

Squeezing his hand once, she pulled free of his hold. "I'm going to speak to them alone."

"Like hell you are."

"Nate—"

"You're not going out there by yourself. They're your parents. I'll follow your lead here, but I am not letting you do this alone."

She glanced to the main door, then back to him. "Okay. Let's go see my parents."

***

A mixture of dejection and dread darted through her as Nate swung open the door. Despite it all, she wished she could fall into her parents' arms and forget the insanity of the last few months, yet it was a fool's hope. They had traveled to Rome to bring her back, to make sure she never used the financial statements she'd taken.

Her parents watched her warily, crossing their arms as she and Nate stepped into the bright Roman sun.

"What in the world are you doing?" asked her mother. "Where's Isabella? We are here to take you home."

Francesca met her mom's familiar gaze. "We are not going back to the Righteous Hearth. You're wasting your time."

"Francesca, Miles is here looking for you," her mother continued. "The Spiritual Leader is concerned about you. He wants you back home, safe. We want you back home, safe. It'll be easier on all of us if you come back with us, of your own accord."

Easier for everyone but her. "The Righteous Hearth isn't my home. Miles has found me already, and I told him the same thing—I won't go back."

"The Spiritual Leader decreed it, and so it shall be," said her dad. But the edge to his voice softened as he continued. "Miles is your chosen betrothed. You can't escape fate, Cessie."

"Miles isn't fate. Miles is a random man who another random man commands I marry. I refuse to do it. Where's Sofia?"

"Sofia misses you." A sad smile broke across her mother's face. "She doesn't understand why you left."

"I want to see her."

"Once you're Miles's lawful wife, you can see her all you want," her father said. "Come back with us, Cessie. Come back because you want to."

"Is she in Rome?"

"Where's your grandmother?" countered her mother.

Before she could answer, her father cut in. "Francesca, where is it?"

Ah... They're here for the file. "Where is what?"

"You know what!" Her father's voice boomed down the cobblestone-lined road, bouncing off the cafes and restaurants along the way.

"Everyone is feeling really tense right now," her mother said. "Let's take a deep breath." Turning to her husband, she frowned. "What are you looking for?"

His jaw set. "Nothing at all."

"You're pregnant again." Francesca changed the subject.

Her mother cupped her stomach. "A baby due this winter."

"You'd want to raise him or her behind barbed wire?"

"The Spiritual Leader wants us safe." Her mother looked at her as one would look at a small child throwing a tantrum in the ice cream aisle. "We are here to take you and Isabella home. First, you refuse the divine plan, and then you take our daughter from us. Enough is enough. You've had your fun. It's time to be an adult now, an upstanding member of our community."

Francesca crossed her arms, mimicking her parents' defensive stance. "You came all the way here to tell me this?"

"We are here to take you home," said her mom.

"You're here because you don't want to go to jail."

Confusion flickered in her mother's eyes. "Why would we go to jail?"

Her dad's body vibrated. "You and Isa return with

us, or we are done. You'll no longer have a relationship with us, Sofia, or the new baby."

"You'd cut off all ties with your own flesh and blood?"

"You betrayed our church," her father replied. "The Spiritual Leader is giving you one chance to return on your own."

"Isa and I want to have a relationship with you and Sofia and the new baby. Maybe we can talk, come up with a plan that works for everyone. Isa and I miss you." She looked at her father. "And that thing that you're here for… you can have it if you let me have Sofia."

Her father's lip curled. "The Righteous Hearth has done so much for you. For us. You owe your life to them."

"She owes her life to no one," Nate finally interrupted.

Her dad blinked, as though he'd only remembered about Nate now. "We have nothing to say to someone who brought back Sodom and Gomorrah."

"You stay away from our daughters," Francesca's mom added. "You're what's wrong with this world. Francesca, get Isa. We are leaving."

"Never."

Nate moved to stand between her and her family, a physical barrier. "They are not going anywhere with you."

Finding herself behind his broad shoulders felt oddly… nice. She could count the number of times someone had stood up for her on one hand, and even then, she'd have fingers to spare. And yet she couldn't let him run roughshod over her insistence she handle her parents herself.

Moving forward until she was even with him, she touched his arm. "Nate, I got this."

She could tell he wanted to shield her from further conversation. The tension gripping his muscles made that clear. Touching his forearm, she infused her smile with all the appreciation she had for his steady presence.

His nostrils flared, but he didn't move to place her behind him again. Nevertheless, he hovered close.

Her father focused on Francesca. "Where are the statements?"

"What statements?" queried her mom, angling her head to better look at her husband.

"In a safe place. Isa and I want a relationship with you both and Sofia and the new baby. If you don't want that, that's fine. But I will do whatever necessary to get Sofia away from there."

A flush of anger colored her mother's face. "You've made your decision then."

"I want to see my sister."

"Out of the question," said her dad. "Your mother wants to settle in our new home before the baby comes. If you wish to see Sofia, you'll come with us now."

"Don't do this. Don't imprison Sofia and the baby like this."

Her father's face remained impassive. "Our new home isn't a prison. It's a haven. When you see it, you'll understand."

Francesca had nothing left to say. She formed the only words she could. "I hope you change your mind."

The corners of her father's mouth drooped. "We hope the same of you."

He started away from them, along the cobblestones. Her mother promptly followed. Francesca watched them turn the corner and disappear from sight.

"They're not done with me or Isa yet." She stepped

back into Nate's body. "They'd never fly this far to back away this quickly. They knew where to hit so it hurts, though."

His arms wrapped around her. "They will have you married to Decker or won't have you at all."

"It's a good thing I make my own decisions."

Not giving him time to respond, Francesca turned, pulled his head down to hers, and kissed him right there in the street… in front of Zohra, curious passersby, and myriad security cameras.

As he kissed her back, thoughts of her parents, of Miles, of the Righteous Hearth evaporated like summer rain in parching desert heat and she lost herself in the kiss, in the feel of his hands smoothing over her body, heating her insides.

She didn't care who saw them. His presence next to her had made her feel—for once—less alone. It hadn't been easy for her to let him join her outside with her parents. And it hadn't been easy for him to stand next to her and not intervene. Yet they managed it. Gratitude mixed with infatuation for this man she'd come to know.

Wishing to continue, knowing they shouldn't, she broke away long enough to say three little words. "Take me upstairs."

Chapter 28

He didn't have to be told twice. Scooping her up in his arms, he strode with her into Zohra, having the foresight to take the side entrance to avoid Isa and Teddy.

The old door creaked, and gave them away.

"Cessie?" Isa called from the ballroom.

"Crap." Francesca sighed.

Nate set her on her feet just as Isa and Teddy found them.

Isa's eyes were huge pools of apprehension and hope. "Did you talk to them? What happened?"

Nate waved them toward the bar. "I'll make more coffee."

Francesca was halfway through the story by the time Nate brought in the cappuccinos. Neither Teddy nor Isa reached for the drinks until Francesca finished the update.

Isa chewed her lip, concern digging a trench between her brows. "Think they'll ever come around?"

"I hope so. Someday."

When Isa's eyes filled with fledgling optimism, Francesca winced. Deep down, she wasn't so sure they ever would. Especially if she had to use the financial records against them.

Nate, as though reading her thoughts, laid his palm on her shoulder and squeezed, leaning close. "We'll figure it out."

Surprisingly, she didn't want to fight his assertion. The *we* felt pleasant—the *we* felt nice, like they were part of one cohesive unit, ready to work through any obstacles together. She told herself not to get used to it, that it could never work, but for a moment, she let herself picture the life they could have together, and let it comfort her.

***

"I know good attorneys," Nate continued. "I'll hire them for you. We'll get your sister away."

Francesca tensed under his palm as though his words had whipped across her skin. "You know I can't accept—"

He felt like he had the top of Mount Everest finally in sight and somehow ended up sliding back down the mountain. All progress, gone. She'd been burned too much in her past to ever trust him fully. The despair thickened, dragged him under, made him lash out. "I can't keep having the same fight."

Trading a glance, Isa and Teddy backed out of the ballroom.

"Listen—"

"No, you listen."

As he swung her to his chest, she yelped. "Nate, what are you doing?"

Striding through the ballroom to the staircase, he took the steps two at a time.

He admired her self-sufficiency and independence. It was what made her, her. But right now, when she was too stubborn to see reason, too blinded by the sins of the Righteous Hearth to understand he needed to help, it irritated.

Francesca's protests died away as they reached his bedroom and stopped at the bed, the bed where he had had her willing and naked under him before. He set her on the edge, marveling at how much she blushed under his stare still, after all the things they'd done together.

Her eyes darkened to a stormy indigo as he tore at his clothes, attacked hers next. Covering her naked body with his, he let her feel his need for her as he possessed her mouth.

He skated his lips over the curve of her jaw, the bridge of her nose, before pulling back to look at her. As he did, the uncertainty, the sadness in her gaze gathered, condensed into a glittering tear, and that tear rolled down her flushed cheek, crushing his heart. With a curse, he moved off her, but she closed her arms and legs around him like a vise and held tight.

"No." She lifted her mouth to his. "Don't go. More. More. I need you."

On a silent prayer of gratitude, he gave in to them both, letting her demand for him feed him, drive him. When he joined with her, and she gasped his name, he could no longer hold back.

"I love you, I love you," he whispered on each deep thrust, luxuriating in the feel of her silky heat closing and fluttering around him. He kissed any part of her he could reach, punctuating the words with wet bites and kisses.

Francesca shut her eyes against the onslaught, as though protecting herself against his words. He didn't give her quarter, terrified he'd lose her forever if he did, so he repeated the words like a mantra while he drove into her, claimed her, took her until she shuddered and bowed under him, coming apart in his arms.

When he found his own release, he whispered the words still, a despairing wish that even a little part of her would accept his feelings… maybe even, someday, return them.

***

"Why did you say that to me?" Francesca demanded as soon as he separated himself from her. She scrambled away from him to the other end of the bed, sitting up on her knees and pulling a pillow in front of her.

He sat up too. "Because it's the truth. I love you."

She scrunched the pillow tighter to her feverish body, wishing he'd stop saying the words. "You don't. You can't."

The sincerity in his eyes stabbed through her. "I moved to Italy to escape a broken heart—and it almost cost me everything I'd ever worked for. But I'm grateful, Francesca—because it brought me to you. Fate brought me to you."

The very word chilled Francesca as effectively as an unexpected ice bath. "Isa stole into your club. That's not fate. I can't take any more talk of fate today."

Nate gave a rueful shake of his head before he shoved his fingers through his hair. "Fate was the wrong thing to say. I know this is overwhelming. But don't shut it off, don't run. We can find a way to make it work."

"You know that it can never work."

She hated the pitiful tone in her voice.

"We are both stubborn, determined people. If we set our minds to it, we can make it happen. I'm willing to try. Are you?"

Why couldn't he understand? "You didn't grow up like me, Nate. Everything I ever wanted has always been blocked from me—this is finally the time for me to pursue a future I want. No matter how I feel about you, I can't give that up."

"I'm not asking you to give up anything."

"Not yet." Unable to continue the conversation perched on the mattress, Francesca tossed aside the pillow and climbed off the bed. "You're too… derailing. Look at this, for example. Isa and Teddy are downstairs, anxious over my parents, and instead of being with them, what did I do? I made love with you! I let my feelings for you overrule everything."

He moved to stand too, the bed now an obstacle between them. "So you do have feelings for me."

"Of course I have feelings for you! But it doesn't matter. I won't let Sofia and the new baby be raised in a cult." Realizing she was yelling, she gentled her voice. "I will never forget you, Nate. You've been so kind and—"

"Kind? You won't forget me because I've been kind to you?"

The dangerous tone caught her off guard.

"You *have* been kind," she pointed out.

"I don't want to be remembered for kindness. I want you to lie in bed at night missing the things I did to your body."

"Nate—"

He prowled toward her and, reaching her, he pounced. "I must have been remiss in that department."

Tumbling her back onto the rumpled surface of the bed, he pinned her with his weight.

"Nate, we don't have time—oh!" The sharp bite on her shoulder surprised more than hurt, and when he soothed the burning spot with his tongue, she shifted restlessly, wanting more.

"I didn't intend to fall in love with you." He slid his hand between her legs.

"You aren't in love with me."

She moaned when he plunged two fingers deep.

"I told myself I'd never fall in love again"—the low rumble of his voice ignited her skin with wildfire—"but you made it impossible for me to keep that promise."

Lightheaded from the pressure his clever fingers built inside her and his overwhelming words, she didn't know whether she wanted to escape or to push closer. His touch twisted the liquid need higher, torqued it until she thought she'd go blind.

She whimpered when his fingers withdrew, and he rolled away to grab protection.

Craving drummed deep inside, and she felt his return with every beat of her heart. They both groaned as he filled her, imprinted himself on her. He withdrew slowly, then sank every inch of him into her again, setting a languorous rhythm until sweat sheened both of their bodies and she cried out for more.

She felt his control unraveling, knew the moment it snapped. He plundered her with the wildness of a mating animal, his hand finding her throbbing clit, pinching, launching her off the ledge into a shimmering darkness and following her over. She barely felt him withdraw and fall to his back next to her. Using up the last dregs of her energy, she closed the small distance between them and wrapped her arm tight around him.

Audibly struggling to catch his own breath too, he threaded his fingers through hers and held tight.

"We should go downstairs before Isa and Teddy

decide to come find us," Francesca said against his sweat-slicked skin.

He pressed a kiss against her hair. "In a minute. I need to hold you just a while longer."

Relaxing against him, she stayed and let the beat of his heart steady her. Just as she felt herself drifting into sleep, she forced herself to move, to leave the comfort of his hold, to seek out the clothes he'd scattered across the floor. The reprieve was over.

Nate found his clothes, pulled them on piecemeal.

She should have been doing the same, but the fingers holding her dress went slack.

She didn't even realize she'd dropped it back to the ground until concern flashed in Nate's eyes. "You okay?"

She shook her head. Even through the mist of tears blurring her vision, she saw alarm in his features. "What—"

Unable to stop herself, she ran toward him and plastered herself to his body, only relaxing when his solid arms closed around her.

He pressed a kiss to the top of her head, his palms drawing soothing circles across her naked back. "What's wrong?"

She burrowed deeper into his soft cotton shirt, inhaling his reassuring, familiar scent. "Say the words again."

The demand scared even herself. She didn't want to hear the words. She couldn't.

He understood immediately. His arms tightened until she was sure her ribs would crack, but she didn't care. "I love you," he said against her hair.

Impossibly, she pressed even closer. "Say it again."

"I love you."

Unable to face him, she spoke into his chest. "I like hearing it."

"I'll say it for as long as you need."

She swallowed against the tight knot in her throat. "My life will complicate yours."

"I know."

"Don't you care?" She chanced a look, wishing to see his face when he responded.

His somber eyes met hers. "I'd rather have a complicated life with you than a simple one without you."

She wished she could say it back to him, say the words as easily as he did, but she couldn't. Not yet. She wanted him to know that he meant a lot to her too, that the feelings weren't one-sided. "I miss you when you're not near." The words tumbled out quickly, tripping over one another on her tongue.

His eyes softened as he processed them, and he pressed a gentle kiss to her lips. When he lifted his head, she wanted to follow him, to demand his mouth on hers again, but she restrained herself, remained still as he spoke. "Then don't make us end this."

"All right… let's see how this goes."

A relieved rush of breath bathed her face, and he tumbled her back onto the bed.

Chapter 29

Later that day, a handful of hours before the club would open for the night's activities, Nate closed off the topmost floor for Teddy and Isa.

He walked the teens through the space reserved for them. "As soon as the first staffer arrives, you better keep your butts in these rooms. I'll post a guard at the stairwell so no one comes up here."

"And so we don't sneak down?"

Nate faced the teen. "You snuck into my party once, and once was more than enough. I've learned my lesson."

The buzzing of his phone had Nate reaching into his pocket. Jackson's name popped up on screen. He answered.

"What. The. Fuck." Jackson's voice came out clipped and angry.

"Hold on a second." Turning on his heel, he took the stairs down to his own room. "What's going on?"

"You didn't see the tabloids?"

"I don't read tabloids."

"Well, you better start. Our Comms team is being inundated with calls from legit papers now too. What did you do?"

"I didn't do anything."

"Read the articles I just sent you."

Setting the phone to speaker, Nate scrolled through the text messages from his half-brother, each one a link to a different tabloid story:

ITALY'S HOT NEW SEX CLUB OR A MONEY-LAUNDERING FRONT FOR THE FRASCATI MAFIA RING?

JACKSON AUCLAIR'S HALF-BROTHER, NATE ICEFALL, LINKED TO ITALIAN ORGANIZED CRIME GROUP FRASCATI

INVESTIGATORS LOOKING INTO TIES BETWEEN ROMAN SEX CLUB ZOHRA AND FRASCATI

DOES NATE ICEFALL, BROTHER OF ZOHRA FOUNDER JACKSON AUCLAIR, WORK FOR FRASCATI MAFIA GROUP?

ZOHRA ROME AND OWNER'S BROTHER NATE ICEFALL CONNECTED TO INTERNATIONAL CRIME SYNDICATE, FRASCATI

NATE ICEFALL AND GIRLFRIEND, FRANCESCA BROOK, INVOLVED WITH GLOBAL CRIME GROUP

WHO IS NATE ICEFALL AND FRANCESCA BROOK, TWO AMERICANS LINKED TO ONE OF ITALY'S MOST POWERFUL CRIME ORGANIZATIONS?

Nate clicked into several articles. Confusion gave way to disbelief, then to anger. The tabloids had run with the story without even a fact check, and included photos of him and Francesca in Italy, including their kiss on the Ponte Vecchio.

"What the fuck?" He repeated Jackson's earlier phrase.

This wasn't happening. He couldn't have a scandal on his hands. Rhyme, Ryan, & Shuster would rescind the offer and, with it, the resources their backing would provide for him to represent Steven. Not that Steven would even want him for an attorney now—what jury would trust someone linked to organized crime? The reps for Clary Guns would have a field day.

The door slitted open, and Francesca peeked inside. "Hey, are you—" Seeing his face, she stepped into the bedroom and shut the door. "What is it?"

Waving her over, he pulled up the articles one more time. "Jackson's on the phone. Look at these."

As Francesca read through the headlines, her hands flew to her face. "This is all my fault. You declared war on the Righteous Hearth. They are fighting back."

"Or the Morettis finally found another way to fuck me over."

Jackson's voice cut through their conversation. "What is going on over there? Do I need to fly out?"

Nate knew his brother would catch the first available flight if he only gave the word. That was how Jackson operated. Yet he had a wife to think about now. Nate wouldn't tear Jackson away from his family.

"Of course not. I'll handle this."

Francesca gnawed on her lip. "I'm going to go find my parents—I'll tell them—"

He snagged her hand before she could leave the room. "You stay put."

"I'm getting Legal involved," said Jackson. "They'll have the stories taken down."

Still holding on to Francesca, Nate replied to his brother, "I refuse to release a statement over tabloid fodder."

"Agreed, but Comms will call you if they feel otherwise. Keep your phone on you."

As Jackson disconnected, Nate tossed his phone to the desk and focused on Francesca.

Her wide eyes looked stricken. "How would Righteous Hearth get these photos of you? Of me? How long had they planned to do this? You're not even part of the church. They want to get me, and you're collateral damage. This is all Miles's doing. If you hadn't threatened him in Venice…"

"The clear first choice is the Morettis. I'm going to track down Giorgio." Nate cursed. "We may have vultures circling the club tonight. Soon as security arrives, tell them to be vigilant. Our members' privacy is of utmost importance. I won't subject them to this. I'll be back once I find Moretti."

"Alone? Out of the question. I'm going with you."

"I'm not letting you come within a mile of him." He took both of her hands now, needing the contact, to feel her safe and near him.

She watched their hands as she spoke. "Do you think he has a connection to the Righteous Hearth?"

He wished he knew. "Hayes would have a way of finding out."

Hayes had connections neither Jackson nor he even fully comprehended. Reluctantly letting her go of Francesca, he dialed his sibling. "I need a favor."

Hayes didn't need the background. "I just spoke with Jackson. What do you need?"

"Find out if the Morettis are linked to the Righteous Hearth."

Not even a pause. "Will do."

"And find out where Giorgio is right now."

After Nate ended the call, Francesca grabbed his hand. "You are not going to confront him."

"I need answers. I intend to get them." He looked at her then, looked until the deep furrow between her brows eased. His thumb soothed across her skin.

His phone rang. Recognizing the caller, he groaned. "Damn. That's the managing partner."

Suspecting that Rhyme, Ryan, & Shuster were cutting ties, he answered.

***

The door swung ajar, and Isa stuck her head through. "Cessie, since the club hasn't opened yet, Teddy and I are going to get gelato. We'll be back soon."

Not wishing to distract Nate from his phone call, Francesca waved Isa out and followed her into the hall, where Teddy waited. "It's not a good idea to leave Zohra right now."

Isa jutted out her chin. "We can't be cooped up inside all day. It's just across the street."

Francesca understood. After being trapped inside Righteous Hearth's directives, Isa chafed at feeling confined. "Just across the street and back. Don't stray far."

"Deal." Isa took Teddy's hand and the two practically skipped down the stairs.

Intent on reading through the tabloid articles, Francesca followed them to the main level and headed to her office, and the laptop. Maybe she'd call Haley. See what she'd heard from the Righteous Hearth's end.

"Cessie!" Isa's voice, then her hasty footsteps, caught her before she reached the office. Isa, panting, sprinted toward her. Grabbing her hand, her sister dragged her toward the side door. "Nate's car! Come look!"

Isa didn't stop tugging until they stopped at Nate's destroyed Fiat, which Teddy was circling.

Someone had taken out their anger with Nate on his poor car. Its windows had been smashed, its shiny red surface wracked by ugly black spray paint. Anger bubbled. *Nate loved this car.*

"Don't move," she tossed at Isa and Teddy on her way back to Zohra. "I'm getting Nate."

***

Nate hung up the call. Rhyme, Ryan, & Shuster had withdrawn the offer, and he couldn't blame them. What law firm would want him now? He called Steven. His mentor wouldn't want an unemployed attorney, or one linked to the fucking Mafia.

After Nate explained what happened, and insisted he find someone else to represent him, his mentor's gentle voice hardened. "I don't care about your firm's resources or about tabloid fodder," Steven said. "I care about you. Are you okay?"

"You need another attorney."

"I don't want another attorney. I want you. We're in this together. We are shutting down Clary Guns."

"Steven—"

"Don't tell me who I want to represent me. I'll see you here when you're ready, and we'll get started."

Too stunned to argue, assuming his mentor needed time to come to a saner decision, he promised to call back just as two texts from his brothers came through simultaneously.

Jackson:

We are releasing a statement denying the claims and

286

pursuing legal action against the tabloids. Check email for draft copy. Need your sign-off.

Hayes:

They hid the trail, but Righteous Hearth's biggest funder? Giorgio's brother. Morettis are behind the articles.

Nate reread Hayes's text.

Giorgio's brother was funding the Righteous Hearth.

Francesca had said Haley's father was the cult's biggest donor. Was Haley a Moretti?

Another text from Hayes pinged through.

Hayes:

Marco Moretti lives in the US. Goes by Micah Johnson. You've heard of him.

Micah Johnson owned Clary Guns.

The chain of shops was run by the Morettis. The Moretti family never wanted a piece of Zohra. They offered him protection to indebt him to them so he'd drop—maybe intentionally lose—Steven's case.

Nate didn't hear the intruder or see the butt of his gun.

Only felt cold, sharp pain as darkness blinded him.

***

Francesca didn't make it far into Zohra when she saw them.

Four strangers, dressed in black, gathered in the ballroom, their nasty-looking weapons trained on her. She absolutely hated guns. She tamped down the fear that burned like nausea. Tried to steady her voice. *Don't show fear. Bullies thrive on fear.*

"Let me guess." She glanced over the men. "You're

with the Morettis." No response from the Four Horsemen. "Where's Nate?"

The four didn't speak, just watched her with dead eyes. She darted for the stairs—

A sharp, earsplitting clap splintered the balustrade near her apart, showering her in wood.

A warning shot.

Ears ringing, she stopped. Faced them.

The front door swung open.

No, no, no.

Isa's pale face as she stepped inside sent Francesca's stomach lurching. Teddy walked in after Isa—face serious and snow-white.

Behind Isa and Teddy, Miles pushed in, a gun aimed at the two kids.

"Miles…" Francesca tried for a calm voice. "Put that down before you hurt someone."

"I don't take orders from you," spat out Miles. "You take orders from me. You're my ordained wife, as chosen for me by God through the Spiritual Leader."

Francesca fought to keep the outrage from her tone. "I'm not your wife. What are you doing, Miles? Put the gun down. We can talk." She encompassed the four men aiming their guns at her. "Are they with you?"

"They won't hurt you—they're here to make sure you cooperate. I've tried talking, tried cajoling. I'm done. You should see the wedding gown your mother made. Little Sofia will be our flower girl. It will be beautiful. You'll see."

Francesca steadied her trembling knees. If she let fear win, she'd collapse right there on the floor in a quivering pile.

"We can do it the easy way or the hard way,"

continued Miles. "My friends here can shoot your sister's little boyfriend. Or you, Isa, and I walk out… no fuss, no muss… and he lives."

"You're resorting to murder now? Think God would approve of that?"

"I'm doing God's bidding—the Spiritual Leader decreed it. Our life has purpose, Francesca… *we* have purpose. The Spiritual Leader sees the great things we are destined to become. Together."

"Miles, I won't marry you. I thought I loved you once, but I can barely look at you now."

"The outside influences have messed with your brain, but that's okay. Nothing a little time in the Sinners Shed can't fix. Leave with me now, or I'll make you regret it."

Miles swung the gun toward Teddy.

Isa stepped in front of her boyfriend. "Don't touch Teddy!"

"Miles," Francesca snapped, hoping the sharpness of her tone would distract him away from the kids. The crazed look in his eyes told her he really could shoot someone. "Let Isa and Teddy go, and I will leave with you."

"Good, goooood," Miles drew out. "Now you're coming around to your true purpose. If you leave with me, Teddy can go, but your sister must come with us. The Spiritual Leader insists you both return."

"Fine," Isa hurried to agree. "Just let Teddy go."

Teddy's pointy jaw set. "I'm not letting you leave with him."

"So brave for a little boy." Miles tsked. "Stand back, Teddy. Isabella and Francesca and I have somewhere to be."

"I suggest you hurry up and leave," came a voice

from the stairs. "I'm not done teaching Signore Icefall a lesson."

Giorgio Moretti strolled down each step without much hurry, a man who knew he'd won.

"*You*," accused Isa. "You paid me to go to Nate's club!"

Giorgio lifted a nonchalant shoulder. "I tried to be helpful to Nate, but he refused my offers. Miles is much smarter than that." He fixed Miles with a bored look. "The car is outside. The driver will take you to my private plane. My brother will meet you at the Nevada airport."

"We are not going anywhere with you now," Francesca told Miles. "How do you two even know each other?"

"Family friend. And afraid you are." Giorgio still lingered near the bottom steps. "A fire broke out upstairs. Your little boyfriend is chained to his bed—one of his silly sex cuffs. Ironic, no?"

Panic veiled her eyesight as she looked up the stairs. She blinked to clear her vision. "What did you do?"

Rage flashed across Giorgio's face. "He's been a thorn in our side for months. Now, Miles, you go on with your fiancée and her sister. I'll deal with Nate and the club. Leave the boy here. I don't need witnesses."

He can't be serious. This can't be real. Francesca glanced back up the staircase again before leveling her gaze on Giorgio. "I'm not leaving Nate and Teddy with you."

Moretti raised his gun. "I can get you to change your mind."

Miles trained his weapon on Francesca too.

Francesca crossed her arms. "I'm staying."

"So am I," Isa piped up, terror in her eyes.

"Can I maim them a little?" Giorgio asked. "They're starting to annoy me."

"No. Spiritual Leader wants them hale and whole. They have a destiny to fulfill."

"That's no fun." Giorgio tsked.

"Why did you hire *me* to compromise Nate?" Isa asked. "Did you know I was from the Righteous Hearth?"

Moretti smiled that oily, slippery grin. "It was easy to follow your activity once we found you online. When you posted on that job site… I couldn't help myself—hiring a Frascati princess amused me. If only you'd taken the photo with him as I'd asked—would have given the tabloid stories much more juice."

Frascati princess? What—

The acrid notes of smoke drifting down the stairs stung her nasal passages. *Oh God.* Giorgio hadn't been lying. He had set the club on fire, and Nate was upstairs, handcuffed and possibly hurt. How long before the smoke suffocated him? Or the fire incinerated the building whole?

Giorgio motioned to the four soldati. "You four, go bring my car before the fire spreads. And take care of the security cameras out there, and any witnesses. Go. This is between a man and his wife. Miles here doesn't need gawkers to a family dispute, and I don't need Trigger Finger over there maiming his bride."

One of the four glanced down at the floor and his ears reddened.

Must be Trigger Finger.

"Miles isn't my family," Francesca said, but as the men filed out, she breathed a sigh of relief. Giorgio and Miles were both armed, but facing off against two men was better than facing off against six.

A sharp clap split the air.

Francesca had no idea from where.

Deafened by the rush of her own blood in her ears, she saw Isa's face contort in a scream.

As if in a silent movie, Giorgio Moretti toppled across the bottom steps, blood pooling.

Francesca swallowed, trying to clear the vibration from her eardrums.

Miles's gun, still trained on Isa and Francesca, faltered.

"Miles." The achingly familiar voice cleared the rest of the ringing. "I suggest you drop your piece. Unless you'd like to join your friend Giorgio in hell."

Miles turned at the directive, gun still raised.

Another shot.

He too fell to the ground.

Dazed, Francesca looked at the newcomer. Or, rather, newcomers.

Isa, beside her, gasped. "Nonna?"

Nonna stood, regally dressed in jewel-toned blue, next to Dante, who lowered his recently fired weapon.

"We need to go." Nonna rushed forward.

"Are they—are they—" Isa stammered.

"They will live," assured Nonna. "But we have to go. The fire is spreading fast—we saw it coming out of the upstairs windows when we drove up. We cannot be here."

Francesca shoved Isa into her grandmother's hands. "Go with Nonna. I have to get Nate."

Before Isa could argue, Francesca scrambled toward the stairs. Giorgio lay sprawled across the bottom steps. She refused to look at him as she sprang past him—

A tight, painful grasp on her ankle hauled her back, tumbling her to the hard steps.

Giorgio.

She kicked at him with all her might, until he let go with a growl.

Not wasting time, she took the stairs almost on all fours.

"Cessie!" Isa called.

"Nonna, take her!" Francesca yelled through the balustrade. "I'll be right out."

"Dante, go with Francesca," Nonna commanded. "Teddy, Isa, let's go."

Francesca didn't wait to see whether Dante followed, but she heard the heavy thud of his footsteps behind her on the staircase.

The higher up the stairs she climbed, the more the smoke and the heat thickened, scalding her lungs with billows of bitter smoke. When she reached Nate's room, the smoke clotted. She fought through it as she ran toward him on the bed. He lay flat on his back, his arms chained to the iron headboard while flames licked along the walls. His name froze in her burning throat.

"What the fuck are you doing here?" He lifted his bloodstained face to growl at her. "*Leave.*"

"Not without you." She grasped for the bobby pin in her hair with shaking fingers and straddled him to get the best angle on the lock. Even though blood soaked the pillows beneath him and one eye had swollen shut, he felt solid and alive under her.

The coagulating smoke stung her eyes, sealed her throat. The heat from the spreading fire kicked her flight instinct into overdrive; her limbs trembled as she fought against it. Her sweaty, unsteady fingers managed to get the pin into the lock regardless.

Nate bucked under her. "For God's sake, Francesca, go."

"I'm not leaving you. I almost got it. Darn it. Hold on, don't distract me."

From the corner of her eye, she watched Dante battle with the flames, but they were spreading too fast. Despite the futility of his task, Dante refused to withdraw.

Francesca managed to undo the handcuffs on the second try.

"There." She sighed as he yanked his bleeding wrists from the fuchsia bindings.

Blood from his head wound hemorrhaged profusely over his beautiful face.

She touched his cheek. "Can you walk?"

He held her gaze from under blood-clumped eyelashes. Cupping her head, he brought her mouth to his for a brief, burning kiss. "Yes."

Dante led the way as they ran toward the stairwell and down the endless steps. The stairs multiplied as they fought to escape the spreading fire, another one appearing just as they thought they'd reached ground.

At the base of the stairs, Moretti waited, his weapon trained on them, his shoulder a spreading crimson splotch.

Without slowing, Dante reached for his gun.

Too late.

Moretti fired.

Nate threw Francesca against the wall, covering her body with his, inserting himself between her and the bullet.

Caught in the projectile's path, Dante hit the wall next to them with a groan, blood spraying. He bumped against Nate, slipping his weapon into Nate's hand before he collapsed.

Nate aimed the piece at Moretti and fired. Moretti dropped to the ground with an ear-piercing shriek, grasping his knee.

"Terrible aim," wheezed Dante.

"Everyone's a critic," said Nate just before lunging

down the steps. He kicked the gun out of Moretti's hands, slamming the butt of his own weapon against Moretti's temple. The man collapsed, prostrate, and didn't move.

Nate ate the distance back to Dante and Francesca, and the two maneuvered Dante down the rest of the stairs and out the door to the glorious outside just as the fire brigade and the police and the medical help arrived.

Medics rushed for Dante, setting him into the ambulance.

"Two more men inside," rasped Nate.

"You need help too," Francesca told him.

"I'm fine." He waved off the medics even as he sank to the ground. "Just a scratch. You?"

She sat next to him on the cobblestone street. "You can barely see from the blood."

Chaos raged around them, but Nate's gaze fixed solely on Francesca. "You stayed in a burning building for me. You could have died."

She bracketed his blood-smeared face with both hands, needing to feel the solid heat of him. "I love you. I wasn't going to let you die."

His mouth gaped. "You love me?"

Did he have to look so shocked?

"Yes, you fool."

Hands shaking with adrenaline, lungs burning from the smoke, she barely noticed the ambulance personnel approach them.

"Hold on," Nate growled at them in irritated Italian. "We're in the middle of an important conversation."

The medics ignored him, and shuffled them both into the waiting ambulance.

Francesca's gaze collided with her parents, who waited on the street next to the many gathering onlookers.

She caught a glimpse of Nonna, Isa, and Teddy as they got into a tinted car and drove off, following the ambulance that took away Dante. Then one of the medics gave her oxygen to breathe and the ambulance doors slammed closed.

Chapter 30

After being poked and prodded by doctors and questioned by the authorities, Nate and Francesca were released, long after night had fallen outside the hospital windows.

Isa and Teddy waited for them in the lobby.

Isa's arms closed tight around Francesca. "I'm so glad you're okay." She gave Nate a brief hug too. "You too, I guess."

He patted the girl's shoulder. "Now, now, no need to be effusive."

Isa studied his swollen eye and the neatly patched gash on his forehead. "Does that hurt?"

"Not as much as Giorgio hurts right now."

"The police who were here earlier told us he's been arrested—Miles too. But Nonna dropped us off here and now isn't answering her phone, and we don't know where the private ambulance took Dante." Isa returned to lean into Francesca. "I told the police everything—about the Righteous Hearth and how Miles tried to kidnap us with Giorgio's help. I left Mom and Dad out of it though. Should I have not done that?"

Francesca didn't know. She wished she could understand the depth of their parents' involvement.

"I told my dad everything," said Teddy. "He will turn the Righteous Hearth into his next project. They won't know what hit them."

Francesca squeezed the boy's shoulder. "Anything to make the world aware of that fucking cult."

"Whoa…" Isa murmured. "You swore."

"Sometimes the occasion calls for it."

"I'll get us a hotel for the night," said Nate. "I'm not ready to see the damage to Zohra today. Not ready to explain anything to Jackson yet either."

A hotel didn't appeal to Francesca. "Let's go to Nonna's."

They took a cab to her grandmother's, but found the apartment empty.

Restless, anxious, Francesca began chopping garlic and tomatoes before she even realized it. Her stomach gurgled as she tossed them onto a sizzling pan.

"I'll put the pasta to boil," offered Nate.

While Isa and Teddy hung out on the couch, Nate and Francesca worked in silence, ladling spaghetti with tomatoes and garlic into bowls.

The four had long finished eating before they heard the scrape of a key. The door swung open, and their grandmother walked inside. She didn't look surprised to see them in her apartment, squished around the small table.

"Nonna!" Isa rushed forward.

Despite everything, her grandmother looked calm and collected.

"How's Dante?" asked Francesca.

"He'll make a full recovery." Her composure cracked as she studied their faces. "How are you all?"

"Nate'll live," Isa replied. "You owe us a huge

explanation. How did you and Dante show up at the club? Why did Dante have a gun?"

When Nonna hesitated, Nate answered for her. "Your grandmother runs Frascati."

The Frascati princess... No. Impossible.

"It is true." Her grandmother pulled up a chair to their table, sinking into it.

Isa returned to her seat at the table. "Nonna… how? Did Dante pull you into a life of crime?"

"Dante did no such thing." Her wise, brown eyes met each one of theirs at the table. "It is time I told you the truth. Dante is not my boyfriend. I'm flattered you even fell for that lie. He's young enough to be my son. He's my bodyguard. I haven't lived in this apartment in decades, not since your mother moved to the States. When you called from the airport, you had caught me off guard. I couldn't take you to my villa. So I brought you here, to where your mom grew up. To tell you the truth, I haven't been inside this place in years. I had to remember how the stove worked."

"What are you saying?" asked Francesca.

"Your grandfather made Frascati what it was—all-powerful. When he died, Frascati needed a leader. That leader had to be me. I didn't want that kind of power at first, but I couldn't let the silly puppies nipping at my heels take over. They'd have destroyed your grandfather's legacy. I had to step up. Marco Moretti refused to work for a woman. He and his brother launched a war. That war lasted for many long, dark months, and blood ran in the streets before Frascati prevailed. The Morettis lost. They're still around— got their grubby paws in businesses here and across several countries, but they were weakened. They're not even our top competitor anymore.

"Your mother was livid when she found out I'd taken over Frascati. She never approved of Frascati, of our lifestyle… had left for the States when she learned the full extent of her father's business. She already lived in Nevada when he died, had met your father… and cut off ties with me. I tried to reconnect, and we did for a bit, but she couldn't get over the fact that your grandfather—and then I—led Frascati."

"When I broke my leg as a kid…"

"I had heard from my people you were hurt. I tried to send money, to pay for your medical bills, but your parents refused. Your mom said she didn't want blood money. They turned to the Righteous Hearth instead. Trust me, that cult will pay. I've collected a lot on them over the years. I haven't used any of it because you were all so ingrained. I couldn't do that to my daughter—or her husband. But the Righteous Hearth crossed a line, and they will regret it."

"The Morettis are linked to the Righteous Hearth," said Nate, his voice casual.

"Yes. Marco claims to be a believer."

"That's Haley's father," Nate clarified.

Francesca shook her head. "Impossible. Her father is Micah Johnson."

Nonna's face said otherwise.

Francesca studied her grandmother. "Haley's dad is Giorgio's brother?"

Nonna reached for Francesca's glass of water and took a sip. "I'm not convinced the Morettis didn't convert your parents into it as a way to fuck with me. Marco says the Spiritual Leader has offered him salvation. I think he found a way to launder money and conveniently convinced himself he's doing it for God. His spiritual leader gets a cut of it."

"Do Mom and Dad know?"

"Your mother would never be a part of something like that. At least, I don't think."

Isa scooted her chair closer to their grandmother. "Have you seen Mom and Dad? They're in Italy."

"I saw them near Zohra, yes. They're staying in a hotel near the Spanish Steps."

"Did they know Moretti planned on killing Nate?" Blood whooshed so loudly in Francesca's ears, she could barely hear her own question.

"I hope not," said Nonna.

But none of them could really know for certain.

Chapter 31

Graziella had given Nate and Francesca her room for the night while she bunked with Isa. The next morning, Francesca woke just before dawn. Peeling Nate's arm away, she crawled out of bed in her sleepshirt and tiptoed to her tote.

Despite her best attempt not to wake Nate, he sat up, immediately alert. "What's wrong?"

"Nothing," she whispered. Pulling the file from the tote, she returned to the bed, sat next to him on the edge. "Here. You can look."

Doubt didn't twist her organs when she handed over the documents. The papers would show the depth of her father's involvement with the Righteous Hearth and—now she knew—the Morettis. She trusted Nate with the truth.

Flipping on the lamp next to the bed, he pulled the papers closer. It didn't take long for him to realize what they were. "This is why your father came to Rome. He wants these back."

"And I can use them to get Sofia."

He looked at her. "You sure you want to do this?"

"No. But I won't let them imprison her. And I'll find a way to get the new baby away too."

A faint knock at the door had her head swiveling. "Francesca, are you awake?"

Why was Nonna up so early? Francesca called for her to come in.

Her grandmother held up her cell phone. "It's your mother. She only had my number, but wants to speak to you."

Nonna handed the phone to Francesca and slipped out the door.

"Mother?"

"Cessie…" Her mother's voice cracked. "Are you okay? Is Isa?"

Francesca squeezed the phone until her knuckles hurt; she'd never expected her mom to call. "We're fine. Where are you?"

"Your father just told me about… Cessie, he'd *never* willingly do anything illegal like that… Don't break apart our family. Don't give those documents to your grandmother. You don't know what she's capable of."

She'd intended to give the papers to US law enforcement, not Nonna, but she saw no need to clarify. "I want Sofia, Mother. I want her out of the Righteous Hearth. You can have the files—just give me my baby sister."

Her mother hesitated. "I'll speak to your father."

"Let him know that I intend to use those files unless I get Sofia back this week."

"All right," said her mother. "You may come and get her. But I don't want her anywhere near your grandmother."

"That's not up to you, Mother. I take Sofia to Italy, and Dad doesn't go to jail. Deal?"

The line muted—Francesca surmised her father and mother were speaking. When her mother's voice came on, it crackled with resentment. "Deal."

The tears came after she hung up, relief and gratitude so powerful she couldn't contain them. "Mom is letting me have Sofia…" She laid her hand on his. "You don't have to go with me to get her, but I'd really like it if you do. She doesn't have a passport, so I'd have to hang around and wait for an expedited one. I don't know how that would impact your plans for Steven's case."

"What if you and Sofia come to Manhattan with me while we wait for her passport? I still have my place there. Isa can come too."

Manhattan…

A place she'd dreamed of visiting for so long… with Nate, and with both of her sisters? It all seemed too good to be true, but for once she didn't question it.

Chapter 32

The next day, Nate and Francesca left Isa with Nonna while they flew to Nevada to get Sofia. Although Francesca hadn't yet grasped the extent of the dark and dangerous empire that her grandmother ruled, she had let Nonna take Isa to her villa. Frankly, it was much safer than Nonna's apartment, and Isa wished to stay with Nonna and Teddy rather than tour New York. Francesca left the files with Nonna too—she didn't quite trust her parents not to renege on their offer if she'd brought them with her. Once she had Sofia, she'd ask Isa and Nonna to destroy them.

It was almost eight p.m. before she and Nate exited Harry Reid International, but the air was still hot enough to sting her skin. Nate's brother and sister-in-law had invited them for a late dinner tonight, before she and Nate met with Francesca's parents early tomorrow morning. Francesca itched to get Sofia sooner, but the drive to Rose Falls would take over an hour, and going into enemy territory that late at night screamed chancy. At least her parents had agreed to meet in the small town, and not at the compound.

When their Uber arrived, Nate held open her door while the driver situated their two bags in the trunk.

As the driver pulled out onto the road, Nate turned to her. "I'm starving."

Despite her best efforts, she couldn't shake her apprehension. "Do your brother and sister-in-law even want to see me? I'm the reason Zohra Rome needs renovations."

"They're dying to meet you." His warm, comforting fingers linked through hers. "You'll love them."

"I guess I'm just… nervous."

He leaned close, so that the driver wouldn't overhear. "I've got just the things for your nerves."

"I'm sure you do." She chuckled and rested her head on his shoulder.

Jackson and Evie's home, in the Green Valley Ranch neighborhood of Henderson, was all glass and modern lines. Date palms lined the wide driveway, and a lit fountain gurgled in the front yard. Approaching the massive front door, they heard the low, appreciative groan of a man followed by a female laugh—and something like the crash of glass breaking.

Francesca jumped. "Should we come back?"

Nate didn't share her concerns; he grinned. "Nah. If we wait until they're not fooling around, we'll never see them."

He rang the doorbell. Quick footsteps approached, and the gargantuan door swung open on silent hinges. A beautiful blonde in a pink dress all but danced in place.

Her smile bathed them in warmth before she launched herself into Nate's arms, then hugged Francesca. "I heard so much about you, I could barely stand until I met you. I'm Evie. Come in, come in."

Instructing Nate to leave the luggage in the hall, she shuffled them through a brightly lit living room to the open-plan kitchen, where Nate's brother was sweeping up glass shards. She couldn't have mistaken Jackson for anyone but Nate's sibling. Even though his dark hair was shorter, his eyes were the same remarkable shade of blue as Nate's.

Jackson flashed a grin and stalked toward Francesca. "We finally meet." He gave her a hug. "You're all Nate talks about."

"Don't embarrass him," chided Evie.

Jackson wrapped his arms around his wife and pressed a kiss to her cheek. "I'm his brother. It's my job."

As Evie relaxed in her husband's hold, Francesca felt like she was intruding. She stammered for something to say. "I'm sorry about Zohra Rome. I'm the reason Moretti started that fire."

Jackson's eyes stayed warm. "It wouldn't be the first time someone tried to burn down one of my sex clubs."

"Jackson's ex once set fire to Zohra Paris," explained Evie. "We're so glad you guys didn't get hurt. That's what matters."

"How can we help with your sister?" asked Jackson.

Overwhelmed by Nate's half-brother's readiness to help her, Francesca paused, uncertain what to say.

"We'll let you know," Nate cut in. "Hopefully her parents will cooperate when we see them tomorrow."

"Is it such a good idea to meet with them?" Evie worried. "What if it's a trap of some sort?"

"I have to trust them to keep their end of the bargain," responded Francesca.

Jackson kissed his wife's cheek before he waved Francesca and Nate to the dinner table. "Let's eat—you guys have an early morning tomorrow."

As the meal progressed, Francesca watched Nate interact with his brother and sister-in-law. The affection among them was evident. Nate had shared that he'd originally met Evie over a decade ago, when Jackson and she had married the first time, just before the two had divorced. She and Jackson had reconnected last May and got remarried soon after that, and the three had quite a story of that reunion. All three were natural storytellers, and Francesca couldn't stop laughing at their—very different—versions of what transpired.

"What are you even talking about?" Jackson accused Nate in mock outrage. "You weren't even in France at that point."

"But Hayes was," Nate pointed out. "And he painted the picture perfectly."

Evie giggled, taking a sip of her water. Her laughing eyes met Francesca's before she tossed her head back dramatically. "But *I* was there. And I'm telling you what really happened."

Laughing, her husband laid his hand over hers, and their gazes met, heated. Their laughter died. The emotion that arced between them almost scalded Francesca. Jackson leaned closer to his wife, kissed her cheek. The brief touch of lips made Evie blush a bright red. She swatted him playfully away, but kept their hands entwined.

Nate turned to Francesca with an exaggerated pained look. "These two."

How easily his family got along. How different from her own family situation.

After dinner, Evie invited Francesca to sit by the pool while Jackson and Nate cleaned up the dishes.

The brothers' laughter reached them through the open French doors as Evie led her to a comfortable-looking outdoor sofa facing the lit pool.

Despite the late hour, the air remained warm; crickets chirped in the oleander that lined one side of the yard, the sound reminding Francesca—too much—of Rose Falls and the desert compound.

"A little girl talk while we can." Evie grinned, settling deeper into the sofa. "I was so curious to meet you. The last time I saw Nate, he wasn't himself… made me worried."

Francesca tucked her feet under her, facing Evie. "What do you mean?"

Evie glanced behind them, watching her husband and brother-in-law clown around in the kitchen. "He's very private, but he was… unhappy. I see the old Nate again now."

Francesca observed them too before she tore her gaze away. She studied the shimmering pool water, the giant stars in the night sky above, as she processed the words. "We have a lot to figure out still."

Evie scooted closer. "I'm going a little stir-crazy trapped in this house with a manuscript deadline, so please don't take offense, and you can tell me to shut up and I won't be offended, but… what do you have to figure out?"

It was a fair question. "I've always wanted to go to college. My parents and our community refused to let me go to school. This is finally my chance. I can't give that up no matter how much… how strong my… how much I love Nate."

"You don't think he'd be supportive?" Evie asked in a gentle voice.

"I can't rip him away from his life so I can pursue mine."

Evie's lips curved up in a warm smile. "You two will make it work. I know it." She laid her hand over Francesca's, and her eyes flooded with compassion. "I heard your mom is pregnant."

"Yes." She sighed. "And that baby may come to live with me too eventually. Evie, how can I ask Nate to take all that on? He should want to run."

"Would you run if the situation were reversed?"

"No." Francesca gave Evie a rueful smile. "I'd insist on taking it all on too, no matter what it costs me."

"Don't fight it. Nate wants to help. We all want to help."

"Why? You don't even know me."

Evie shrugged, as though it were a no-brainer. "That's what families do."

Later, after checking into their Green Valley Ranch hotel, they stepped into the elevator that would shoot them up to their floor.

Nate pulled her close against him. "Jackson and Evie loved you."

She let her head rest against his shoulder. "I loved them too."

"I love you," Nate whispered, pressing his lips to her neck.

Turning in his arms, she offered her mouth. "I love you."

Maybe they really could figure it out.

Chapter 33

Rose Falls, Nevada, was located an hour northwest of Las Vegas, with a single road leading through the Old West town. As they drove down the narrow main street in a car they'd borrowed from Jackson, Francesca remembered grabbing dinner in town on a Friday night or a movie during a Tuesday matinee—before Righteous Hearth banned its members from cinema.

"You ready?" Nate asked her as they parked next to the inn where her parents agreed to meet them.

"I can't wait."

Nate's gaze shifted beyond Francesca. "I see your mother."

Francesca's heart clutched with anticipation. When she realized her mom strode out of the inn alone, dread freeze-burned her from the inside out.

She unbuckled her seat belt and exited the vehicle. Nate came around to join her, his solid hand closing around hers as they waited for her mother at the car. Much as Isa tended to lean into her when she was scared or nervous, Francesca found herself doing so to Nate, pressing into his warm, familiar heat as nerves loped inside her.

Hands held tight, they presented a solid front. The realization washed a fresh surge of love through her.

Her mother looked pale and withdrawn as she stopped a good ten feet away. "Cessie."

The crisp tone stung. "Where's Sofia?"

"Sofia is with your father."

"Mom—"

"I thought we had an understanding. Now there are rumors of an upcoming investigation—talk that you've broken apart our community."

"Miles was arrested—of course there's an investigation. Mom, the Righteous Hearth is funded by the Morettis. Don't you care about that?"

"*That's not true.* None of that is true. It's all your grandmother's machinations. This is why I wanted her out of our lives."

"Nonna loves us. She loves you too. Please, leave that prison. Let Sofia leave."

"I thought we had a deal, but not if the police are already involved—you know how the outsiders feel about us. There will never be a fair trial. I don't even know why I'm speaking with you." Although her mother's face remained impassive, her voice broke halfway through the sentence.

The hairline fracture was more than Francesca could have wished for. It gave her hope.

"Please, Mom. Please come with us. Get Dad and Sofia."

For a split second, her mother's eyes filled with yearning. Then she blinked, erasing every trace of emotion. "I can't give you Sofia. Not if they are already looking into your father, into our community. You should go. I don't want you to ever return."

***

Francesca slipped away from him with every mile they put between them and Rose Falls. First, she'd withdrawn her hand, then stopped responding to his carefully worded statements.

As they pulled up in front of their hotel, the valet helped with her door. She climbed out of the seat like a deflated birthday balloon, a shadow of her old self as she followed him to the room. He tried taking her hand, but she snatched hers away.

Using the keycard, he let them into their room. "Let's talk about what happened."

Shoulders low, she shook her head and stalked to the shower, closing the bathroom door before he could follow.

The snick of the lock spoke for her.

Her sobs broke through the hiss of the water, reaching him even through the bathroom wall.

When she emerged, wrapped in a fluffy towel, she didn't let her red, swollen eyes meet his. Pulling on her old cotton shirt, she climbed into the king-sized bed and tugged the covers over her head. She tried to stifle her sobs, but they broke free anyway, shaking her slim frame under the thick duvet.

His heart splitting for her, he climbed in bed with her, wrapping her body with his. She froze but didn't struggle. After a tense moment, she relaxed into his hold and burrowed closer. He planted a kiss into her hair, inhaled her beautiful scent, and rejoiced as she twisted in his arms and tucked her head under his chin.

Her tears came, raw and hot, and fell onto his chest. He held her tight as she cried.

"She'll never give up Sofia," said Francesca against his neck. "She'll never let me have her."

He rubbed circles along her cotton-covered skin. "She's not blind to the cracks in the Righteous Hearth. Give her time. Let her see its faults."

"How long will that take?"

"I don't know. Do you want us to go to the compound tomorrow and try to speak to her and your dad?"

Francesca lifted her face then, and her tear-reddened eyes met his. "You don't want any of this. Go to New York. You had a job lined up, and the Righteous Hearth took it away from you. I've dragged you to the desert and heaped a ton of my own problems on your shoulders. You need to go. Focus on Steven. I can handle this."

Unfathomable anger seized his muscles like a midnight cramp. "Can you? You want to handle this all alone, do you? All by yourself? Because you don't need anyone and don't want to depend on anyone? Love be damned. My feelings be damned. You don't want to owe anyone anything."

She struggled out of his hold, sitting up to glare at him. "I'm giving you an out."

"I don't want a fucking out. I love you. How many times do I have to say it? Show it? What will make you finally realize all I want is you. If we have to move here and wait for your parents to come to their senses, I will. If we have to find attorneys and fight, I'll do it. I love you, Francesca. I want to be with you. Why the fuck are you always trying to push me away?"

Heartbreak gathered in her eyes. "Because I love you too. I want to see you happy. How is living with me going to make you happy? I have Isa I have to parent, and hopefully soon—somehow—Sofia too. And the new baby. I want to see my parents leave that cult once and for all. And I want to go to college. How can I ask you to be with me when my life is a mess, and it's going to remain complicated for a very long time?"

"Easy. You just have to let me. I want you. No matter how complicated you are. I love you. I'll help you get your siblings. I'll meet you after school and walk you home. Whatever you need, whatever you want."

She sniffed back the gathering tears. "Just like that?"

"Yes, damn you."

The tears spilled again as he pulled her close. "I'm scared," she sobbed against him. "I'm so scared. I want it all. I want you, and I want school, and I want my family out of the cult. But I'm so frightened, and I don't want to be selfish and—"

"Stop." He pulled back to look at her. The tears slid down her cheeks, and he kissed them away, one after the other, even as more fell. "You're not selfish. Do you want me here?"

Her arms locked hard around him, held tight. "You know I do."

"Then we will figure it out together."

On a shaky breath, she lifted her head, met his gaze. "I want you to be happy too."

"You make me happy."

"You make me happy too."

She closed the rest of the distance between them, took his mouth in a hungry kiss. He gave to her what she wanted, demanded from her what he needed, until they caught each other's groans and melted together in surrender.

Epilogue

Unlike the Righteous Hearth and the Morettis, Graziella Rizzi didn't turn to gossip rags. She went straight for the jugular.

For years, she had been collecting evidence against the Righteous Hearth and their connection to the Moretti crime family, holding off using it because it would incriminate her son-in-law. Now that Giorgio had almost gotten Francesca and Isa killed, Graziella no longer saw the need to be lenient.

Francesca never used the financial records she had taken from her parents. Nonna already had them, and more. She sent decades' worth of documents to the US Attorney's Office, the Department of Defense, the DEA, the DOJ, the IRS, the CPS, the EPA—even the USDA.

The evidence was overwhelming and, six months later, in a coordinated anti-Mafia operation with the Italian authorities, Giorgio Moretti, Marco Moretti, and the Spiritual Leader—whose real name was Eric—were arrested, together with a dozen associates. Charges included racketeering, money laundering, human trafficking, drug trafficking, and tax fraud, among others.

The Righteous Hearth members were questioned, and several were arrested, including Miles, Francesca's dad, and Haley's husband. The three had helped the

Morettis and Eric commit millions of dollars in tax fraud using the chain of gas stations Francesca's father operated. Francesca's mother hadn't known about her husband's involvement with the Mafia, and accepting his participation was difficult.

The various businesses linked to the Righteous Hearth and Marco Moretti, aka Micah Johnson, were shut down. Nate, refusing to sit back where Clary Guns was concerned, worked out a consulting deal with the Department of Justice and partnered with them to close down the Clary Guns chain of arms shops permanently. It hadn't been simple, and required him to spend most of his time in Manhattan. After promoting Giacomo to run Zohra Rome, Francesca had moved to New York City with Nate so he could focus on the case and she could concentrate on the custody battle over Sofia.

Once Clary Guns came down, Nate and Francesca celebrated with Steven.

Not even a full month after Francesca's father's arrest, an unanticipated call changed the trajectory of their custody case. Francesca's mom wanted to talk. She'd just had the baby and wanted to speak to Francesca; Francesca and Nate flew back to Nevada.

On their way to the compound, they stopped by Haley's home at the edge of Rose Falls. Haley waited for them outside and dashed to the car before they'd even parked. Francesca bounded out, hugging Haley as hard as Haley hugged her.

"I'm sorry Greg got arrested," whispered Francesca against her friend's hair.

"He got what he deserved," Haley assured her, holding on to the hug.

"Your dad—"

Haley's eyes filled with tears. "I swear I didn't know. He never once said anything. Neither did Mom. I had no idea that he was even involved in… that my family… much less… You have to believe me. I'd never have—"

"I know," Francesca assured her. "I know."

"I'd have told you if I knew. How could I have not known? About my own father? My own husband?"

They shared ice-cold sodas with Haley and then drove deeper into the desert to meet Francesca's mom just outside the old compound.

Her mother agreed to give Francesca temporary custody of Sofia as she fought through the many confusing truths that began to emerge with the upcoming trial and the new documentary.

Francesca trembled with anticipation while they waited for Sofia to cross to them through the compound fence. As her baby sister passed the boundary, she began to run. Francesca met her halfway, scooping her into her arms and spinning her around, their laughter and tears mingling.

Nate and Francesca rented a house a half mile from Jackson and Evie in Henderson so Sofia could have a solid home while also remaining close enough to her mother for occasional visits. Her mother still refused to speak to Nonna, but she had been asking Francesca more questions about her grandmother. It would be a long road to reconciliation all around, but Francesca trusted they would eventually get there.

Because her father had agreed to a plea deal in exchange for testifying against the Spiritual Leader, he'd be released in two years' time. Francesca hoped both her parents would find it within themselves to leave the Righteous Hearth and their beliefs once and for all by then. For themselves, and for her new baby brother, Nico.

Although her mother hadn't yet disavowed the Righteous Hearth fully, she and the baby did move away from the compound and into a Rose Falls home. It was progress. Slow progress, but progress nevertheless.

Isa joined Francesca and Nate in Nevada as soon as they'd furnished their new home, and they settled into a comfortable routine.

After receiving her GED, Francesca enrolled at a local community college, with the eventual goal of transferring to a nearby university. Inspired, Isa signed up for a few classes at the same community college and was doing well. Francesca and Nate hired several tutors for Sofia to get her caught up before they'd enroll her in school next fall, and they had found her a trustworthy therapist. Francesca and Isa sought therapy too, and Francesca hoped someday her parents would follow suit.

Every Sunday, they had dinner with Jackson and Evie and whichever family members Jackson and Evie had in town—and, Francesca learned, they had a lot of family members.

Francesca had worried that Nate would find himself restless in Nevada. However, within weeks of moving to the state he, as a favor to a former colleague, took on a pro bono case in New York, working remotely from Henderson for most of it and commuting to Manhattan when he had to. After he won it, he took on another.

A few months later, Nonna came to visit. Sofia was cautious around the grandmother she'd never met, but Isa practically crawled into her lap when she saw her. As a gift to Nate and Francesca, Nonna whisked away Isa and Sofia for a long weekend in Palm Springs, giving the couple some much-needed privacy.

Francesca and Nate had gone outside to see the

group off, but a phone call dragged Nate into the house. Francesca watched the group drive away, waved one more time, and returned to the house to seek out Nate. If he were done with the call, they could get their long weekend started.

Even though he'd closed his office door, she heard his voice through it.

"You don't know how sorry I am to turn this down, Jake," Nate said. "No, it's out of the question right now. I traveled there for a few cases, but I can't move there permanently. My girlfriend goes to school here. Her sisters are here. We may have her baby brother with us soon. I can't drag them all cross-country."

He hadn't heard her come in, staring at his phone long after the conversation ended.

"What was that about?" asked Francesca.

He set the phone aside. "Nothing."

"Tell me." She came around the desk and stopped near him.

Quick as a cat, he pulled her into his lap, planted a kiss to her shoulder. "That was the former managing partner at Rhyme, Ryan, & Shuster. He's at another firm now, the one I've been helping with the cases. He wants me to come on board full-time. But it's in New York, so it wouldn't work."

She sifted through the silk strands of his hair, cupped his cheek. "You want the job."

"Someday." He covered her hand with his. "I'll never work the same crazy hours again, but I do eventually want to get back into it full-time."

"And the only reason you're turning it down is me?"

He shrugged. "I can't commute daily to New York from here, and you and Isa just started school. I can't ask you to move."

Drowning in love for him, she kissed him lightly on the lips. "You should take it."

He patted her thigh. "Not right now. Someday, maybe, when we're ready."

"No… I mean it. I'm okay with us all moving to New York. You still have your place there, and living in a metropolitan area will be good for Isa and Sofia. I can go to college there. We can do this, Nate. I think we should move. This isn't about me wanting you to sacrifice everything so I can have my way. I'd never want you to give up yourself for me. I didn't trust that we could compromise before, but I do now. We can do this."

He framed her face, studied her eyes. "You're sure?"

With a wide smile, she nodded.

"What about your mother and the baby?"

"She's asking the right questions, taking a step back from the church. She has a long road ahead of her, but I think the baby is good for her. I think he's making her see the world with a fresh perspective. Loitering here just in case she backslides isn't healthy for anyone. And, I heard Dad is asking the right questions too. I don't need to hover."

"We'll fly back here as often as you want so Isa and Sofia can see your parents."

She kissed him again. Brushing his hair away from his brow, she let her palm linger. "I have no doubt about that. I love you, Nate Icefall."

It was his turn to kiss her, and he did it so thoroughly her head began to spin. When he pulled back, tenderness swamped his face. "I love you more than I can express, Francesca Brook. Here, stand a moment." He lifted her to her feet, and rose from his chair.

With unsteady hands, he yanked open his desk's bottom drawer, pulled something out of it, kept it behind his back as he dragged the chair out of the way. "I wanted to wait until tomorrow night, take you to a fancy Italian dinner, but I need to do this now."

He dropped to one knee in front of her, whipped out the small box, and opened it to reveal a ring nestled in velvet.

***

Nate watched as shock came over the love of his life before her eyes went soft and misty.

"You're proposing?" she asked, as though she needed to clarify.

"Francesca Brook, marry me because I can't imagine spending a single day without you."

She dragged him up then. "I never, ever wanted to get married, Nate. Or at least, not until I got my degrees and started a career. I'd never, ever say yes to anyone else, but yes, yes to you. Yes, because I love you and you love me, and I know you'll support me no matter what, like I'll support you. And because I can't imagine spending a single day without you either."

His heart burst open and all the love he felt for her flooded him like perfect, tropical waters. He kissed her first, hard and deep, and then slid the ring on her finger.

She looked at the sparkling diamond. "It's a perfect fit."

"Isa helped me pick it out for you—gave me her blessing and everything."

"You asked her? Wow, you're full of surprises today," she said, as he lifted her into his arms. "I can't believe I found you."

"If you hadn't, I'd have found you," he promised, and sealed his mouth to hers.

About the Author

Anya London resides in California. When she's not writing, she enjoys running, hiking, reading, and traveling. Please contact her at www.anya-london.com.

Also by Anya London

A Very French Scandal
Once Upon a New York Summer
A Very Italian Scandal